A Citac

A Citadel of Ice

By

Anne Thomas

Dedicated to

William Cave Thomas

A man of faith, courage and service

&

to all who, for the sake of others,
commit themselves to a task
and driven by sound principles,
determine to see that task
through to the end...
no matter how difficult the path
nor how great the personal cost.

A Citadel of Ice

Published in 2020 by FeedARead.com Publishing

A CIP catalogue record for this title is available from the British Library.

This book is based upon a true story. However, the characters and their adventures are a mixture of truth and fiction. The journey to St Petersburg, with a cargo of gold, was undertaken by the artist, William Cave Thomas, early in 1854. The three Quaker gentlemen mentioned in the story made their way there at about the same time. They, and Mr Cattley were real people, as were Christina Robertson. John and Jane Durdin, George and Emily Laws, William Thomas Snr, Cave Thomas's Pre-Raphaelite friends and the major figures of state. However, all other characters, and plot embellishments, were formed in the imagination of the author.

Discover more about William Cave Thomas and his relationship with John and Jane Durdin in *At A Stroke*
Published in two volumes by feedaread.com:

Vol. 1   *Deceit of Riches*   Vol. 2   *Fortune's Spite*

Spanning fifty years between the 1820s and 1870s, *At A Stroke* follows John Durdin's career, domestic life and downfall.
In 1861, as the Durdin family is thrown into chaos, William Cave Thomas, a close family friend, emerges as a talented artist, a loyal friend and a principled and generous man.

6

Author's Note

 *'In the depth of winter, and before the outbreak of war in the Crimea, William Cave Thomas undertook a hazardous journey to St Petersburg with a large sum of money in gold on behalf of a mercantile firm.'*

This footnote in *The Diary of Ford Madox Brown,* edited by Virginia Surtees (Yale University Press, 1981) appears under an entry for August 30th 1854. I happened upon it whilst researching for my book about the fraudulent banker's clerk, John Durdin – published in 2 volumes by feedaread.com (2018) under the title *At A Stroke* - in which Cave Thomas first encounters John's wife, Jane, who is the source of much fictional heart-searching in this book.

There is no doubt that the journey took place. At a Sunday lunch with William and Lucy Rossetti as late as 1885, William Cave Thomas kept them entertained with tales of his journey to Russia – more than thirty years later!

A Citadel of Ice seeks to tell the story of this journey.

I cannot be certain how much gold Cave Thomas took, nor on whose behalf – other than a 'mercantile firm' - but I matched the figures to those in the British Factory accounts for the period – which show that their income fell dramatically with the onset of war and to practically nothing by the end of 1856.

Letters written to the Czar by Queen Victoria made interesting reading – they were surprisingly personal considering that Britain was on the point of going to war with Russia. The fact that William Cave Thomas's father had reframed the Royal Collection only a few years previously, and that Cave Thomas himself had had dealings with Prince Albert regarding what should be done with the 'Crystal Palace' after the Great Exhibition of 1851, raised an interesting possibility – for which I found absolutely no proof. But both William Thomas senior and Cave Thomas certainly met the Prince Consort on several occasions, raising the question 'was Royal interest behind this journey?' I leave this as a tantalising possibility.

8

Discovering the Quaker peace mission was a gift – they travelled at about the same time as Cave Thomas – so they pop up in the story. The Times newspapers of the time were also instructive.

William Cave Thomas's portrait entitled *A Russian Dealer of the Gostinvorder* appeared in the 'Exhibition of Art and Industry' in Paris in 1855. George Wallis wrote of it: *'the fur around the man's neck is a most seductive reality'*.

Perhaps it was a study for this the painting of which Ford Madox Brown wrote in his diary *'He showed me a study of a Russian Merchant that quite astonished me, a most noble painting equal to anything modern or ancient. Thomas will paint great works yet I am now convinced'*. (sic)

Christina Robertson was a notable portrait artist who painted for the Czar and other Russian nobles. She had family in England but the James Robertson in this story is a figment of my imagination.

Mr Cattley, at the English Church, combined his role as Church Warden with that of managing the British Factory – a conglomerate of merchant families more than 2000 people strong, who dealt in commodities much desired by the West. Previously known as the Muscovy Company, they had moved to St Petersburg from Moscow and made a good living there. They enjoyed favourable treatment by the Czar and benefitted from charters stretching back several hundred years. The relationship between the Czar and the English Church was good – although the minutes of a meeting in early 1854 show that whilst appearing grateful for the Czar's promises of free passage and unmolested ships, the British Factory staff were busy making plans to defend the church and cut themselves off from the city.

As late as spring 1854 the Czar and his son attended the funeral at the English Church of Sir James Wylie, senior medical officer to the Russian Army and to the Czar himself – a native of Scotland, born and raised only a few miles from Christina Robertson.

Into this tangled web I poured a mixture of espionage and romance… all my own!

Acknowledgements

My thanks go to Tricia, my friend and editor, who gave generously of her time and talent, to keep me on the straight and narrow with this book.

To Peter, for his endless encouragement, refreshments, advice and patience, and to all my family and friends, who have been so supportive - especially those who helped proof-read the manuscript.

To the late Virginia Surtees, art historian and author, whose footnote in *The Diary of Ford Madox Brown*, Yale University Press, 1981, set me off on this journey.

And to all the other sources I used for the facts behind this story, especially:

- Griselda Fox Mason (1925-89) for *Sleigh Ride to Russia* The Ebor Press, 1985, which tells the story of the Quaker men who went to talk to the Czar - and helped me with details of the journey.
- Mr Bradshaw, for his excellent Continental Railway Guide 1853, republished by Harper Collins in 2016, without which we might have missed a train.
- The London Metropolitan Archives and the Bank of England Archives – where I went in search of the story behind the gold.
- Dorich House Museum – where I encountered WCT's Portrait of a Russian Merchant.
- Orlando Figes – for his history of the war in the Crimea in his book: *Crimea*, Penguin 2010.
- Dafforne, James, Art Journal, 1839-1912; Jul 1869; 91; British Periodicals pg. 217 *British Artists: their style and Character:* details of WCT's life and work.
- The Times Newspaper archive.
- Queen Victoria's Letters: Vol. II 1844-1853 www,gutenberg,org

Anne Thomas, October 2020

Notes on the Crimean War

(5th October 1853 – 30th March 1856)

Orlando Figes, in the introduction to his book *Crimea* (Allen Lane 2010 and Penguin 2011), refers to the Crimean War as *'the major conflict of the nineteenth century'* and tells us that it was of *'huge significance for Europe, Russia and that area of the world – stretching from the Balkans to Jerusalem, from Constantinople to the Caucasus'*. He explains that *'the Crimean War was a crucial watershed. It broke the old conservative alliance between Russia and the Austrians that had upheld the existing order on the European continent, allowing the emergence of new nation states in Italy, Romania and Germany. It left the Russians with a deep sense of resentment of the West, a feeling of betrayal that the other Christian states had sided with the Turks, and with frustrated ambitions between the powers in the 1870s and the crises leading to the outbreak of the First World War'*.

Figes analyses the motives behind each nation's entry into the war. Of the Turks, he writes *'it was a question of fighting for their crumbling empire in Europe, of defending their imperial sovereignty against Russia's claims to represent the Orthodox Christians of the Ottoman Empire'*. The British, he says *'claimed they went to war to defend the Turks against Russia's bullying, but in fact they were more concerned to strike a blow against the Russian Empire, which they feared as a rival to Asia, and to use the war to advance their own free-trade and religious interests in the Ottoman Empire'*. The French had their own motives, not least *'to restore France to a position of respect and influence abroad'*.

For Russia, dominance in the Mediterranean had become a pressing issue. With limited access to international waters (the Baltic Sea ports being closed by ice for much of the year) they sought a base from which to maintain their strong presence in the East. However, Figes points out that for Russia and its proud and arrogant Czar, this was above all a religious war – *'a crusade, to fulfil Russia's mission to defend the Christians of the Ottoman Empire'* – and by so doing *'extend his* (the Czar's) *empire of the Orthodox as far as Constantinople and Jerusalem'*.

As we begin *A Citadel of Ice,* Europe is balanced on a knife edge and about to become embroiled in the conflict already taking place in the East. All countries are unsure what the future will bring, and for the British Factory in St Petersburg, every new snippet of news is read and scrutinised in an atmosphere of fear and tension.

Meanwhile, peace talks go on in Vienna, Russia gathers her forces, the British and French muster their armies, and brave men polish their swords.

The War in the East, the Crimean War, is about to explode. Soon, names such as Sevastopol, Inkerman, Alma, Balaklava will trip off people's tongues; Florence Nightingale, and later Mary Seacole, will earn international respect, and the valiant and hopeless 'charge of the Light Brigade' (October 25th 1854) will define sacrificial British heroism. Figes writes that *'at least three-quarters of a million soldiers were killed in battle (during the two and a half-year war) or lost through illness or disease, two-thirds of them Russian. The French lost around 100,000 men, the British...about 20,000....'* and *'nobody has counted the civilian casualties'* Figes goes on to say, citing *'starvation, disease, massacres, and organised campaigns of ethnic cleansing'* as being responsible for the additional loss of life.

The journey of three and a half thousand miles made by the men in this story was truly heroic – particularly that of the three Quaker gentlemen, none of them young, whose motives were genuine and courageous. The journeys can be compared to sailing in a tempestuous sea and placing oneself at the mercy of the unpredictable elements. None knew whether they would be successful, whether they would see home once more. All felt driven to do what they considered right, in the face of great danger. History brings perspective, but for our adventurers, the way ahead was totally unknown. APT

Sketch maps of the 3,500-mile round trip undertaken by William Cave Thomas

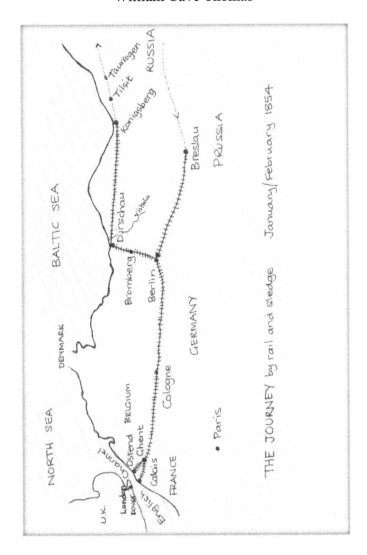

THE JOURNEY by rail and sledge   January/February 1854

(not to scale)

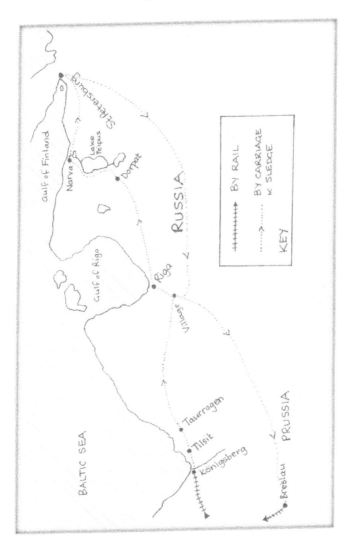

The words of this much-loved hymn by Charles Wesley (1709 – 1788) seem to define the spirit in which William Cave Thomas set out on this journey and could well have framed his prayer along the way.

Forth in thy Name, O Lord, I go,
my daily labour to pursue;
thee, only thee, resolved to know
in all I think or speak or do.

The task thy wisdom hath assigned,
O let me cheerfully fulfil;
in all my works thy presence find,
and prove thy good and perfect will.

Thee may I set at my right hand,
whose eyes mine in-most substance see,
and labour on at thy command,
and offer all my works to thee.

Give me to bear thy easy yoke,
and every moment watch and pray,
and still to things eternal look,
and hasten to thy glorious day.

For thee delightfully employ
whate'er thy bounteous grace hath given;
and run my course with even joy,
and closely walk with thee to heav'n.

Contents

1

Wars and Rumours of Wars
Sunday 8th January 1854

Herbert Ellis and his superior, Sir Henry Loughton, emerged from the anonymous Government building in which they had spent the last six hours, still locked in deep discussion. They paused on the steps, alone now – the others had left for home or club some time earlier. A distant clock struck eleven. The bitter wind, carrying a drop or two of icy rain, whipped upriver and around the corner, tugging at their clothing. There was likely snow to come.

"No good standing here," said Sir Henry. "Best get home."

"Are you happy with the outcome of the meeting, sir?"

"Happy is not the word. These are perilous times, Ellis. Reports from the Continent are so contradictory that it's hard to know how best to act."

"But someone must go to Russia."

"Yes, indeed they must. Our people there are in great danger. Without aid from this country, I shudder to think what might become of them."

"The journey will involve great risks, especially with such a cargo..." Sir Henry frowned, silencing Ellis with an irritable gesture.

"Don't speak of it. Confidentiality must be maintained at all times."

Ellis apologised. Then added: "This man – Thomas – you are confident he's up to the task?"

"I have my reasons for believing so. His background is impeccable, his business an excellent cover and he speaks good Russian. Now it's up to you to persuade him to act."

"I intend to see him tonight, late though it is. I'll report back to you in the morning."

"I'll see you at nine. Good luck to you."

"Thank you, sir, and good night."

The two men parted, Sir Henry to walk the short distance to his club, and Ellis to carry out Sir Henry's orders. He tightened the knot in his scarf and, wishing he could afford a thicker coat, set off in search of a cab to take him to the man's lodgings. William Cave

Thomas had rooms at his studio. On a night like this, he was likely to be there. Ellis hoped Sir Henry had been right and that the man would agree to join them.

Two hours earlier

William Cave Thomas was weary and cold. He had laboured hard all afternoon and evening, forgetting food, so engrossed was he in his work. As he closed the shutters in his studio, against the bitter night, he remembered his supper and went in search of the tray Mrs Trent, his daily help, had left him. It was cold in his quarters, so he took his supper of bread and cheese back to the studio. He made up the fire in the iron stove which heated the large room, pushed a pile of sketchbooks off a chair and settled down to eat. He had a great deal on his mind. His paintings were selling, and he had promise of a place in the forthcoming Royal Academy exhibition. With friends, a decent studio, money for materials, and family ever ready to help him with framing and exhibiting, he was making an impression on people in high places. But…

His mind travelled over the well-worn path he'd been visiting and revisiting over the past three months. He'd spent the previous summer travelling on the Continent, trying to escape the tangle of his London life. On his return from Munich, his troubles had greeted him, unchanged. No matter how assiduously he applied himself to his painting, his unsettled frame of mind continued to rob him of sleep. There were few he could confide in. Only his close friend, Ford Madox Brown, knew of his distress, and his advice had been to 'work, man, work' - advice Cave Thomas had taken. But work had failed to numb his pain and so he remained locked in an impossible position, at war with himself.

His supper finished, he put the tray on a table and looked about the studio. His natural love of order was offended by the mess and muddle all about him. This could not go on. He left the warm circle of the stove and began to tidy up, returning pigments and brushes to their rightful places, folding rags, and tidying discarded sketches into a folder. He glanced at the corner where his recently completed canvasses lay. Against his better judgement, he walked over, picked up the nearest and, yielding to temptation, turned it around. The broad brow and steady gaze transfixed him. The eyes, painted from memory, held his. It was his best work, but it could never be shown. A secret shame. He took it with him to the fire and sat down, still holding it. Holding her, Jane, captured in his mind's eye and superimposed on the figure he had paid to sit. One of many. How could he overcome this shameful weakness?

It had all started a couple of years earlier. In '51 and '52, after the Great Exhibition, he'd thrown himself enthusiastically into plans for converting the huge exhibition halls into a college for artists and artisans; engineers, architects and draughtsmen. With the Prince Consort's approval, he'd devoted much time and energy to the project. He'd shared his plans with his friends – with Brown, Rice and Durdin, with his sisters, Maria and Emily, and… with Jane. But Royal interest had failed to become Royal patronage, and nothing came of it. The Prince had transferred his attention to other projects.

A disappointed man is vulnerable to a soft voice. In need of a sympathetic ear, he'd spent more and more time with his sister, Emily, and was drawn even deeper into her circle of friends. Jane's gentle friendship, her pleasant smile and beguiling, innocent attention had stirred feelings which had taken him by surprise.

Warned by his younger sister that he was likely to cause embarrassment, he'd drawn back. Entanglements with married women were not for him. His trip to Munich was intended to put an end to any such temptation, but he'd returned to find himself ever more strongly connected with the family – invited to be godfather to their youngest child – a trusted friend, an avuncular presence, included in every family occasion and made welcome at their table.

What he regarded as the unacceptable behaviour of men like Dante Gabriel Rossetti were not for him. He was made of a different metal, brought up to more exacting standards. Mere whim must not lead him into the betrayal of friendship and trust. Goaded by this never-ending circle of thought, he picked up the poker and riddled the stove with unnecessary vigour.

Long walks with Madox Brown helped, he conceded. Striding out across rough fields and along country lanes, they'd thrash out their ideas about art and aspiration, present toil and hoped-for future fame, walking in all weathers and returning, energy renewed, to work with increased application and vigour. Or, exhausted by their discourse and exercise, they'd slump by the fire, sharing a pipe in tranquil harmony. But, once alone, his mood would change and yet again he'd throw himself into his work, seeking solace there.

Cave Thomas stood up, admitting defeat. Alone, here in the studio, once his brushes were clean, and painting put aside for the

21

day, his troubles had once more crowded in. Confronted by his unchanged situation, his thoughts treading an unending circle, he knew he was beaten. He found it impossible to put Jane entirely from his mind. She crept into his thoughts and slipped between sleep and wakefulness. Something more drastic must be done, or he would be driven mad.

As the clock struck ten, Cave Thomas returned the portrait to its corner, resolutely turning its face to the wall. He closed the damper on the stove, lit a candle, extinguished the lamp and made his way up to bed. A faithful Christian, he knelt, as his mother had taught him in early childhood, and prayed. The familiar words somehow soothed him, and he lay down a calmer man. He had confessed his faults and sought divine guidance. His burden lifted, he drifted into sleep, hoping to wake refreshed… even if no nearer a solution to his problem.

Midnight

At first, Cave Thomas couldn't understand why he'd woken. He'd been asleep only an hour or so when persistent knocking on the front door broke into his dreams. He sat up, wondering who could need him at this hour. Leaving the warmth of his bed, he pulled on his dressing gown, went to the window and threw up the sash. He leaned out to see who stood on the step. The knocking ceased. The man below stepped back, so that the light of a nearby lamp shone upon his upturned face. It was a face Cave Thomas knew, but he couldn't recall the man's name.

"Mr Cave Thomas? Sorry to disturb you. It's important. Sir Henry sent me. Sir Henry Loughton."

"Loughton, did you say?"

"Yes."

"I'll come down." Cave Thomas lowered the sash. Sir Henry Loughton was a name he knew well – a man he'd met several times, always in elevated company; always a little mysterious. He understood that he was something high up in Government circles. It could mean many things, but, as he slipped his feet into a pair of slippers, Cave Thomas's first reactions were ones of interest rather than irritation. He was intrigued to know what had brought the man here at midnight. Perhaps his prayers were about to be answered.

He drew back the bolts and opened the door, revealing a man about his own age. His visitor doffed his hat and introduced himself.

"Herbert Ellis. Sorry to disturb you so late at night, sir. You may recall our meeting before – at the time of the Great Exhibition. As I said, I'm here on behalf of Sir Henry Loughton. May I come in?"

Cave Thomas regarded his visitor for a moment, recognising him as one of the men involved in the closure of the 'Crystal Palace' and plans for its removal to a new site. Ellis – yes, that had been his name – a public servant or part of the Prince's household? Seeing nothing to cause him concern, he opened the door wide.

"Of course. You'd better come into my studio. There should be some heat left in the stove. I'd not long retired to bed."

He led the way to the studio, lit the lamp and gestured to Mr Ellis to sit down. He attended to the stove whilst Ellis removed his hat and scarf and sat in the chair Cave Thomas had vacated only a couple of hours earlier.

"The matter is most urgent, and confidential, or I wouldn't be bothering you at this hour," Ellis began. "Sir Henry is working on behalf of the Government and," he paused slightly, "…and of others, who cannot be named."

"Really?"

"Your name has been mentioned as one who could offer help at this…er… delicate time."

Cave Thomas pulled a second chair towards the open stove and warmed his hands by its growing flames.

"Delicate?" Cave Thomas questioned. "How do you mean?"

"You've lived much abroad." The statement appeared to require an answer.

"Yes, I studied in Italy, France and Germany, before settling here in London."

"You have a grasp of these languages?"

"I'm fluent in German and French and can make myself understood in Italian and Russian."

"I can see why you might know three of those languages, but why Russian?"

"From my time in Bavaria. I came to know people who had left Russia after the Decembrist uprising – mostly artists. I take an interest in languages, so it was natural for me to learn their tongue."

"Good. Very useful." Ellis took out a notebook and opened it. Cave Thomas could see what appeared to be notes, written in an illegible scrawl. "You've no wife?"

"No, I'm single and I live here alone – except for a servant who comes in by the day, Mrs Trent, who cleans and cooks for me. What is the purpose of these questions?"

"Forgive me. I should have come to the point more quickly. The matter is of great urgency and is of a delicate nature."

"As you said, earlier." Cave Thomas eyed the man thoughtfully, his customary warmth ebbing. "Forgive me, but you've woken me in the middle of the night, told me you've been sent by a man I know to be of great importance to this country, then proceeded to ask me a string of questions. It would be better, I think, if you were to tell me what you've come to tell me, and then I can say what I think of it."

Ellis smiled bleakly. "I apologise. I'm new to this and, to be perfectly frank, a little out of my depth."

Cave Thomas went to the cupboard, took out two glasses and poured them both a brandy.

He handed a glass to Ellis and cradled the other in his hands, his back to the stove.

"So?"

Steadied by the brandy, Ellis began.

"How much do you know about Russian activity in the East?"

"I read the papers. The Turks seem to have been in belligerent mood for months."

"There's far more to it all than appears in print. The situation in the Balkans has been causing us some concern for nearly two years. It was clear from the start that Czar Nicolas had ambitions to expand his power and influence over the Ottoman Empire. His ports in the Baltic are unusable in the winter, so he's been looking for something in the south, to give him free access to the Mediterranean."

"So, you consider that all this alarm about Jerusalem and the Holy Places is merely a ruse?"

"Exactly; an excuse to threaten Turkey and take Constantinople. Now the Turks are at war with Russia, it can only be a matter of weeks before France and Britain are dragged into the conflict."

"Yes, I've read all this in the papers."

"Indeed, but what you will not know is that our people in St Petersburg are now in great peril. Some two thousand or more souls – men, women and children who look to this country for support, will face penury, and possible imprisonment and starvation, should matters come to the worst."

"Victims of war?"

24

"Yes. The British Factory – you may recall its former name, the Muscovy Company – relies entirely on Russian exports for its survival. A war with the West will almost certainly cut them off from commerce. With no income, they'll have little or no provision for their most basic needs. Add to this the likelihood of aggressive treatment by the Russian military, and… well you can supply the rest."

"I see." Cave Thomas filled his pipe and lit it. "So, where do I fit in?"

"Our usual avenues won't work. I've been given the task of finding an alternative. Sir Henry mentioned your name. I believe he knows your father."

'Of course,' Cave Thomas thought, 'that's where I first met Sir Henry – when Father was framing the Royal portrait collection.' He wondered whether the 'others who cannot be mentioned' had Royal connections.

"Your familiarity with European travel, your grasp of languages and, to be blunt, your availability, stand in your favour." Ellis went on. "As an artist, you'd be free to travel where a man in a more official position might find it difficult."

"With war coming…"

"Exactly."

"And the recommendation came from...?"

"I'd prefer you not to ask, Mr Thomas."

"Because you can't answer?"

"Precisely."

Cave Thomas transferred his attention to his pipe, using the time to organise his thoughts.

"Sir Henry Loughton sent you?"

"Yes."

"I met him once – when I was assisting my father."

"Is that so?"

"Yes. We were measuring some paintings he'd agreed to frame for one of his most esteemed patrons."

"Ah, he's a frame-maker." Ellis clearly already knew this.

"I recall that we were surprised in our work by two or three gentlemen coming to watch us. Sir Henry was one. He spoke to his companions in German. He was surprised when I used the same language to ask him if the painting was straight."

"And the other men?"

"I believe that one of them would be unhappy to think his name was being bandied about in a lowly artist's studio. And the other? I understood that he was visiting from Eastern Europe."

"You're no fool Cave Thomas."

"Not fool enough to be drawn into such a venture blindfolded. What, or whom, would I be taking with me?"

"I cannot say 'who' would go with you at present, as no-one has yet been chosen, but regarding the 'what', that is easy. We want you to carry the British Factory's port dues to St Petersburg: all this year's money and some from last year. It will be at least a couple of thousand pounds." He paused, searching Cave Thomas's face for signs of his character: what kind of man he was, whether he was trustworthy and up to the task. Appearing to find what he sought, Ellis stood up.

"The money will be all in gold. With war about to engulf them, nothing else will be of any use to our compatriots."

"Gold!" Cave Thomas looked at Mr Ellis aghast as he considered what it would mean in terms of complexity and peril. He slowly rose to his feet then, fixing Ellis with a steady gaze, fired a string of questions at him.

"How heavy will it be...?"

"How will it be packed...?"

"How will I conceal it...?"

"How much extra money will I be given in order to bribe my way across Europe...?"

And, after a slight pause, in which his look of consternation changed to a smile,

"When must I start?"

Ellis, who'd remained transfixed as he watched Cave Thomas wrestle with the implications of the task, sat back and laughed.

"Too many questions, Mr Thomas. I don't have the answers, but I'll take your questions to Sir Henry... and tell him you are willing to help?"

"Yes. I'll help. I can do no less for people who are in such peril." He smiled and held out his hand. Ellis took it, and their handshake confirmed their shared commitment to the mission.

"I would like to choose my companion – a man I can trust. Would that be possible?" Cave Thomas was reluctant to lose all control over arrangements.

"I have someone in mind who might be just the man for such a journey," he continued. "I'm confident that he's trustworthy – of course, you'll want to confirm that - and I think he can use a revolver. As for myself, it's a while since I used one, so I'll need to practise; although I hope it won't be needed."

"That makes sense. I have it in my notes." Ellis returned Cave Thomas's smile, "I wish I could be the man to accompany you, but my face might be known."

"When must I be ready?"

"As soon as possible. I'll return in the morning. You will need papers."

Ellis left, promising to call again by eleven o'clock, his appointment with Sir Henry being at nine.

Cave Thomas locked the door behind Ellis and returned to the studio. He realised that if they were to be ready to travel within a short space of time, arrangements would need to proceed at a pace. When living in Germany, he'd encountered men who'd travelled in Prussia and beyond. He had a good idea of the magnitude of the task and the kind of terrain he'd have to cross. A great deal must be achieved before he could go.

Before seeking his bed, he opened a wall cupboard and took out a small bundle. Inside was a handgun. He tested its weight and then reached in again and pulled a box from the back of the cupboard. It held the empty powder flask and lead balls he'd placed there two years earlier, hoping never to need them again. He folded the cloth around the gun and put it back in the cupboard. He'd oil it in the morning.

2

A Reliable Friend
Monday 9th January 1854

Ellis arrived just as the clock struck eleven. The few hours' sleep, and had refreshed both men, and Ellis had already fitted in an hour-long meeting with Sir Henry. Cave Thomas showed him through to the studio. The newly oiled revolver lay on the table. Ellis walked over and picked up the gun, feeling its weight.

"A Navy Colt," he said. "How did you get hold of this?"

"I acquired it when I was in Munich some time ago. There was a little local trouble.

I was encouraged to arm myself before going south into the mountains."

"A little local trouble?"

"Nothing with which you need to concern yourself. But the gun was useful."

"Did you use it?"

"Only as a warning."

"And now?"

"It's been locked away for two years but seems to be in good condition. I'm confident I could still use it. I'll only carry it as a precaution."

"We certainly don't wish you to shoot your way into St Petersburg. However, with matters as they are, we can't tell what you might have to face."

Ellis began to question him again about a choice of companion but stopped as Cave Thomas's expression reminded him that less than twelve hours had elapsed since the artist had agreed to the task. Ellis watched as he wrapped the revolver in its cloth and placed it back in the cupboard, together with the flask and lead shot.

"I'll need powder and percussion caps. Perhaps you could get them for me?"

Ellis nodded in acknowledgement of Thomas's proficiency. Cave Thomas decided to press him for more details.

"Mr Ellis, this mission has clearly been discussed at length. If you already have a plan, why not tell me what it is? My own

28

thoughts are still quite fluid, but I'm happy to share them with you."

Ellis regarded Cave Thomas. 'The man has a quiet assurance about him,' he'd told Sir Henry. 'He's a man who can take stock of a situation, consider his options and then make a firm decision: a strength, but his lack of experience and training might count against him, if placed in sudden peril and required to act quickly.' Setting these thoughts aside, he said,

"We've looked into the best way of approaching the problem. Any mission must be informal, small, and able to find its way into Russia far away from any conflict. We expect confrontation to be in the south and east, so you should ideally travel in through the Baltic."

"Impossible, I'd say, at this time of year!"

"The time of year is definitely against us – the sea will be frozen hard by now. You must go by land."

"My own thoughts," Cave Thomas smiled. He took a large atlas from a shelf and the two men sat down to pore over its pages. Taking an old paintbrush, Cave Thomas pointed out the route he had selected. Would Ellis agree?

"The first part is easy: Paris, then across to Germany. My preferred route would be via Berlin, a place I know well. I'd be able to buy provisions there, then take the train to the Russian border… well, as near to it as possible."

"Via Warsaw or Königsberg?"

"Königsberg, I think. The road beyond there will be more reliable – the ice should be solid and the river crossings easier."

"But surely the ice will be more compromised nearer to the sea? Wouldn't it be better to cross the rivers further upstream?"

"No, Ellis. Trust me on this – the crossings at Tilsit and Riga are likely to be more dependable. It has to be Königsberg."

"Very well. I'll take your word for it," Ellis showed just a little scepticism. "I'll arrange for tickets for the ferry across to Calais. The best route from there would be via Ghent where you could rest overnight before going on to Dusseldorf. Our man would meet you there."

"Why?"

"You'll need papers. I can get most of them together before you leave London, but there will be others. These, you'll have to collect along the way."

"Will that not draw attention to me?"

"I think not. It's customary practice. You would stand out more if you didn't have to stop." Recalling his previous journeys on the continent, Cave Thomas saw some sense in this. Ellis was right.

"My companion; he would need to be approved, of course."

"We must know who he is and that he can be trusted."

"As I mentioned yesterday, I have someone in mind to ask. If he's prepared to join me, I'll pass on his name at once, but I'd prefer to have a free hand at this point, if that is in order?"

"Sound him out, by all means, but avoid going into detail until…"

"Of course." Cave Thomas looked at the map and made a few calculations. Four days to Berlin, then Königsberg, another twelve hours or so to the Russian border, by road, and then… And the sights along the way! He must make sure there was room for his sketchbook. Already, the treadmill of worry was sliding from his shoulders. What better cure for love than such an adventure?

Ellis traced a line across the map. "Berlin – Königsberg – Riga, and then?" He raised his eyes to Cave Thomas's.

"Riga is 250 miles from Königsberg, I believe. Then another 400 to St Petersburg. I imagine that leg will be by sledge – or rather, carriage and runners. You know how they fix these things to run on road or ice and snow?" Ellis nodded.

"If all goes well, the journey could be made in ten or eleven days – but might take a little longer, in view of the recent thaws."

"No quicker?" Ellis stood up and moved over to the large studio window. He gazed out of it to the grey scene below. Cave Thomas joined him. The January cold sucked heat from his hand, where it rested on the sill. If it was as cold as this, here in London, what dreadful cold would await him in Russia? In all, two weeks or more to reach St Petersburg 'if all goes well' – and how long, if possible, to return?

"We must reconsider the date of your departure," Ellis said, turning to Cave Thomas. "I had thought Friday 20th would be soon enough, but we must bring it forward. Can you be ready by Monday next?"

Cave Thomas returned to the atlas, closed it and replaced it on the shelf.

"Yes," he answered simply. "But I'd prefer to go on Tuesday. I cannot carry the gold in a strongbox – it must be concealed. That will take time. I will need a full week."

"If all is ready and your companion approved, let us try for Tuesday then – as early as possible."

The two men went through all the other arrangements and Ellis parted from Cave Thomas, apparently confident in his choice and with a full list of what must be put together to take to his meeting with Sir Henry.

Left to himself, Cave Thomas began his preparations. He would need warm clothes from the start, and was careful to pick out scarves, socks and gloves, and the many layers of clothing that would be necessary. By the time he crossed the Russian frontier, he'd need them all. Satisfied, he packed everything in a sturdy leather case and tried its weight in his hand. It would do, for now.

Remembering his duty to his sister, Emily, he scribbled her a note, warning her that he might be late for her tea party that afternoon. He had promised to attend but it would make an encounter with Jane Durdin inevitable. With a sigh, he sealed the envelope and then he went out to post the note before continuing through the icy streets to his club.

The club doorman welcomed Cave Thomas and relieved him of his hat and coat.

"Snow on the way, sir, I shouldn't wonder."

Cave Thomas smiled.

"Warmer in here, though," he said, and passed through the open doorway into the main room, where he joined the informal group gathered round a good fire. He scanned the room looking for the man he'd hoped to meet. He was there but tucked in a corner; their encounter would have to wait awhile.

"Good day to you, Thomas!" Madox Brown greeted his friend warmly. "No need for introductions; you know everyone here, I think," he said, with a sweeping gesture. Cave Thomas acknowledged the nods of welcome. Most were well known to him.

"Done any good work recently, Thomas?" It was young Stephens, who fancied himself as something of an art critic. "I hear you've taken to portraiture."

"I've been working hard on a variety of pieces – not just portraits. I hope to have something worth showing in the exhibition this year."

Madox Brown, who had seen the painting, looked pleased. "It's exceptionally fine work, Stephens. You must come along and see it as soon as Thomas can be persuaded to show the piece to anyone."

"I hope that will be soon," Stephens replied.

31

Cave Thomas sat down by Madox Brown. He had nothing to fear from Stephens. He'd known him for years – ever since the days of *The Germ* magazine, back in '49. They'd both had a hand in that, but it had been Cave Thomas's favoured name for the Arts and Poetry magazine which had been chosen. A pity that the publication had lasted so short a time; another of the Pre-Raphaelite Brotherhood's ideas which had fallen by the wayside. The trouble was, that the group was made up of such opposing figures. He glanced across at Rossetti. He avoided him when he could, but there could be no avoiding him this afternoon. Cave Thomas couldn't forgive him for the way he'd squandered Ford Madox Brown's money when he'd lived with him as a student. He'd repaid his teacher's kindness by leaving him cold and hungry, at a time when he'd been in much need.

Rossetti, who was standing at the edge of the group, laughed. "Maybe he'll beat you, Fred – his painting completed before your poem! How many lines does it stretch to now – nine, is it?"

Frederick Stephens looked annoyed. "You know exactly how long the poem is, Rossetti – you were there when I read it. But you're a fine one to start casting stones."

Now it was Rossetti's turn to look annoyed, but he drank his coffee and kept silent. Eventually, he set down his cup and left, hoping, perhaps, to find a more sympathetic audience at home.

Meanwhile, the group had split up, and several people moved away to continue their discussion in another room. Cave Thomas stayed by the fire. As the clamour of voices slowly faded, he judged the time was right to make his move. James Robertson, a quiet man, dressed sombrely in black, cut a solemn figure. He'd kept out of the group conversation. Seeing him alone with his newspaper, Cave Thomas left Madox Brown and walked over to him.

"Good day to you Robertson. How are you keeping?"

The man looked up. "I'm well, thank you, Cave Thomas. It's kind of you to ask." He closed the paper and put it down. He and Cave Thomas had struck up a friendship four years previously, during the Great Exhibition. Their ideas about art and science ran along similar lines.

"I was sorry to hear about your father." Cave Thomas noted that Robertson still wore a jet pin in his cravat.

"His death was a great loss. My sisters sorely miss him."

Cave Thomas knew only a little about Robertson's family. He'd not seen much of James Robertson since '52, and then, only in connection with his work. However, he knew that Robertson's mother was a talented artist, living in Russia. Hence his current interest in her son.

"And how is your mother? She was unable to return home for the funeral, I understand."

"It was impossible last year, but my father's death has forced her hand. With Father gone, she's needed at home."

"A difficult time for her to travel. It's a pity that she didn't return earlier. Surely there's been time since last summer?"

"She'd have come, but she had commitments at the Russian court: several portraits to be finished. She couldn't leave before they were in the hands of her patrons." Cave Thomas picked up the discarded paper.

"Is there much in here about Russia?"

"Enough to concern me. I hate to think of her there, alone."

So, matters stood exactly as Cave Thomas had been led to believe. The comments he'd heard, here and there, had pointed to this.

Mrs Robertson's story had interested him for years. She'd spent more time in Russia, in recent years, than at home in London with her family. Her husband had apparently looked upon his wife's career, as a portrait artist, with a kindly eye.

"It's high time she returned to England," Robertson continued, "but with war increasingly likely, it's becoming more difficult." He paused, "I intend to go to St Petersburg and bring her home."

Cave Thomas looked at him. "That won't be a simple matter. Are your plans in place?"

"Nothing definite," Robertson replied, "but the sooner I go, the better. In two-months' time, war might have closed the roads into Russia."

"How well do you know the territory?" Cave Thomas was curious. He knew that Robertson had travelled a little but was uncertain how extensively.

"I've spent time in France and Italy," Robertson continued, "but I've never been into Russia."

Ellis had told Cave Thomas to be cautious. It was important that he didn't betray the true reason for his trip until Robertson had been approved by Sir Henry. However, Cave Thomas felt free to explore a little further.

"I've been thinking of making a trip out that way, myself. I've friends in Berlin and Munich whom I'd like to see while it's still possible to travel. How would you like a companion? You ought not to go into Russia alone. I could certainly travel with you as far as Germany and, if you like, come with you and take a look at St Petersburg. I speak Russian, you know, which might be useful."

James Robertson's eyes widened in disbelief. "Are you seriously making such an offer? I can think of no-one better to have with me, if I were in a tight corner! My own Russian is very limited – I've never visited there."

"I've become restless, Robertson. I need to be on the move. London is stultifying. If I'm to expand my work and my understanding, I need to see more than a few smoke-blackened streets, in the rain. I'd be delighted to come with you."

"A trip to St Petersburg will hardly be easy." Robertson's initial enthusiasm faltered as he considered all the journey might entail. "There will doubtless be some danger in making it now, in the winter. The distance, the transport, the poor roads, and the severe cold will be enemy enough, setting aside the political situation."

Cave Thomas needed to convince him of the genuine nature of his offer. Maybe his sister, Emily, could help persuade him.

"What are you doing this afternoon, Robertson? I've been invited to join my sister, for tea. Why not come along with me? Emily would like to see you, and George might drop in for a while. They're not long back from their honeymoon and eager to see old friends."

Robertson accepted at once. He'd dreaded the task of fetching his mother home, but if Thomas was serious in his offer, the journey would lose some of its terror. It would be good to discuss it at greater length. The two men left the club together, deep in conversation.

3

Thin Ice
Monday 9th January 1854 (afternoon)

It was a couple of miles to the address in Camden, so they had plenty of time to talk about the different ways of travelling to and in the land of the Czar. Robertson, it emerged, was now well versed in the differences between troikas and carriage sleds. Cave Thomas was tempted to take the conversation further, but recalling Ellis's warnings, shut it down as they turned into the street where Emily and George now lived. Cave Thomas explained that his sister lodged with friends. The afternoon would have two hostesses: Emily, and Jane Durdin, the wife of John Durdin, Cave Thomas's friend, who was a banker.

They reached the house just in time for tea. The door was opened by a maid, who greeted Cave Thomas by name.

"Good afternoon Mr Thomas. Mrs Durdin and Mrs Law are expecting you."

"I've brought a friend – I'm sure Mrs Law will be pleased to see him."

The two men left their coats with the maid and passed through the narrow hall into a parlour which seemed full of people. A child separated himself from the throng and grabbed Cave Thomas by the hand.

"Uncle Thomas, Uncle Thomas, come and see!" He dragged Cave Thomas across the room to where his Christmas present stood in place of honour on a table. "Look! I have a box of soldiers!"

The child pointed at the lead figures, begging Cave Thomas to take a closer look.

"Well Harry, what a lucky boy you are! I hope you will take good care of them. You could make a parade ground for them to march on."

"Yes, Maggie said she would help me."

Harry's older sister, Margaret, approached them.

"Good afternoon, Uncle Thomas. Mama would like to see you. Can you come?"

She distracted Harry, who would have monopolised Cave Thomas, by suggesting that the other gentleman might like to see his soldiers. Then she led Cave Thomas through to another room, which looked out over the narrow garden. Here, Jane Durdin had just finished nursing baby William, and was enjoying a few moments' peace.

"Here he is, Mama."

Margaret tickled her baby brother affectionately under the chin as he sat on his mother's lap, then slipped out of the room.

"How are you, Jane?" Cave Thomas asked, eyes fixed on his baby godson.

"I'm well, as is young William. See, he takes an interest in everything," she added as the baby grabbed at her locket and tried to stuff it in his mouth. She gently disengaged his hand and distracted him with a toy. "It's good to see you. I feared you were unwell when you failed to join us last week."

Cave Thomas recalled the day. He'd sent a note, feeling unable to join the family and watch John carve yet another Sunday roast. Jane clearly had no idea of the agony he endured, acting one part and battling with another. He apologised for his absence and sought to avoid further discussion of the matter.

"I hope you don't object. I've brought a friend with me," he said. "I left him admiring Harry's soldiers and being welcomed by Emily, whom he knows."

"Who is he?"

"James Robertson."

"Mr Robertson? Yes, I remember him. He was part of the group who worked with you on your schemes for the Great Exhibition Hall, was he not?"

'She has such a good memory,' thought Cave Thomas. 'How much more does she see?' He wondered whether she'd noted his irregular visits, his sudden trip abroad, his reluctance to be left alone with her.

"Let me fetch him," he said, and stepped back into the parlour. There he rescued Robertson from Harry's attentions and took him to meet Jane.

"Good afternoon, Mr Robertson. Welcome to Kingston Russell Place. I was so deeply sorry to learn about your father. A sad loss to your family."

Once again, Cave Thomas was surprised by Jane's knowledge. Little evaded her quiet observation.

"You're exceedingly kind, Mrs Durdin. Thank you for your concern. I hadn't realised that Mr and Mrs Law lodged with you – Cave Thomas only mentioned it on the way here."

"Where is your mother, Mr Robertson?" asked Jane "Surely not still in Russia?"

"I'm afraid she is. It's my aim to travel there as soon as possible and escort her home. With all this talk of war, I don't like to think of her being out of the country."

Jane rang for the servant, "Baby William is tired and needs his nap," she said. "Mr Robertson, you must go back to the tea party, or all the cake will have gone."

The nursery maid entered the room and baby William stretched his arms out to her. She carried him away to his cot. Robertson returned to the parlour, but Jane touched Cave Thomas's arm, wishing to detain him.

"William," she said. "Why did you bring Mr Robertson?"

"I met him at my club. He seemed sad and alone. I thought it would cheer him to meet old friends."

"You were quiet when he told me about his intended trip. Do you intend to go with him?"

Once again, Cave Thomas was struck by Jane's insight.

"Yes, I do," he said.

"Why?"

"I need a change. My work is becoming stale. The travel will refresh me. And Robertson needs a friend."

"Four exceptionally good reasons, William. I wonder how long you've had to practise them."

"Ah, Jane, I'm discovered!" Cave Thomas returned. "I am, of course, either a spy or a man addicted to Russian tea and samovars."

Jane laughed. "You're making fun of me now," she said. "Come, let's return to the party. But promise me you'll take care of yourself and come back safely to your godson - and his family."

"I'll do my best," Cave Thomas replied. It was unlike Jane to probe so deeply. He was left with the uneasy feeling that he had missed something – that there was more to Jane's detaining him than at first met the eye. He must be careful – and observant, too.

Re-entering the parlour, the pair separated – Jane to help host the tea and William to seek out his sister, who was deep in conversation with Robertson. Emily looked radiant. Her happiness was infectious and her look of pure joy as her husband George joined them, was a delight to see. They lacked sufficient funds to move into their own home, at present, but it wouldn't take long for them to save enough. Emily, loving and gentle, with a slight shyness which made her an excellent listener and an astute judge of character, was delighted that her brother had joined the party. She moved across to him whilst George went to talk to Jane.

"Jane is so kind," Emily confided to her brother. "We only have rooms in her house, but she treats us like a sister and brother. Look at her now! You'd never guess that I'm her lodger. She makes this party mine as much as hers."

"Well, it is yours Emily – we're met to hear about your honeymoon in the Lakes and to see that you and George are not at one another's throats."

Emily laughed. "William, you're a dreadful tease. Can't you see how happy I am?"

"Of course, I can, Emily! I brought Robertson here to cheer him up. He's still grieving for his father and now finds he must go to St Petersburg to bring his mother home."

"Oh, poor man!" Emily's natural sympathy was roused. "What a terrible journey – and now, in winter. Oh, William!"

"So, you see, I cannot let him go alone…"

Emily took his hand. "No, surely not! William, are you mad?"

"I'm familiar with much of the way. Of course, the last part of the journey won't be easy, but I've always had a wish to see St Petersburg."

"Oh, William, not now! Not with war coming?" Anxiety clouded her face as her happiness was suddenly overshadowed by fear.

"Emily, you must see that I can't let him go alone. He needs a friend and I'm not tied down. I'm free to go tomorrow if it pleases me."

"If you must, then you must," Emily replied, as near to being cross as she'd ever come with this much-loved brother. "George!" she called, seeing him nearby, "come here and persuade William to be sensible."

George joined them. "I've never known him to be otherwise. What's the trouble?"

"I'm planning a short trip to Russia, with Robertson, to bring home his elderly mother. He could do with a translator."

"Are you, indeed? Well I envy you the adventure. I'd come with you if I were still single."

"Oh, George!" Emily knew she was beaten. "Very well, William, go with our blessing, but be sure to write to us and let us know that you've not been eaten by bears."

She smiled bravely and squeezed Cave Thomas's hand. Then, for his ear only, she said,

"Just so long as it's not because of Jane. She has heard about the painting you know – George let it slip."

Emily left him and went to attend to her other guests, leaving her brother to consider her words of warning. There was only one painting that Emily could have meant. Cave Thomas's heart flinched as he considered the possible repercussions were Jane – or John – to see his portrait of *The Goddess*.

Thankfully, the rest of the afternoon passed without incident. Cave Thomas and Robertson, having arrived together, left together. Robertson seemed much more cheerful than earlier in the day. An afternoon in pleasant company had raised his spirits.

"Emily and George seem happy together," he said. "Your sister was singing your praises. According to her, there's nothing you cannot do!"

Emily had always looked up to her brother, believing him to be utterly dependable. Her comments had obviously affected Robertson. As conversation returned to Russia, the trip now seemed to be an accepted fact. Robertson was going and he would like Cave Thomas to go with him.

The two men returned to Cave Thomas's studio and had supper together. Cave Thomas used the time to familiarise himself with Robertson's preoccupations and connections, gently probing to make sure that he really was the right companion for the mission. They parted as friends, Robertson believing he'd found a travelling companion and Cave Thomas keen to contact Ellis with the news that Robertson would provide the perfect cover. He sent his promised note to Ellis, telling him that Robertson would be at the studio at noon the following day. If Ellis found problems with Robertson, there could be difficulties – but Cave Thomas refused to meet trouble halfway.

4

Too Much Gold
Tuesday 10th January 1854

Cave Thomas hadn't slept well, and Tuesday morning came all too soon. Since Herbert Ellis had knocked on his door, late on Sunday night, he'd hardly stopped. His brain was on fire as he went over his lists again and again. There were all the preparations for the journey, the packing to be completed, the travel papers and tickets to gather together (no, Ellis would do that), communication home to be established, friends and relations to be told, and so many more things competing for his attention. He'd also minutely dissected the events of the past few days, questioning everything that had happened. Why had he been chosen? Who had suggested his name? Cave Thomas felt certain that he'd missed something there. Was there more to the connection with his father than he'd worked out? One way to discover would be to go and ask him - but how to do this without divulging the true purpose for his journey? Aware that he might have gone ahead of himself with Robertson he didn't want to make the same mistake regarding his own father.

His thoughts ran over his initial meeting with Robertson. There'd been nothing strange about his name coming into Cave Thomas's mind, or in their meeting at the club. He was certain that the encounter hadn't been orchestrated, so that was a shadow he could chase from his mind. He knew enough of the man and, come to that, of the people gathered at the club that day, to feel sure that there'd been no unseen hand behind the meeting. Ellis worked for the government, but in what capacity Cave Thomas wasn't sure. He'd assumed that Sir Henry was a man to be trusted, but how could he be certain? His mind went back the time he'd helped his father hang paintings in the Royal gallery. It was suddenly all very mysterious and filled him with foreboding. He wondered who Sir Henry was really working for? And how much Ellis knew.

Ellis arrived at noon, but a note delivered at a quarter past eleven had warned Cave Thomas that Robertson would be late. He'd been to buy foreign currency and the bank had insisted on asking countless questions. The note said that he'd be with Cave Thomas as soon as he could. Ellis seemed unconcerned.

"A pity we have to let him do all this. We could have furnished him with the money, but it would look suspicious if he didn't do it for himself. You'll need to do the same, Mr Thomas. You will, of course, be recompensed for all you expend… upon your return."

Cave Thomas smiled. His doubts about Ellis disappeared. Only a government department would quibble over money. This should have caused Cave Thomas some anxiety but had the opposite effect. He felt certain that he'd survive to send in his bill.

Once Robertson had joined them, Ellis took the lead. He introduced himself to Robertson as Cave Thomas's friend, saying that they'd met a few years ago when they were working abroad.

"Since returning to England, I've been kept busy with work, but I was delighted to meet up with Cave Thomas again. It's been good to reminisce about our time in Munich."

Robertson glanced at Cave Thomas, who picked up on Ellis's theme.

"Happy days, but we're in sadder times now. Russian greed is driving a wedge between nations."

"I gather you have reason to be anxious about the prospect of war," Ellis directed his words to Robertson. "Cave Thomas tells me your mother is in St Petersburg." Robertson turned to Cave Thomas with a questioning look.

"Yes. My mother has lived there for some years."

"I was telling Ellis of your difficulties," Cave Thomas explained. "And how I hoped to assist you in bringing your mother back to England."

Robertson seemed to hesitate, weighing up how much to reveal.

"My mother is far from well. She's lived in St Petersburg for some years, working as a portrait artist. Her style was once popular and she received many good commissions, but lately, she's fallen upon hard times. It doesn't take much for public taste to change."

"Sick, and in need?" said Ellis sympathetically. "I can understand your concern. Do you think that things might go against her in St Petersburg, Mr Robertson? I thought our people there had good friends among the most influential people in the city. But perhaps you know more than I do?"

If Ellis had laid a careful trap to discover how much Robertson knew, he appeared happy with the man's subsequent answer.

"Those influential people – the Russian elite," Robertson said, with a certain amount of bitterness, "are the very people whose lack of concern for my mother have led to her difficulties. The British community has been kind, but she's owed a great deal of

41

money by Russian patrons. My mother's always been a diligent letter writer. From what she's written it's clear that the British living in St Petersburg form an important part of society in the city. But war is always uncertain. I wouldn't like to think of my mother trapped there and finding herself a prisoner."

Cave Thomas watched Ellis. From his manner, it was clear that he'd made up his mind about Robertson. He turned to Cave Thomas and said,

"I think our friend should hear what we know about our compatriots in St Petersburg, don't you?"

Cave Thomas nodded, then sat back and let Ellis do his job, which he did very well. By the time he'd finished, Robertson was all for boarding the next train to Dover.

"Mr Robertson," Ellis calmed him down. "We need to plan in detail, and I would appreciate your ideas about this…"

With these words, he drew a small bag from his pocket and dropped it on the table. It burst open and about three dozen gold coins rolled across the table.

"There are coins worth thirty guineas there. Gather them up, put them back into the bag and then feel the weight of it."

Cave Thomas followed Ellis's instructions and then handed the leather bag to Robertson. Both were forcibly struck by its weight.

"Our people in St Petersburg, who work as part of the British Factory, are owed a total of over two thousand pounds in port dues." Ellis allowed this figure to sink in. "We were approached by the Mercantile company concerned with a request for assistance. At present, we have the Emperor of Russia's promise that all conditions of the existing (and historical) treaty with the company will be honoured. But we all know what that means."

"Very little!" Robertson interjected. Ellis nodded grimly.

"In time of war, nothing is sacred. At the very least, it will become impossible to get the money to St Petersburg. At worst, the treaty will be torn up and our people thrown upon the mercy of God. We must do our best to get the money owed to the British Factory to St Petersburg, while it can still be done. This means smuggling it in."

Cave Thomas watched as the truth of what was being asked of them dawned upon Robertson, who realised after a few seconds that Cave Thomas had known this all along. The signs of his inner turmoil were obvious. He looked from one man to the other, uncertain whom to trust. Cave Thomas had the sense to stay silent.

Ellis went on, "It comes to you as a shock, I can see that. But you must see that we need men of probity and honour, men who are not known by certain factions in Russia, who can be trusted to help our countrymen and women there. You fit this description perfectly." He paused. "You are ideally qualified to take the money to St Petersburg."

Robertson turned to Cave Thomas. "You knew," was all he said.

"Yes. Mr Ellis came to see me just a few days ago. Like you, I was shocked and perturbed. Take a little time, James. Think it over. Nobody can make you do this."

"I thought you wished to help me, but all the time you had this in mind."

"The one doesn't exclude the other. I couldn't speak of this until Mr Ellis gave me leave. We are all men under authority. Our ultimate authority is God. So, take your time and pray, as I did." Cave Thomas held out his hand to his friend. "If you decide against this, I won't hold it against you."

Robertson accepted Cave Thomas's hand and shook it firmly but couldn't speak. Cave Thomas turned to Ellis. "I'll vouch for this man. Whatever he decides, your secret is safe with him."

Ellis stood up and walked over to the window. The first flakes of the winter's snow were beginning to fall, an apt reminder of the terrible circumstances in which all concerned with the British Factory stood. But he didn't comment upon it; he merely said,

"I trust you entirely Mr Robertson. Take what time you need but, I beg you, be as quick in your deliberations as you can. Many lives depend upon it."

Robertson rose and went to join him by the window.

"I don't need time to think about it. You forget, I have an elderly mother there. I will go, and I will help Cave Thomas take the money to the people there. I've heard of their goodness, the way they helped during the great flood, and more recently, when the foreign workers were in need. They gave generously to the relief work, often giving more than they could afford. They need our help now. We cannot let them down."

"Good man." It was Ellis's turn to shake Robertson by the hand.

"There's just one problem," said Cave Thomas, thoughtfully as the dangers of the task ahead dawned upon him. He was still seated at the table, playing with the bag of gold, shifting it from one hand to the other. "Two thousand pounds, in gold will be a considerable weight! How are we to conceal and carry it all – and at what peril?"

43

5

The Devil in the Detail
Wednesday 11th – Thursday 12th January 1854

The next two days passed by in a race to prepare everything. Ellis arranged for both men to meet Sir Henry Loughton. This had to be done discreetly. They met on Thursday evening, at an address just off the Strand. A man Cave Thomas didn't recognise admitted them. He led them up two flights of stairs and opened the door to a room which looked out towards the back of the building. Sir Henry, together with Ellis and another man (whose name they were never to learn) were already there.

"Come in," Sir Henry welcomed them. "Sit down, won't you?" They took the seats indicated and waited for him to continue. "Ellis tells me that you are both willing to perform a vital service on behalf of our compatriots in St Petersburg."

Cave Thomas and Robertson nodded.

"I see you have both travelled on the Continent and know your way about. Do you both have experience with firearms? I believe you do, Mr Thomas."

"Yes, and Mr Robertson is not a stranger to a hunting rifle."

"I'll practise with a handgun," said Robertson. Sir Henry seemed satisfied with this.

"You both have several languages, including Russian," he went on. "You are both single and free to go immediately?"

"Yes," they said together.

"Good. Your cover, as artists, could prove useful. The financial support we intend to send is to be kept secret, you understand. We can't have any Tom, Dick or Harry learning that there's gold on the move. I'd much prefer to use my own men – experts in secret work, but your names have been placed before me as more suitable. It won't be easy. Do you think you're up to the task?"

The questioning went on. It became clear to Cave Thomas that there were others pulling strings here – men above Sir Henry. Again, his thoughts ran to the framing of the Royal portraits. The Prince Consort was a Prussian.

At length, Sir Henry came to a halt. He coughed loudly, as if finalising his decision.

"We'd better get on with telling you what exactly we want you to do."

Sir Henry laid out a broad plan of the mission. He made it clear that the men would have to look to their own safety for much of the journey, but that there would be agents of the Crown ready to help them, at least as far as the border with Russia.

"I must remind you of the importance of conducting yourselves as artists, at all times. On no account must you permit anyone to think that you're travelling for any other purpose. You must appear to be two artists on your way to meet another artist, Mr Robertson's mother. This will help you to behave more naturally and avoid unwanted attention. To this end, it might be wise to conceal just how fluent you are in the language."

His reasons for stressing all of this were clear enough. If anything went wrong, the British Government would wash its hands of them. They couldn't be permitted to affect matters on the wider stage, this close to international conflict. It wasn't spelt out in so many words, but neither man was a fool; each knew that they must fend for themselves if Britain, and the other members of the Four Powers,[1] became embroiled in war.

They both agreed.

Sir Henry turned to Ellis. "Mr Ellis will go over your travel arrangements. Mr Robertson, I gather you have already seen the bank about money. Mr Thomas, you will do the same tomorrow. I should remind you that it won't do for you to be seen together from now on – until you travel. Mr Ellis…"

Ellis stood up and traced out the route on a large map, which lay spread out across the desk.

"The difficult part," he said, "will be judging the roads across the Russian border. Until then, everything should run quite smoothly, as transport has not yet been affected by hostilities. There's been something of a thaw in part of the region, so the river crossings may be suspect. We can't advise you at this stage but will pass on any information we receive before you leave Germany, so that you can alter your route if necessary."

"The first part should be easy enough," said Cave Thomas. "Once we've bought winter furs and food in Berlin, we should be able to get ourselves and our luggage as far as Riga. What has been

---

[1] The Four Powers: an alliance made up of the Ottoman Empire*, France, the United Kingdom and Sardinia *Modern day Turkey – the Empire, which had covered much of the Mediterranean coast was much reduced in size by 1854.

decided about wheeled transport?" Hiring or buying a conveyance fit for the Russian part of the journey still needed agreement.

"There are clear advantages to purchasing an equipage to take you into Russia," said Ellis. "One of the carriage things that can be bolted to runners. What do you call them?"

"I'm not sure they have a name," said Cave Thomas, "a 'post carriage on a sledge' seems all the description we'll need. It must be large enough to hold us and all our luggage safely. A troika wouldn't do."

"A post carriage it will be, then," Ellis agreed. "Once your luggage is aboard, it can remain with the carriage and thus avoid too much talk. Taking passage on a public carriage would open you to a whole range of possible hazards. The only concern I have is that the financial outlay may draw attention to you." Ellis turned to Sir Henry. "Sir?"

Sir Henry cleared his throat. "As I've made clear from the start, it was not my idea to use untrained men. But, since it appears that we must, we'll do our best to keep you away from any unnecessary exposure to danger. My own belief is that the security and privacy of the personal carriage outweighs disadvantages of cost. However, you may wish to carry up to two more passengers. We could, if you like, find a couple of hand-picked men to join you; as strangers, you understand."

"How would that add to our safety? It would make us a more obvious target." Robertson was worried. Sir Henry's evident unease had sapped his confidence. He continued, "I'm not sure how we'll be received by our drivers and the horse stations along the way. Surely, if we carry our own men with us, it's possible that we might be thought to be spies."

"And I'm not sure there'd be room," said Cave Thomas. "After all, we'll have a fair quantity of luggage."

The conversation went on for some time, each new concern being thrashed out and decisions made. Then, at last, they reached the subject of how to conceal the gold. This is where Cave Thomas was able to lead the discussion.

"You've told us that we'll be carrying the money as coins. I've worked out the weight," he passed a sheet of calculations to Mr Ellis, who read it, then handed it to Sir Henry. "As you can see, it will be no mean feat to carry it undetected. My suggestion is that we should divide the money into several discrete packages. I've tested my luggage and calculate that I could carry up to about three or four pounds in weight, well packed, without anything appearing

46

unusual; that is, if I split my clothing between two bags. Robertson could do the same. If we do that, we could carry over half a stone in our personal bags alone."

"But that's not much more than a fifth of the weight," Sir Henry pointed out.

"Yes, and in some ways the most vulnerable. Anyone suspecting us of carrying valuables would expect them to be with us all the time. The very first place they would look would be in our bags."

Ellis and Sir Henry nodded in agreement.

"So, we must conceal the greater part of the money in our other luggage, where it would be less likely to be discovered."

Robertson took over here. "As you know, my mother is a portrait artist, living and working in St Petersburg. What could be more natural for a son to visit his mother and to bring a friend - also a portrait artist - to meet her? And what could be less suspicious than these two men carrying materials to her: materials she has requested?"

He drew out a small sketch book and opened it to a page covered in careful drawings, depicting the cross-section of two packing cases, in which were drawn layers of artists' materials interspersed with dummy pigment boxes: each to contain a cache of coins, concealed in plaster of Paris. He passed the book around.

"I believe that another twenty or thirty pounds of coins could be concealed in these crates.

But Cave Thomas has the most ingenious plan…"

It was Cave Thomas's turn to stand up. He pulled a folded sheet of paper from his pocket and spread it out on the table, on top of the maps.

"As you know, gentlemen, my family is famed for its work in gilding and moulding, particularly in connection with frame making. Here are some of our recent designs. The frames are strongly made. They are held together by pegs – butterfly pegs – which combine strength with the ease of removal in order to adjust the pressure in the frame. Our most popular line – in, shall we say royal circles? - is this flat frame. It has an oval aperture for the portrait, with ornate gesso work on a raised and moulded base, in each of the corners. The whole is then gilded and packed in such a way that the gilding is not damaged in transit."

"Surely you are not suggesting you will carry the rest of the gold as *gilding*?" Sir Henry's disbelief was almost comical.

"No sir, that would be impractical." Cave Thomas smothered a smile. "No, my suggestion is that the gold should be concealed within the frames. Each of these corners could take two or three pounds of gold, hidden underneath the moulding and the gesso scrolls. We could even fit another couple of pounds along the edges of the frame. So long as the coins are firmly held in place and the weight evenly distributed, there'd be no suspicion that anything was amiss. We'll carry a little quantity of gold leaf for the gilding. If necessary, we could use it to distract thieves. Make it easy to steal and they'd be satisfied with that. It would be worth losing a little, in order to save the rest."

"How heavy would each frame be?" Ellis voiced everyone's thoughts.

"If we managed to conceal fourteen pounds of gold in each frame, the frames would weigh something like double that. Their style is misleading – they weigh less than one would think."

"So, the Russians would be fooled!" Sir Henry rubbed his hands together in delight, conceding that Cave Thomas was, after all, the perfect man for the task. The plan was ingenious. "How long will it take you to do this?"

"My father has a number of frames left over from a commission for… perhaps I should not mention the name. I could hollow out the sections, pack them and remould them in three days. It will take that long for the material to set hard. If my father or my brother could help, it could be done in two days."

"Your father, yes, but not your brother. Your father is known to us. But our enemies have eyes everywhere. Your family business must go on as if nothing were amiss. Let your brother take over the running of the business for a few days." Sir Henry was adamant.

"Very well. I'll ask my father."

"There's no need. I'll see him myself."

So, Sir Henry knew William Thomas senior. This confirmed what Cave Thomas had begun to think. His father's work for the royal palaces had placed him near to some very influential people. He began to see how his father was regarded by them. His mind flicked to the occasion when he'd encountered German speakers, the time he accompanied his father to the Palace. Yes, there was something deeper here – something of significance, perhaps, now that war was imminent.

The meeting ended. Each man knew what he had to do and was ready to perform his part. Robertson and Cave Thomas each felt reassured by the degree of detail put into the planning, although there were still many unknown problems to be overcome. They parted with handshakes all round and clear, unwritten, but memorised instructions regarding when and where to meet next. They left casually, as if departing from a social event. Anyone watching would have no idea of the business which had brought the men together.

Cave Thomas walked away from Covent Garden towards his parents' home. He knocked at the door and was admitted by Molly, their servant. Supper was still on the table. The delicious smell of the rich beef stew reminded Cave Thomas that he'd not eaten since morning. A place was made for him and his mother put a generous plateful before him. The family chatted around him, telling him their news, whilst Cave Thomas ate. He was able to bring news of Emily and George, having seen them so recently. Mrs Thomas intended to call upon them the next day if she wasn't needed in the workshop. Her husband smiled and told her to go 'and take the young couple my promise to come to see them soon.'

Chairs were pushed back, and William Thomas led his son through to the workshop to look at his new designs. The others, who'd heard him talk of little else for days, were happy to let Cave Thomas go alone. So it was, that the pair had the time they needed together, uninterrupted.

On entering the workshop, William Thomas closed and bolted the door, walked across to a corner and drew back a curtain, behind which lay several of the unwanted royal frames.

"You'll have come about these," he said.

"How did you know?"

"Never you mind, but let it be shown that the Thomas family lacks nothing in skill or in courage. I am proud of you. I'll do all I can to help. Have you brought the drawings?"

So, he knew about those, too. Cave Thomas handed his father the sketches.

"I see," he said. "Yes, I would go about it much the same way, although I have reservations about the filler. Plaster of Paris, you suggest – I think I can do better than that. I'll test a light-weight filler – one that will hold the coins in place and not add over-much to the weight of the frame. Could you come to me in the morning? With two of us working on the task, we could have the carving done by the afternoon and that would give plenty of time for the filler to dry before we apply the top finish."

"I'll need to arrange for the gold to be delivered."

"It's already arranged. Thirty-five pounds weight of gold coinage will be delivered – disguised as gesso powder, tomorrow morning. Sir Henry doesn't waste time."

"Father, do I have your blessing?"

"Of course." His father strove to hide his anxieties. "But promise me one thing – don't take more risks than you need to. Your mother must know nothing of your true purpose until you return. And make sure you do. As her eldest, you were ever her favourite."

Cave Thomas chuckled. "She had a strange way of marking the preference. I never felt myself her favourite." As he recalled, James, his younger by several years, had always had an easier time.

"That just shows you how even-handed she is – for James says that she favoured you!"

When Cave Thomas eventually sought his bed that night, his mind was racing with the speed at which matters were progressing. However, he felt curiously more confident than he had done hitherto and slept without dreaming. Perhaps to be active was the only way to escape his emotional torment.

He woke at six, refreshed and ready for the long day ahead. He washed, dressed in his work clothes and set off for the family workshop, to start the painstaking work of concealment.

6

Concealment
Friday 13th January 1854

William Thomas had been hard at work since before five. He greeted his son with a satisfied grunt.

"It's going better than I thought. I've completed the preparation of four frames and, as you see, am well on with the fifth."

Cave Thomas hung his coat on a peg and donned one of the workmen's aprons. He examined the frames his father had prepared, running a thumb over the carving. There were no rough edges. The work was impeccably executed.

"I'll complete the frames," his father went on. "Take a look at the other items. I have marked where you must cut into the wood."

The 'items' were piled up in a corner of the workshop: several stretchers, an easel and the boxes of pigment, discussed at their last meeting. Each bore signs of the master framer's hand.

"Whatever time did you start work this morning?" Cave Thomas asked, in wonder at the advances his father had made on the task.

"I couldn't sleep," was the simple reply. He glanced up and immediately looked away, under his son's questioning gaze. "If these are to be ready in time, the carving must be completed by mid-day, so that we can start work on concealing the gold this afternoon. The filler will take time to harden, and all must be perfect before you sail."

Cave Thomas saw the sense in this and, with only a few questions as to how he should approach the other pieces, set to work. There would be time enough later to gauge his father's mood. He was soon totally absorbed in the task, applying the skills he'd learnt as a boy, keen to match his father in his attention to detail. No-one bothered them. The family had been instructed to leave them alone; a changed schedule, exacting clients, pressure of work and so on, providing the excuse.

The morning slipped away steadily, the sounds of tools against wood measuring each passing minute. Piece by piece, the different items were worked upon, cleaned, placed to one side. First, they had to rough chisel away the wood, where the compartment was to be made, taking care that the wood didn't splinter, and that the frame or box remained intact. Once satisfied with this, finer tools were needed to cut away and finish the interior of the compartment, leaving just enough roughness for the filler to grip the wood securely. Each process required its own specific tool to gouge, plane, clean and finish. William Thomas's hand instinctively reached for the perfect piece, matching tool to task with unerring skill. His son occasionally fumbled, uncertain, changing one gouge for another, larger for smaller, square for pointed, new for old. But the skills of his youth gradually returned and by noon he had succeeded in catching up his father. The two men finished together, wiping cramped and dirty fingers down their aprons and stretching stiff backs.

"Good," was William Thomas's assessment of the work. "We've done it."

He handed Cave Thomas a broom and took another himself. Together, the two men cleared away the evidence of their work, set the workshop back to its usual appearance and placed the items they had been working on behind a curtain in the corner. There would be no need for further concealment until later that day.

Ellis arrived after their mid-day meal, accompanied by one of the men who'd been present when they met with Sir Henry. Cave Thomas didn't know his name and he remained unintroduced. With a nod from Ellis, the man checked the doors and slipped through to the main house, leaving them in the workshop. William Thomas raised no objection. His son watched the procedure thoughtfully.

"You will understand," Ellis said, quietly, "We must proceed with the utmost confidentiality and security. Everything depends upon that."

"Of course," William Thomas replied. "We're alone. The rest of the household is out. No-one is likely to return before five. We should have three good hours to work unobserved."

The man returned, having confirmed that the house was empty, and then set about checking the workshop. He walked round peering behind curtains, under work benches and inside cupboards, and opening and shutting doors. Apparently satisfied, he slipped out into the yard and round to the street. A moment or two later, there was a low rumble in the yard. Ellis signalled to Cave Thomas's father to open the workshop door, which he did, revealing two men, dressed in heavy overcoats, shifting packing cases in a covered cart. A third man stood guard, armed, Cave Thomas suspected, with a firearm, as well. There were other men, working for Ellis's department, placed at intervals around building and street, but none of those present were aware of how many, or where they were located – not even Ellis, himself.

The packing cases, of which there were six, were not large, but were clearly heavy. The gold! The men carried them, one by one, into the workshop and placed them on the floor. They took up much of the available space.

"Please sign for them." It was not a request. Ellis brought out a sheet of paper and laid it on the workbench, placing a pen and portable inkwell beside it.

William Thomas looked at the sheet and then eyed Ellis thoughtfully.

"I would prefer to inspect the delivery first, but I imagine that time is of the essence."

"It is."

"Very well." He signed.

"And you…" Ellis held out the pen to Cave Thomas.

Cave Thomas exchanged a glance with his father, who nodded slightly. He signed.

"Thank you, gentlemen. We'll allow you to return to your work. You will understand that evidence must be supplied, proving that you've done what you've undertaken to do. Until the… merchandise… is beyond these shores, it is my responsibility to ensure its safety. Once you set foot on the ferry, the responsibility will be yours." He turned to Cave Thomas. "By signing this paper, you've agreed to this arrangement. However, should any harm come to the merchandise once you've left England, neither you nor I are likely to be held to account for its retrieval. It's entirely possible that the vicissitudes of war might prove too great for a successful completion of the errand."

'An odd choice of word,' thought Cave Thomas.

"This man," the quiet, nameless man who'd checked the place was secure, "will remain here until he is satisfied that the initial task is completed. He, or his colleague, will stay with you until Tuesday. He will not inconvenience you."

Cave Thomas doubted that but kept silent.

Ellis pocketed the paper and writing materials, shook hands with them both, and left by the workshop door, which his agent closed and bolted behind him. The man turned to the Thomases and spoke for the first time.

"Sorry about the cloak and dagger nature of this business. All rather staged, I think. I can't give you my real name, but you may call me Martin. He's a saint I've always rather admired."

"Welcome to our workshop, Martin," said William Thomas. "Have you eaten?"

"No." The man looked sheepish. "Didn't have time."

"Fetch the man a plate of bread and cheese, and some of the porter, and I'll explain what happens next."

Cave Thomas did as his father asked and returned to find them both, sleeves rolled up, lifting a crate onto the workbench. Thomas senior had no intention of touching the gold until it had been counted, recorded, and the record signed and witnessed. The next hour was spent in itemising the contents of each crate, labelling it and getting Martin to witness the accuracy of the count. When they were done, William Thomas brought out sealing wax and sealed all but one of the crates, marking them with his unique cypher. He locked the signed papers in his desk and then sat down with the other two men to describe what he intended to do next.

Martin was a man of action. Standing about doing nothing was the part of his job he detested. He made it clear from the start that he would like to help in the work of concealment, so (apart from the regular patrols he had to make, to fulfil his role as guard and to reassure the unseen minions of the Service, who had the premises under watch, that all was well) he became their eager apprentice. He was quick to learn, admitting that he'd enjoyed helping his father with odd jobs, as a lad.

William Thomas amazed his son by bringing out several examples of filler, prepared earlier for testing purposes, using his own money as the hidden gold. When his father had said he'd been unable to sleep, he'd not exaggerated. He could only have snatched a couple of hours between his filler experiments and beginning the carving work. His companions watched in fascination as the carver and gilder checked each sample for strength, weight, any sign of movement, and ease of destruction. The samples had been made from offcuts, with compartments gouged out in the same way that father and son had used earlier. Each cavity had been filled with a sample of filler, which had set overnight. Each bore a number, denoting the mix. William Thomas stamped on them, dropped them, hit them with hammers, even poured water on them. He would pause periodically to shake them and to listen. One after another they began to disintegrate, some succumbing to rough treatment, others to prodding with chisels. Gradually, one sample emerged as superior to the rest. It had withstood all bad treatment and proved itself both light and strong. They all agreed. It was the one to use.

"Here is a list of the ingredients and their proportions." He handed it to Cave Thomas. "We'll make it up by the pint. I'd have liked time to test the correct thickness of gesso and the effect of gilding, but there isn't time, so we'll just have to hope that it lasts the journey. Cold as the weather is here, it will be far colder on the Continent. Again, we'll have to hope that the work is good enough."

"You've thought of most things, Father. The rest we must trust to God."

Martin grinned. "It looks good to me. Come on, show me how to make the mixture and I can be preparing it for you to use."

Before long, the men worked out a system which made the work go along easily. Martin was a practical man. He quickly determined how much filler was needed and when to fit in his tours of the property. By the time the light began to fade, they were well on with their task. The other members of the household were due at any time now.

"How much more have we to do?" Cave Thomas asked his father.

"Not much. We must try to finish and get everything put away before five. No-one in the house must know of this."

They laboured on with increased urgency. Every unexpected sound promised potential detection. Eventually, they completed the work on all the prepared frames, the stretchers and the easel. There just remained the pigment boxes, which would be quicker to do and easier to conceal. They forced their tired hands to work faster. At last, the final pint of filler was used up.

The men were cleaning their hands when Mrs Thomas called from the kitchen.

"Cook's back from her half day, and supper will be ready in half an hour. Can I come in?"

Martin nodded. Cave Thomas was nearest the door. He turned the key and flung it open in a clumsy clatter, hiding the fact that it had been locked against her.

"Meet our latest apprentice, my dear," said her husband. "Mr Martin is a friend of our son, keen to learn the trade. I invited him to come and work with me for a spell, before making up his mind."

"You're most welcome, sir," Mrs Thomas, who was always pleased to meet new people. "Will you join us for supper?"

"It would be a pleasure, Mrs Thomas." Martin slipped into this new role with ease. "As long as it's no trouble?"

"None at all, sir," came the reply, and Mrs Thomas returned to the kitchen to warn the cook.

Concealment, of many kinds, was well under way.

7

The Last of England
Tuesday 17th - Thursday 19th January 1854

All their luggage was safely stowed. The ship's moorings had been slipped and they were heading out to sea. Robertson stayed below, to guard their boxes and bags, but Cave Thomas went up on deck to watch the cliffs of England slowly recede. The past few days had been a jumble of work, meetings and preparation, during which time their undertaking had relentlessly grown in complexity and layers of secrecy. At every turn, a new problem arose, to be considered, discussed and a plan of action set in place. Each day had made him more aware of how exposed to danger he and Robertson would be. It felt good to be at sea, cut off from the intensity of so much intrigue.

He cast his mind back over the time spent with his father, earlier that week. Concealing the gold had proved arduous. His father, a perfectionist, had refused to rest until all was completed to his satisfaction. As he'd pointed out, the life of his first-born son might depend upon the job being done properly. Cave Thomas was grateful. No matter what he thought of his father's part in all of this (and he had yet to discover just how deep was his connection with Sir Henry) he knew he could rely on his father's meticulous work. When Ellis had checked the consignment, he'd been amazed. The balance and weight of the frames were right. He'd wondered at their skill and questioned whether the gold was really there. It was good to have Martin, to vouch for that.

The remaining gold - fitted into the false bottoms in their bags, squeezed into padded cavities in the packing cases and even into a spare pair of boots - would escape detection by all but the most probing of searches. Now they must trust to their planning and foresight, and to the reliability of Sir Henry's men, primed to meet them along the way. Cave Thomas was no fool. He'd sensed that they'd been watched throughout the period of preparation, by men hidden in plain sight. He'd not detected who they were but was certain they'd been there. It was curious how easily one became accustomed to the thought, even if it made for sleepless nights. He smiled. In all likelihood, he was following in his father's footsteps, entering the secret world of the government agent. He'd enjoy smoking a pipe or two with his father, one day, as they chewed over their exploits.

Once in Europe, Cave Thomas expected further scrutiny. The chance of their spotting any watchers would be slim, and he suspected that some of the eyes upon them might not be friendly ones. They would be exposed to danger from every angle, throughout the whole length of their journey. It wouldn't do to become complacent.

He gazed at the receding coastline. Busy though this past week had been, he'd failed to completely bury his troubles. His inner turmoil, although overshadowed by all that had happened, had not slept. In quiet moments, his treadmill thoughts returned, powerful as ever. Jane's face was quickly before him, crowded by images of her husband and children. It would not do, his conscience told him. He freely admitted to himself that this journey was, in part, an attempt to escape from his moral dilemma, as well as taking help to the beleaguered merchants in St Petersburg. Maybe, as he travelled, he would find the answers he was looking for, and return with a clearer view of his future. He could only hope so.

At length, when all sight of England was gone, he joined Robertson below decks, determined to concentrate on the journey ahead.

The weather was kind, for January, and the steam ferry swift, but Robertson sadly discovered that his stomach was no stronger than the last time he'd sailed. This didn't bode well at the beginning of so arduous a journey. However, they arrived in Calais only a little after two in the afternoon and the transfer from ferry to train, including the inevitable inspection by Customs officers, was undertaken without incident. Both men were still adjusting to the need for vigilance. It was difficult to guard their precious burden without appearing conspicuous. However, all went well, and they reached Ghent by evening. Their belongings were safely unloaded and placed in a large four-wheeler cab. They passed through chill streets to the modest hotel where they were to spend their first night. It lay in a side street, off the main thoroughfare, not far from the Hotel de Flandre. Slightly down at heel, it was accustomed to a clientele of salesmen, clerks and travellers with modest purses. It was perfectly suited to two artists travelling with a load of art materials, and the ideal place to recover before the next stage of the journey. Their bags were brought up to their room and, after a brief conversation in which money changed hands, their packing

58

cases, and the carefully boxed frames, as well. Rather than going out, they ordered a simple supper of bread, cheese and beer to be sent to up to them, blaming an early start for their avoidance of late hours. Any exploration of Ghent could wait for the return journey.

The two men had no way of knowing whether their movements were being followed, or if the criminal underworld had caught wind of the movement of so great a sum of money, so they settled into the disciplined routine outlined for them in London. Cave Thomas wondered whether Ellis's instructions regarding security were a little excessive – never leaving their luggage unguarded by day or night, ensuring it was sealed in the guard's van on the train, carrying their guns at all times - but since he'd agreed to follow these rules, he sent Robertson to bed and made himself as comfortable as he could, for the first watch. He had no idea what lay ahead, no sense of perspective regarding the risk – it must all be guesswork unless, or until, something happened to prove Ellis right.

The town gradually quietened down, the roads cleared, and the sounds of the night intensified. The minutest creak of the hotel, settling gently as the temperature dropped, a cat yowling at a distance or the scratching of a mouse in the attic above their heads, gained significance. Cave Thomas, who'd volunteered for the first watch, pulled his coat tightly round him and thrust his hands into his pockets, wishing he'd remembered to retrieve his gloves from the bag into which he'd pushed them when they first arrived. His revolver lay on the packing case beside him, primed and ready. A clock on a nearby building sounded the hour, with a single stroke. The hardest hours still lay ahead. Cave Thomas shifted in his chair and drew the shutter back just a fraction. Not much light was shed by the gas lamps below, and the waning moon provided little more. With his thoughts flitting between past worries, present preoccupations and future hurdles, Cave Thomas tried to school his mind into some kind of order. He couldn't shorten his journey by worrying about it, neither could he put his life right when all that concerned him lay on the other side of the Channel. At length, he took up a pencil and a small notebook, and in the dim light began to draw. This was something he understood. He drew from memory – the ferry by the harbour, the throng of passengers, the clouds above the cliffs. The shapes took form under his hand and his mind became focused. Time fell away and concentration conquered drowsiness and worry. The clock struck again. To his surprise, Cave Thomas counted three. It was time to hand over to Robertson. He touched the man's shoulder. Robertson stirred.

"Mother…" He woke from the dream. Lost for a moment, he grabbed Cave Thomas's arm. "Where am I?"

"At the hotel in Ghent. It's your turn to keep watch."

Robertson came to his senses. "Sorry," he began. Signing to him to be silent, Cave Thomas gave a whispered report of his watch. Robertson knew what to do. The two changed places. Robertson placed his own revolver where Cave Thomas's had lain, and Cave Thomas, having made his gun safe, put it under the bolster and was soon asleep.

Wednesday morning came and it was still dark as the men washed in cold water and prepared for the next stage of their journey. Robertson went down to find the concierge and to pay the bill. A cab was summoned from the rank by the marketplace and soon the two men and all their luggage were once more on their way. At the station they bought scalding coffee and freshly baked bread, standing by the bar to eat, surrounded by bags and crates. A couple of porters helped them across the station to their train. They had paid in advance for secure storage for all their luggage, and saw it safely stowed in a locked compartment, before finding their seats. The carriage was fairly new, and the seats well upholstered. A good start to the day. The train set off promptly, as dawn broke. They were relieved to be on their way.

At Brussels they had time to stretch their legs, buying more coffee, and food for later. Whilst Cave Thomas was gone in search of refreshments, Robertson wandered down to the luggage van to see that all was safe and that nothing had shifted with the motion of the train. Finding everything as it should be, he re-joined Cave Thomas. The whistle blew and the train pulled slowly out of the station. Their next stop would be Liege. Yielding to the steady rhythm of the train, they took it in turns to make up for the previous night's interrupted rest. At Liege, hot food was available, so they took advantage of this in case their arrival in Dusseldorf was delayed.

They reached Aix-la-Chapelle in daylight, but, as the train left the station, clouds, which had been building for some time, covered the sun. Evening fell upon them with surprising rapidity. However, the sky cleared after a while, and the moon rose above a countryside at present almost completely free of snow. As they neared the Rhine, it was possible to see the steady flow of the river

– no ice in sight. It was with mixed feelings that the two men took their final walk to stretch their legs at Cologne station. The bitter cold of London and Ghent had been replaced by a dank chill here in Cologne. Neither man spoke of it, but each was thinking of the difficult journey ahead, when their way would depend upon ancient roads, rather than the reliable iron rails of the railway.

The train pulled into Dusseldorf at about eight o'clock that evening. It had been a long day's travel, and they had yet to make their precious load safe for the night, but each felt satisfied that the day had gone according to plan. They repeated the arrangements which had worked so well in Ghent and were welcomed at the hotel by a genial concierge. At Ellis's suggestion, they'd reserved a room ahead, so they were expected. Their luggage was transferred without comment and the concierge, a short man, whose enjoyment of kitchen benefits had begun to attack his waist, handed them a letter with an elaborate flourish.

"This come this afternoon. It arrive by hand." He bowed and left the room, closing the door softly behind him.

Cave Thomas opened the envelope. It was from one of Sir Henry's men and carried the agreed code word in the first sentence. Their contact, Herr Finkel would wait upon them in the morning.

The two men settled down to a second night of vigilance. They made themselves as comfortable as the room would allow, with Robertson taking the first watch. He selected an upright chair by the window, pulled his coat across his knees and set the revolver on a packing case. The shutters were half-closed, and with an old curtain draped conveniently, he could see out without being seen.

The fire was nearly out, so Cave Thomas pulled the bedcovers round his shoulders and fell asleep. He was so tired that even the hardness of the bed couldn't keep him awake.

Each took his turn to watch, the uneventfulness of the long night playing upon their taut nerves. Cave Thomas had said nothing, but his interest in Herr Finkel was growing. The more he thought about him, the wilder his imaginings became. Was the man a friend, an enemy, a danger? Would he guide them or trick them? How should he manage the encounter? Herr Finkel's prompt arrival, at eight, put an end to these fruitless questions. Robertson answered the door to the concierge's knock.

"A Herr Finkel to see you sirs."

Herr Finkel, a slender man of about twenty-nine or thirty, entered the room, bowed and stepped aside quickly as a waiter followed him in, pushing a trolley with breakfast for three upon it. There was some upheaval as a chair was brought in from the corridor and the table prepared. With the concierge's eye upon him the waiter arranged the meal carefully on the table and removed the trolley. The concierge followed him. pausing at the door to assure them he would be with them in a moment should they need anything more, then left. Herr Finkel shook hands with Cave Thomas and Robertson, sat down at the table and helped himself to coffee, before offering it to his hosts.

"Forgive the fancy dress," he said, in an English accent learnt on the playing fields of some minor public school. "Sir Henry insisted on my using a certain amount of discretion in contacting you. To the world, Herr Finkel is an art dealer who wishes to purchase Russian art – before it becomes impossible to deal across the border." He sipped his coffee by way of punctuation and sat back in his chair.

"You're not English?" asked Cave Thomas. Herr Finkel's dress wasn't fancy but certainly foreign and the man's hair had a touch of the dandy about it.

"No, I'm Prussian, but my mother was English and so I learnt the language as a child. I was educated in the home counties and met our mutual acquaintance whilst I was working in London. I now work here, in Dusseldorf – and in Cologne, Brunswick and Berlin."

"You have instructions for us?" It was Robertson's turn to inquire.

"I have papers, to add to your passport. They give you permission to travel beyond Prussia, as artists and suppliers of painting materials." He drew a sheaf of papers from a pocket and handed them to Cave Thomas. "I think you will find them all in order."

Herr Finkel watched as Cave Thomas cast a quick eye over the papers. They appeared to genuine and carried the requisite stamps and signatures.

"And we must show these when we get to the border?" he asked.

"Yes, together with your passports and the letters of introduction. You will then be issued with further papers which you'll need for the next part of the journey. With the current tension, you may find it difficult to cross the border, but it's more likely to involve delay then refusal."

Cave Thomas passed the papers to Robertson, who took his time reading them carefully, before folding them neatly and passing them back. As Cave Thomas placed the papers in his wallet, Robertson turned to Herr Finkel.

"I understand, from my mother, that there are advantages in reaching the border in the early morning – when a fresh guard is in place. Is this true?"

Herr Finkel nodded. "It is commonly believed that travellers arriving in the evening encounter more difficulties than those who arrive earlier in the day. Maybe it is the weariness of the guards, or they perhaps have intelligence that foreign powers are more likely to infiltrate in the evening? Who knows?"

"Are we likely to encounter checks anywhere else?" Robertson had been wondering about the safety measures they should take for property left with the Guard.

"Perhaps, but the most thorough searches of property and papers will occur at the border – or rather, at Tauroggen, some miles further on. Perhaps we run ahead of ourselves - there are many miles to travel before you reach the border. If you leave here on the morning train, you should arrive in Berlin tomorrow evening. Would a day be sufficient to purchase supplies there?" He raised an eyebrow and Cave Thomas signalled that this would be all the time they'd need.

"However," he said, "it's frustrating to lose a day here in Dusseldorf. Is there no train we can catch today?" Cave Thomas wanted to waste as little time as possible.

"It would be of no benefit to you, Mr Thomas." Herr Finkel's tone was relaxed. "Take today to explore Dusseldorf. We have some historic buildings here, of great interest."

"Very well. We'll be guided by you." Cave Thomas saw no point in prolonging the discussion.

"Good. That being so, you could leave Berlin on Saturday evening. There's a train which leaves at about 10.40. It would bring you to Königsberg between ten and eleven the next evening."

"Why so long?" asked Robertson.

"The train doesn't go the whole way," Cave Thomas reminded him. "We'll have to cross the Vistula on the ice. That's ten miles or more by carriage, pulled by horses shod for the purpose."

"Of course," said Robertson. "I was forgetting. I had Königsberg fixed in my head as the end of the railway."

63

"Once the bridges are constructed, the journey will be easier – but with matters as they are, it could be a long time before they are completed." Herr Finkel put down his cup. "I must leave you. I believe someone will meet you at Tilsit before you cross the border. He will know how matters stand and will tell you where to buy your permits to use the Russian staging posts. It should be straight-forward, but we live in unpredictable times."

He stood up and shook both men by the hand.

"God speed you and good luck. Be vigilant. Every station is watched now. It cannot be long before we are dragged into this conflict."

Mention of war sobered them all. It was a reminder to Cave Thomas and Robertson that they were part of a grim venture – a desperate throw to save the British Factory community in St Petersburg. It was not an adventure. It was a secret mission, with all that that phrase meant.

Cave Thomas thanked Herr Finkel for his help and saw him to the door. Closing it after him, he turned the key once more.

"Perhaps we should heed Herr Finkel's advice," he said. "There are forces at work that we've barely glimpsed – they may wish our mission to fail. We've not only the threat of theft to deal with but, perhaps more seriously, of arrest as spies. We must question everything, take nothing for granted, be vigilant. We're not in England now."

8

To Berlin
Thursday 19th – Friday 20th January 1854

As soon as Herr Finkel had left the room, Cave Thomas stationed himself by the window. He wanted to see where Herr Finkel went when he left the hotel. For some reason, he felt that Finkel had been a little too good to be true. Probably nothing to worry about, but he didn't want to take risks. A couple of minutes passed, and a figure emerged from the hotel entrance - Herr Finkel. Cave Thomas stepped back, timing his movement to evade Finkel's upward glance. A moment or two later, he cautiously moved forward again and was rewarded with a clear view of the man, who crossed the road and walked swiftly away, towards the square. A few seconds later, a man stepped out of a doorway and fell into step beside Finkel. He was wearing a thick overcoat, his hat pulled down obscuring his face. A carriage pulled up beside them, and they were hidden from sight. It pulled away almost immediately. The men had disappeared. He couldn't be sure, but something suggested to Cave Thomas that Finkel may have been bundled into the carriage - that he'd not entered it of his own volition.

"James, pack your bag. We're leaving."

"But Herr Finkel encouraged us to explore Dusseldorf today."

"If I'm not mistaken, Herr Finkel has just fallen into the hands of our enemy. Unless, of course, he's working with them. Either way, this place is no longer safe for us. We must go."

Robertson's grim expression said all that needed saying.

The two men packed swiftly. Cave Thomas slipped his revolver into his pocket and went down to pay the bill and to request assistance with the luggage. In less than fifteen minutes, having scanned the room to make sure they had missed nothing, the two men and all they carried with them, were in a carriage, heading for the station.

Robertson remained with the luggage whilst Cave Thomas saw to the tickets. A train was leaving for Berlin within the hour - Herr Finkel had misinformed them. Before re-joining Robertson, Cave Thomas found his way to the telegraph office. He sent a message, in code, to Herbert Ellis, who needed to know of Finkel's disappearance. That done, he returned to Robertson, who reported that all was well, so far as he could tell.

"I've sent a message to our friend in London," Cave Thomas said in a low voice.

"Perhaps we'll have fresh instructions by the time we reach Berlin."

The wait was nerve-racking. The revolver hung heavily against Cave Thomas's side, but he knew he was unlikely to use it, here on a crowded station. The two men struggled to appear nonchalant although taut with nervous energy, watching everyone, ready to respond to anything suspicious. With so many people hanging around waiting - porters leaning on their carts, other officials standing about or walking smartly to an unknown duty - the enemy could be in full sight. There was nothing they could do but hope for the best.

At last the train came into the station. Cave Thomas hailed a porter from the shabby group gathered on the platform, accepting the services of the second one to step forward. He noted that the first was soon summoned elsewhere. The packing cases were placed securely in the guard's van, and the two men chose an empty carriage, stowed their hand luggage, and took their guard. The train eased out of the station and gathered speed. Left alone, they relaxed. Cave Thomas gave Robertson more details about the telegraph, and how he expected it to be answered.

"We'll need to check for a reply when we get to Berlin. I'm not happy about any of this. Either Finkel is working for us – in which case, God help him if he has fallen into enemy hands – or he's a spy, working for the other side. If that's so, the papers he's given us might lead us into a trap."

"It might be a trap either way," said Robertson. "You're right. We need advice from Ellis – if our security services have been infiltrated, we can't trust anyone at all!"

"Ellis promised us support all the way to the end of the railway. He seemed confident that his men could be trusted. But, if I'm right about Herr Finkel, that makes little difference. The man may be genuine, but it counts for nothing if he's fallen into enemy hands."

"Sir Henry wouldn't allow a man like Finkel to know much about the mission," said Robertson. "The less people know, the less they can reveal under questioning."

Cave Thomas shrugged. "There's nothing we can do for a bit, in any case. I suggest we get some sleep, while we can. We'll need to be alert at every stop from now until the end of the line."

James Robertson found no fault with that suggestion. Since they had the carriage to themselves, they took advantage of their temporary safety and closed their eyes as the train rattled on towards Berlin. Their sleep was neither deep nor long, but they woke later feeling much refreshed.

Their first stop was at Essen. The two men watched uneasily as passengers left and joined the train, but, mercifully, nobody joined them, so they were able to relax once more.

At Dortmund, they had a few minutes to stretch their legs, time which they used to check the luggage and buy coffee, bread and sausage. On they went, ever further East, measuring the minutes and the hours that took them closer to their goal. The sense of being watched increased as, with nothing to do, the two men had ample time to brood upon what might lie ahead.

At Hanover, their tickets were checked. The inspector took his time and looked at them with unconcealed interest. He spoke to them in German, inquiring about their luggage. Robertson answered easily and the man seemed satisfied. He left them. Having bought more food, they returned to their compartment to find they now had company. A pinch-faced woman and her daughter had taken possession of the seats in which they had been sitting. The mother prodded Cave Thomas's newspaper and muttered something in German. Cave Thomas bowed politely and, picking up the paper, laid it on the seat beside him, neatly folded. He tucked his feet out of the way of the other passengers, opened a book and steadfastly read. Robertson, meanwhile, slouched in his corner, hat pulled down, and tried to go back to sleep. The daughter sniffed and turned to her mother. The words *Mutter* and *Damenwagen* were just discernible. Cave Thomas wondered whether it was an exercise in deception, or whether the girl really did want to sit in a Ladies' carriage. It would be interesting to know if such things were available, but impossible to find out whilst they were moving, since there was no way of accessing other parts of the train.

The day wore on. As the light faded, they travelled on into darkness. The weather was colder now, and heavy clouds threatened rain ahead of them. At Brunswick they were informed that their departure was to be delayed by half an hour. In some agitation, the mother and daughter left the carriage in search of a meal. A good idea. Robertson stayed with their bags and Cave Thomas went to check the luggage was still secure, before ordering a meal. All this took twenty minutes. He returned to the carriage to find Robertson white with shock.

"Whatever's happened? Are you hurt?"

"No, no. Cave Thomas, I've been a fool!"

"Calm down and tell me, slowly, what happened."

Cave Thomas set the meal down on a seat. All evidence of their companions was gone, he noticed.

"The woman and her daughter – you'll remember, they left the carriage, before you did, in search of food. I stayed put. I didn't move. After a few minutes, they returned with a picnic basket. Just outside the compartment, they stopped. There was a scream - the girl, I think. Her mother was lying on the platform. She appeared to have been knocked down and robbed. A crowd gathered. I left my seat to see if I could help. One of the railway officials started asking questions, so I thought it best to return to the carriage. Then I noticed – all their bags had gone."

Cave Thomas glanced up at the rack. Empty, apart from their own bags.

"Did you see who took them?"

"No. They didn't take them when they went in search of refreshment," Robertson's colour was returning and with it, his memory.

"Do you think someone else took them?" Cave Thomas pressed him.

"I don't see how. I looked out and the platform had cleared. There was no sign of the woman or her daughter. Do you think it was a trick?"

The two men looked at one another, aghast. Cave Thomas reached up to pull down his two bags, but Robertson grabbed his arm.

"Look first," he said. "Any signs of tampering?"

"I think not. However, we'd better check more closely."

They dragged their bags down and examined the fastenings minutely. There was no sign of them being forced.

"I should have stayed put. What was I thinking of, leaving everything, taken in by the scene on the platform?"

The slamming of doors, the sound of the engine and the guard's whistle warned that they were on their way once more. As the train slowly drew out of the station, Robertson lowered the blinds. He opened his bag, and unpacked it, to reveal the secret compartment. It was untouched. Cave Thomas did the same. All appeared to be well. In all probability, the woman and her daughter had been innocent travellers. Thank God!

They pushed the bags back into place and slumped on the seats with the exhaustion of relief. Robertson pulled out a flask and poured them each a tot of brandy.

"For our nerves," he said.

Cave Thomas downed his quickly, surprised to see his hand was shaking.

"How near we came to disaster!"

"Yes, but we were lucky," Robertson replied. "We'd better learn from this and make sure we don't get so tired that we cease to be vigilant. We'll take proper rests from now on. We'll need clear minds for Berlin."

Cave Thomas took first watch. Robertson slept for nearly an hour, then returned the favour. Berlin was reached just before midnight, after a hold-up somewhere outside the city. The two men were ready to alight as soon as the train came to a halt. Robertson, now tutored in the art of porter selection, commandeered a man with a trolley, whilst Cave Thomas went to retrieve their luggage from the van. He counted the packing cases with a sense of relief. All were there and none had been tampered with. All was well. Cave Thomas left Robertson with the luggage and went to check when the telegraph office would reopen. Not tonight. Perhaps a message would await them at the hotel.

The cab set off through gas-lit streets, shining from the recent rain, soon reaching their hotel. They then went through the usual ritual of off-loading their luggage, insisting on staying with it as it was carried to their room. The Hotel de Saxe was the sort of place that dealt with every kind of traveller. The quantity of their luggage appeared to raise no questions, nor the late hour of their arrival. The kitchen was closed, but the man at the desk offered them a cold supper, to be brought to their room. They accepted gladly and asked for beer to go with it.

"*Natürlich, Mein Herr.* Of course, sir."

"Thank you. You are too kind. *Vielen Dank.*"

This, accompanied by a generous tip, made them friends at the hotel, where the English had a reputation for not bothering to try speaking German.

They set about stowing their luggage at one side of the room, throwing their coats across the boxes to conceal them a little.

69

Exhaustion was making every task harder. Cave Thomas took pity on Robertson and offered to take first watch. The man was white with fatigue. Anxiety for his mother was added to all the other stresses of the journey. It took a while to waken him at three thirty, but Cave Thomas was too tired himself to stay up longer.

Thankfully, it was a quiet night. Cave Thomas woke at seven to find Robertson in good spirits. They'd ordered breakfast in their room, the easier to guard their precious packages, and it arrived just as Cave Thomas was washing. There were two letters for him, brought up with the meal. The first one he opened was from Ellis and contained names and addresses of three contacts in the city. There was also another sheet of instructions.

"It was posted on Monday. Amazing! But I wonder why he didn't just hand it to us before we left."

"Testing the system, perhaps." Robertson was eating his breakfast, more interested in that than in the post.

The second letter, posted later, had nevertheless arrived in Berlin with the same speed as themselves. A mystery!

This one was from Cave Thomas's father. It was full of advice and admonitions, clearly influenced by his mother. Cave Thomas looked closely. Yes, they were there – all the coded words which he and his father had agreed.

"My father tells me that they have been under surveillance since we left, but not by Loughton's men. He suspects that there are enemy agents in London, and he warns me to be alert."

"He entrusted that to the mail service?" Robertson was amazed.

Cave Thomas handed him the letter. Robertson read it and handed it back.

"It's a lot of information about framing orders and the problems with the servants. How do you read anything from it?"

"Code," was Cave Thomas's simple reply. "We agreed it before I came away. Each phrase has a particular meaning. For example, 'the kitchen maid failed to return from her half day' means that he's been in touch with Sir Henry and is awaiting a reply."

"It's an effective one. Nobody would read anything into it."

Cave Thomas kept his thoughts to himself, but the ease with which his father had produced the code, had left him with no doubts as to how deeply he was involved with the shadowy world of national security.

Their breakfast complete, the pair discussed how best to go about the day's work. Cave Thomas's experience of living in Germany and travelling in winter, some years before, suggested that he was the right person to purchase what they would need for their onward journey. So, he set out with a long list of items, returning at lunch time with furs, food and money. The lad who'd helped him bring his parcels upstairs, stood hopefully by the door. A few coins satisfied him, and he left with a polite salute.

"I hope I've thought of everything," Cave Thomas said, as Robertson opened the first of the parcels.

"There seems to be plenty here." He lifted out a fur coat and tried it for size. Its weight came as a shock to him. "My word! That's heavy."

"You'll be glad enough of it before we're done. How was your morning?"

"Uneventful, apart from these messages, dropped off at the reception desk." He handed Cave Thomas a sheaf of telegraphs, glad to be able to share his concerns about their contents.

Cave Thomas read and re-read them carefully.

"Well, what do you make of them?" Robertson was eager to know.

"First, it's good to know the truth about Herr Finkel. 'Arrested', rather than 'snatched'. The police – or whoever they were – kept him for several hours, but then let him go. There's still no explanation of why he tried to delay our departure. Perhaps it was a genuine mistake, or maybe there's something we're missing."

"And the papers – the letters of introduction and the contacts here?"

"All bona fide, as far as I can tell."

"Do you intend to make the visits you'd planned?"

"I see no reason why not. Are you happy to stay here and sort these?" Cave Thomas indicated the parcels, strewn all over the bed.

"Certainly. But remember, we must wear the furs – or be charged tax on them at the border." He stood up and followed Cave Thomas to the door. "Take care, Thomas. I still feel uneasy about the way things went at Dusseldorf."

"So, do I," Cave Thomas smiled grimly. "We both need to be cautious. Open the door to no-one until I return. We must be on our way this evening, come what may."

Leaving Robertson in charge of packing and security, Cave Thomas set off to the telegraph office, where he sent seemingly bland messages to Ellis and to his father. Another telegraph awaited his collection – it brought news from Ellis that the weather was good and the ice frozen. They could proceed with confidence.

Cave Thomas put the message into his wallet and went in search of the first name on his list of contacts, to collect the letters of introduction, so necessary in Russia.

He was welcomed warmly and found his host had been expecting him.

"I won't waste your time, Herr Thomas." The man, whose name was clearly a cover, was calm and precise.

"Here are the letters of introduction you've been promised. These men are to be trusted."

Cave Thomas looked at the names. They meant nothing to him, but he noted the addresses, which were all in the centre of St Petersburg.

"However," the man went on, "do not trust the men along the way, in the staging posts. Keep to your carriage and never let your belongings leave your sight. Be prepared to be generous with your tips; nobody will accuse you of bribery," he paused, fixing Cave Thomas with an expectant look. Cave Thomas passed him a folded note, the amount Ellis had instructed him. The man smiled and slipped the money into his pocket.

"Given good weather, the journey can be made within a week." With that, the man moved to the door and opened it for Cave Thomas to leave.

The 'week' didn't encourage Cave Thomas, but he parted from the man with thanks for his advice. He was confident he wouldn't meet him again.

His other calls elicited a travel permit, some roubles, a couple more letters of introduction and the names of three more people to see when they arrived in St Petersburg.

He hurried back to Robertson, conscious that he'd been away for nearly four hours. He was as much concerned for Robertson's frame of mind as he was for his own wellbeing, cold and weary though he was. The stresses of the journey so far, the mistake at Brunswick, the uncertainty about Herr Finkel were weighing on them both, but Robertson had the concern for his mother, on top of this. Cave Thomas was worried that he might crumble under the pressure of their task. It made it even more vital that they shouldn't be parted for too long.

He went directly upstairs, to find Robertson slumped in the armchair by the window, ostensibly keeping watch. Signs of how he had spent the time were evident in the ordered room. It was meticulously tidy, and all their bags were lined up ready to go. A meal had been ordered, to arrive at seven, and they were to go to the station to catch the 10.40 train.

Cave Thomas placed the documents and money in his satchel and then settled down with his pipe, having sought Robertson's permission to smoke. Once the pipe was lit, Cave Thomas drew on it and leaned back in his armchair, glad to relax for a while. A few minutes passed and Robertson was clearly preoccupied. Something must have happened during Cave Thomas's absence. He tried a soft approach.

"So," he said, "Why so pensive?"

Robertson drew a letter from his pocket and handed it to his friend. It was a reply to a letter Robertson had written to his mother. He'd given the Hotel de Saxe as a place to contact him.

The letter was short and written by his mother's maid. Madame Robertson had asked her to write. Her lady was ill, in bed – too ill to write, herself. Please would Monsieur Robertson visit as soon as he arrived in St Petersburg? Madame was uncertain how well she would be, on his arrival. Their plans might have to change. If Mrs Robertson were too ill to travel, there would be no question of her returning to England. It was signed Marie-Claire Monceaux.

Small wonder the poor man was troubled. If his mother was too ill to write for herself, matters were more serious than he'd feared.

"Cave Thomas," Robertson brought himself to speak at last, "Have I left it too late?"

9

To the end of the line
Friday 20th (evening) – Sunday 22nd January 1854

Cave Thomas had little to say that could reduce his friend's anxiety. Until he saw his mother, Robertson couldn't possibly assess whether or not she was fit to travel. However, if the maid had written truthfully, things didn't look good. Mrs Robertson was far from young, and the rigours of the journey might well be beyond her strength; in which case, Cave Thomas would have to face the return journey alone. Whatever the outcome, they'd probably be in St Petersburg much longer than planned.

Banishing such thoughts, Cave Thomas gave his attention to the present and their safe embarkation on the evening train. He went out of his way to spare Robertson, discreetly double-checking everything his friend had done, in case worry for his mother had affected Robertson's efficiency. The train left on time, and the men were once more on their way. Robertson took first watch, having made it clear that he couldn't sleep. Cave Thomas woke around three, legs stiff with cold, and aware that a sharp nudge in his ribs had roused him. He sat up and took out his handkerchief, pressing it against his face to hide his discrete scrutiny of the other passengers.

"Sorry, my friend," Robertson avoided using Cave Thomas's name. "Must have disturbed you when I took out my spectacles."

Cave Thomas grunted a surly riposte and settled down in feigned sleep. So, Robertson had noticed something untoward amongst their companions. The use of the word 'spectacles' was one of their coded signals. Robertson carried spectacles, but rarely used them, so reference to them had seemed a useful ruse. Sitting in the corner, Robertson beside him, Cave Thomas ran the other passengers' faces through his mind. An artist's eye misses little. He noted their peculiarities in a mental list:

- Opposite him, a man in a worn overcoat, hand-knitted scarf, slightly shiny hat, gloves, trousers – worn at the knee. Heavy boots, scuffed, and in need of polish. Looked as if they had been in snow.

- Next to this man, another, slighter than the first, and younger. He'd arrived with a small satchel and a heavy leather bag – possibly English, but the man hadn't spoken.

- In the far corner, opposite, a man of middle years. Stocky, well made, with a tendency to fat. Looked like a man who enjoyed his food. He wore a fine set of whiskers. His clothing suggested that he was a man of business – trade? Certainly not high management – maybe a salesman? His bag might contain samples, perhaps?

- The other side of Robertson, beyond Cave Thomas's line of sight, another, similarly dressed. He recalled the two in conversation. German, he thought – certainly, that was the language they'd used, but something about their dress made him think that they were perhaps from France. Yes, a slight aroma of French tobacco appeared to confirm his suspicions.

So, what had caused Robertson alarm? Cave Thomas, still feigning sleep, shifted a little in his seat, so that Robertson's profile came into view. He sat, slumped, his spectacles low upon his nose, one hand limply holding his newspaper, the thumb nail digging into the page. He appeared to be asleep. Cave Thomas 'woke up', blew his nose, pocketed his handkerchief and eased himself into a more upright position. He glanced down at Robertson's lap. One brief look and it was clear what he'd been trying to communicate. The thumbnail, so carefully placed, underlined a word: 'Following'.

Bromberg was their next stop. As the train drew into the station, Robertson woke, stretched, yawned and stood up. He set the newspaper down on the seat and felt in his pocket for his gloves.

"Shall I fetch some food?" he asked Cave Thomas, again avoiding names.

"That would be welcome – and a hot drink if you can find one. I'll stop here and catch up with the news." Cave Thomas picked up the paper and flipped it so that the indented word could not be seen by others.

"It's a few days old," said Robertson. "I'll look for something more recent."

He left the carriage, followed by one of the two 'salesmen'. The other stayed in the carriage. The youngest man picked up his satchel and left the compartment. Cave Thomas watched him dawdle along the platform, uncertain of which way to go. Then he was lost from sight. The remaining man, the one with the scuffed boots, addressed Cave Thomas.

"You travel far?"

Cave Thomas couldn't immediately place the accent.

"Yes, to the end of the line." There was little point in pretending otherwise as their tickets would be checked at any moment.

"Ah, a hazardous journey. I hear the Vistula has been experiencing a thaw."

"Has it?"

"Yes. This make the journey more arduous and uncertain."

"I expect we will be advised at Dirschau," Cave Thomas replied.

"We will. We will."

"And you, sir. Do you travel far?" he asked.

"Like you, to the end of the line."

"Then we will travel together for a while."

"Yes. If you need advice when we reach Dirschau, I will be honoured to assist you, and your friend." The man was persistent.

"I'm uncertain of my plans. But thank you for your offer."

"It is nothing, nothing at all."

Conversation lapsed. Was it imagined, or had he felt the attention of the salesman, throughout this conversation? And the man's his faulty grammar - did that betray anything about his origins, or, at the very least, the way he'd acquired his English? As for the salesman, Cave Thomas would be glad to know whose side he was on, if any.

Even as he was thinking this, he recognised that his growing experience and powers as a British agent were accompanied, in equal measure, by a distaste for the business. He was glad when Robertson reappeared, laden with food and drink, and with two newspapers tucked under his arm.

"Sorry to take so long," he said, "The place was crowded. There's snow on the line ahead, but the feeling is that the blockage will be cleared before we reach it. News of the Vistula is good. The ice has reformed and the road across has been declared safe to travel."

The man opposite him, caught Cave Thomas's eye for a moment. Could he read disappointment there or was he just imagining it?

Robertson sat down and shared out the food and papers between the two of them. As he handed his friend a paper, Cave Thomas noticed that he held it a split second longer than necessary, and that two fingers were gripping the side. He put the paper on his lap and placing the opened food parcel on top of it, concentrated on his meal. The other passengers returned and, as the train moved on, all gradually returned to its previous calm. Once they had all finished eating, most settled to read or doze. Cave Thomas chose to read. Robertson closed his eyes.

Page two of the newspaper held a series of news items about the situation in Europe and how matters lay between the Czar and the Four Powers. Cave Thomas flipped the paper to check its date – just four days old and written about things as they'd stood several days earlier. It was mostly stale news. However, for Cave Thomas and Robertson, whose awareness was heightened by their mission, there were nuances which could not be missed. The most obvious was that an extension of the war, to include the Four Powers, appeared inevitable, albeit couched in terms which seemed to allow for hope. It was clear that the war of words would go on a little longer, but each day of prevarication would bring them one step closer to conflict.

Cave Thomas was about to fold the newspaper once more when he became aware of some irregularities in the page. He looked again, and saw that Robertson's thumb nail, soiled by train travel, had underscored eight words.

Two ~ with ~ us ~ one ~ against ~ other ~ not ~ known

Two with us.   One against.   Other not known.

So, Robertson had worked it out. But who were the two and who was the one? Cave Thomas no longer felt tired. Instead, he set himself to work out how they could safely leave the train at Dirschau, with the gold intact.

Time passed. The train progressed through an increasingly wintery landscape, revealed, bit by bit, with the dawn. It was clear that the river crossing ahead would be on solid ice. The thaw was over. The countryside was covered by a fresh fall of snow. The few figures in the landscape were bundled up in so many layers of clothing that they looked like small trees, without proper human form. Cave Thomas was glad of his fur coat. He was ready for the next, bitter stage of the journey.

They pulled into Dirschau in time for breakfast. There was little more than a moment for Robertson and Cave Thomas to exchange glances, but each sensed the heightened awareness of the other. They set in motion the plan discussed in Dusseldorf when they first

77

felt themselves under scrutiny. They stood little chance of flushing out the enemy. If Robertson had judged correctly, they were four against one - or two but Cave Thomas couldn't be sure that Robertson was right. Which passengers did he think were with them? The odds might be quite different, with maybe only one of the passengers on their side - or even all four ranged against the two of them! So, in the absence of any further guidance, Cave Thomas and Robertson carried on as normal. They took their bags from the rack, descended from the train and made their way to the guard's van. Their luggage lay untouched. Porters appeared from the room where a fire had kept them warm through the night. This time, Cave Thomas selected the third to approach. The man worked hard, piling the packing cases onto a trolley and then indicated where they might arrange for a carriage. They followed him to the place. As they went, one of the 'salesmen' walked up behind them. He intercepted Cave Thomas and spoke in a low voice.

"Ellis sends his regards."

Cave Thomas inclined his head and awaited the pre-arranged safe words.

"I have The Germ[2] of an idea. Might I and my friend, ride with you? Costs to be shared, you understand."

"Of course. My pleasure."

Robertson smiled. "You are welcome; you and your friend," he added as the other 'salesman' approached the group.

"They've gone. For now."

"They?" Cave Thomas noted the plural.

"The man and the student. They're working together. We know them by name, but we don't think they know us."

"They'll not leave us now. It's obvious where we're going."

"It is, but none of us is entirely safe. Accidents can happen along the way. And there may be others on the trail, too, or awaiting us somewhere before the frontier. Nothing is certain."

Robertson and Cave Thomas didn't like the sound of this.

"Very well. Which is our carriage?" They'd decided against using a public diligence; it wouldn't have accommodated their luggage.

---

[2] As mentioned in chapter 2, *The Germ* was the name favoured by William Cave Thomas for the short-lived Pre-Raphaelite magazine: 'safe words' which Cave Thomas had good reason to remember, and others to forget.

"This one." The 'salesmen' helped Cave Thomas and Robertson load their luggage. They crammed as much as possible inside the carriage, but a couple of cases had to be strapped to the roof.

"Let's hope we remain upright."

With this chilling thought, they climbed into the carriage. The driver whipped up the horses and away they went, towards the river crossing. A shower of thin snow, blowing in from the north, obscured the view for the first part of the journey, but ceased before they had gone far, revealing a bleak landscape.

The crossing itself would be on ice, marked with birch saplings, showing the safe route, but the road leading to the river was cut deep into the snow and the unevenness of the surface made for an uncomfortable ride. However, once they were safely underway and the chances of being overheard reduced to nothing by the trundle of wheels across ridged ice, the two 'salesmen', who now proved to be British agents, began to bring Cave Thomas and Robertson up to date regarding Intelligence. The elder of the pair spoke first.

"My name is Russell, George Russell. I've been working for Sir Henry for four or five years, and for Mr Ellis for the past six months or so. My friend here joined the department more recently."

"Arthur Evans. Pleased to meet you." Evans shook hands with them both.

"We'd planned to intercept you at Tilsit but events overtook us and so we decided to join you after Dusseldorf," his friend went on. "A nasty mess there. Herr Finkel was informed against – a subtle ploy of our enemies. He's one of us."

"Then why did he misinform us about the train?" This had niggled Cave Thomas ever since Dusseldorf.

"We don't know. We suspect that he'd received a false message warning him to keep you out of danger – a ruse to keep you in Berlin. Our codes are not entirely fool-proof, and, in any case, our enemies are far from fools."

"What of the pair on the train?"

"The older man's known to us. He's worked for Russian interests for some years. The younger man is exactly what he appears to be – a student. He's what we call a Zealot. He works for the glory of the Cause, not for a pension."

"More dangerous?"

"Not necessarily. He'd certainly be more likely to make a grand gesture, and would fight like a tiger if cornered, but he lacks experience and doesn't blend in easily. He's the more likely of the pair to make mistakes. His mate can be likened to a dog with a rat – he doesn't let go. But then he's slower and more predictable. If cornered, he'd look to his own skin and forget the Czar."

"Are we sure it's the Czar they're working for?"

"Good question, Mr Thomas. We're as sure as we can be, but you're right, there are other forces at work here. Wherever there is a Power, there are those who would see it fall, who wait in the shadows to take over if they can."

"Look, we're at the river!" cried Robertson, much excited by this new experience.

The four men peered out of the dirty window. The flat, wind and tide-rippled water of the Vistula lay frozen before them, caught in winter's grip, the recent snow blown into drifts along its bank. The river was vast – a broad landscape of ice, the impenetrable channels of a major waterway. Scattered along river, towards the sea, lay a motley assortment of shipping, locked in the ice. When the thaw came, the waters would churn with fury as they raced to the sea, breaking the land link with the West.

The sound of the carriage wheels changed as they rumbled onto the ice. Its wide expanse gleamed before them in the weak winter sunshine. They joined the procession of vehicles crossing the river. The carriages were spread out at safe intervals, the experienced drivers knowing exactly how to negotiate the different channels, keeping a wary eye for any changes as they approached the centre of each branch. Cave Thomas could understand the caution men took in negotiating the crossing. He pondered the ambition to bridge it. What a task! A bridge, or bridges, would be years in the making and must withstand the extremes of climate. It would take a gifted engineer to work out a safe way of doing it.

They eventually reached the opposite bank, without incident, and proceeded to the isolated station platform. Their train stood ready, belching smoke and steam as it awaited the signal to go. Russell and Evans boarded the train separately, deciding to keep watch from the carriages either side of Robertson and Cave Thomas. Their farewells and thanks for sharing the diligence, were made on the platform, where plenty of people could witness them. The agents would continue to follow them in Königsberg and hoped to travel in a public diligence as far as Tilsit. Their plans thereafter would remain flexible, but the four men agreed that they should stick to Sir Henry's instructions regarding entry to Russia. The two artists would proceed to the Russian border alone, in order to reduce the danger of arrest.

With luggage stowed once more, Cave Thomas and Robertson made the last part of their rail journey, arriving in Königsberg in the early evening. If their 'shadows' were still with them, they kept well hidden. There was no sign of them.

Königsberg would be their last stay in the comfort of the West, before plunging into the frozen wastes of Russia. They made the most of it. With Russell and Evans keeping a discreet watch over them, they took a room at the hotel, transferring their luggage as before, confident that they were being protected by friendly eyes. Although they maintained their system of watches, they managed to get several hours' sleep. The next day would be the beginning of the more physically challenging part of their long journey, and the most unpredictable. They would need all their strength.

Cave Thomas was still unsure of Ellis's thoughts regarding this final stage. The plan had always been that they would proceed alone, but the advent of Russell and Evans and the arrest of Finkel had changed everything. It would be good to receive new instructions from Ellis. Cave Thomas's last waking thought was 'I hope there'll be a telegraph tomorrow'.

He was not disappointed. Morning brought with it three telegraphs, two of which had come from London. The first addressed the matter of carriage hire. Nothing had changed regarding the choice of conveyance, but the budget had been increased. The second, also from Ellis, mentioned Russell and Evans, though not by name, stating their purpose and assuring Cave Thomas that the two men would be contacted separately with further instructions. The third, a brief message, was from Herr Finkel. Cave Thomas reached for his notebook and examined the message carefully. The hidden words were present. The message clear. They were being followed – but not by an enemy; three Quaker gentlemen were on their way to ask the Czar to choose peace. Herr Finkel had met them. They were exactly what they said they were, but their unsanctioned interference might affect Russian attitudes to the English community in St Petersburg, and even to bring down the wrath of the Czar upon them. Their mission might now be even harder. They could no longer expect to slip into Russia unnoticed. They were no longer alone. There were three more Britons behind them, and they were all intent upon entering Russia discreetly.

In London, on January 22nd, news of the Quaker mission was relayed to Sir Henry Loughton. He received it badly. Incandescent with rage, he berated the messenger.

"What's this? What do you mean? The fools! The utter imbeciles!" He turned puce with frustrated fury. "Whatever are they thinking of? If they prejudice the safety of my mission, I'll, I'll…" But no-one ever learnt what Sir Henry would do. He'd allowed his ire to rule his judgement one time too many. The past weeks had placed an intolerable strain upon him, with pressure exerted from all sides. His usual apparent incisive calm had concealed his inner stress. He half rose in his chair as pain seared his chest and his heart failed him. He fell sideways, taking the chair with him. He was dead before he met the floor.

Herbert Ellis, with barely a year's experience in the department, was now in charge of the mission.

10

Russia
Sunday 22nd (evening) – Wednesday 25th January 1854

Königsberg was the last link with the western Europe. It stood like Janus, one face to the west and the other to the east. From there, each mile would draw Cave Thomas and Robertson further away from all they knew. There'd be no news from home, no warnings of what they might meet along the way; they'd be on their own until they reached St Petersburg. Even if Russell and Evans succeeded in following them in the many bleak miles which lay ahead, they were bound to be separated. Their presence might be to no purpose – until, perhaps, they reached St Petersburg.

Both Cave Thomas and Robertson understood the magnitude of the next stage of the journey. They could now almost smell and taste the tension. Burying their anxiety, they busied themselves with final preparations. A carriage must be found. Cave Thomas left Robertson in charge of the luggage and went out to hire one. Contrary to expectation, this proved to be relatively easy, and he found a willing driver at the second place he visited. A bargain was struck, and Sunday or not, the box-like carriage would be brought to the hotel at about six that evening. He hoped that the luggage would all fit inside it.

Russell and Evans kept at a distance. They had received instructions, also by telegraph. They must allow the two artists to proceed alone and follow several hours behind them, as far as Tilsit or even Tauroggen.

Cave Thomas hoped to reach the Russian border by morning. If all went well for them, they'd reach Riga, perhaps by nightfall, in three days' time. It would mean non-stop travelling, pausing at post stations only to change horses and take on provisions.

They paid their hotel bill and were ready in the entry hall, surrounded by their possessions, when the carriage drew up. The driver jumped down, leaving his mate and a couple of lads to hold the horses. He stacked the luggage into the carriage with surprising care. By the time he'd finished there was only just room for the two passengers. Cave Thomas and Robertson were about to take their places when the driver held up his hand. He wasn't happy with the weight of the load. It would cost them more. How much? A sum was mentioned. Robertson growled his disapproval, but Cave Thomas, more calmly, argued the sum down a little, agreeing upon a surcharge of about £5 – well within the new budget. The driver took the money without a word. They climbed up into the carriage and he checked that the door was tightly fastened before swinging up to sit beside his companion. A crack of the whip and a cry, and they were away, at a speed that surprised both Cave Thomas and Robertson. With four restless horses, it was impossible to proceed slowly, even in the busy street.

The first part of the journey would be made on wheels. There was snow about, but thin and powdery, leaving the road relatively clear. It was also rutted and rough in places, so they were introduced to the kind of buffeting they must endure for the remainder of their journey. They looked back to their rail journey with fond memories of its relative luxury.

The speed with which they covered the ground increased as they left the town. In the open country the horses could spread out into the more effective fan formation. The hours passed, with regular changes of horse at the post stations. Most places had hot water available for the passengers, and rough but wholesome food to add to their stores. They'd taken Herr Finkel's advice and purchased a samovar. It enabled them to make tea when they wished, helping to stave off the cold and digest the assortment of bread and biscuits they'd brought with them.

The first big river crossing was at Tilsit, where they crossed the Niemen on ice as thick as that of the Vistula, the safe road marked by branches of fir and birch. This past, the smaller rivers dwarfed to insignificance. They were becoming accustomed to the country.

They left Tilsit with spirits high but, nevertheless, anxious about the ordeal of the frontier post ahead. Their carriage had been joined by a horse soldier, who kept his horse at an easy distance, occasionally calling greetings to others of his kind, accompanying carriages in the opposite direction. Travellers into Russia appeared to be under scrutiny. It was not clear whether this was a symptom of war preparations or normal procedure. The rider seemed relaxed and friendly enough, but it became clear to the two men that Russell and Evans would find it hard to travel unremarked under such conditions. They were glad to be alone – four Englishmen travelling together would certainly have attracted unwanted attention.

Some miles after Tilsit, they reached Tauroggen and the border. They'd travelled through the night and it was now late morning on the 23rd. They approached the check point slowly and stopped when commanded, while border officials examined the carriage and identified the nationality of the passengers. Their papers were examined and returned to them, then they were beckoned on. The road ahead was clear, and they travelled at a modest pace until they reached the customs buildings which lay at quite a distance from the frontier itself. More officials appeared, to check their baggage. Cave Thomas felt a tic start in his cheek. He was confident that they carried no incriminating material. Having been warned that anything suspect would be confiscated, they'd left their newspapers behind in Königsberg and destroyed the coded letters. They'd nothing to hide… other than the gold.

This was the moment of truth. Would their work of concealment prove good enough?

The customs men invited them politely to descend from the carriage. Their luggage was unloaded and carried into a large building and they followed. They stood helplessly as other officials pored over their papers. The packages were counted and tallied against the list Cave Thomas had handed them.

"You come this way," said one of the men. He led them to a wooden hut and indicated they should enter.

"You sit."

He left, and they sat down on one of the rough wooden benches. There was nothing to do but wait. After the best part of an hour, Robertson stood up to stamp the circulation back into his cold feet. He looked through the window. Some men were approaching the hut.

"Here they come," he said.

"Best not to let them know how well we speak Russian," said Cave Thomas. Robertson nodded his agreement.

Three men entered the room. Two, wearing military uniform, remained by the door. The other man, dressed in a heavy coat and clearly their senior, approached them.

"You come with us," he said.

They followed him out, followed by the men in uniform, and walked across to the shed where their luggage was waiting for them, unopened. The questions, when they came, were polite and in English.

"You visit St Petersburg, Monsieur Thomas?"

"Yes."

"And you?" The question was directed to Robertson.

"Yes. I visit my sick mother."

The senior officer consulted with one of the guards, in Russian. Then, he turned to Robertson and said,

"Your mother, she is Christina Robertson?"

Robertson was amazed that the man had heard of her.

"Yes. She is a painter."

The officer nodded.

"I know of this woman. It is bad that she is ill."

The uniformed men looked carefully at the packages and re-counted them.

"You open a package for us?" one of them said.

"Of course. Which one would you like to see?"

"This one?" The officer pointed at random.

"Shall I?" Robertson took a step towards it, but the senior officer stopped him.

"No!" he snapped, abruptly. Then softening his voice, added, "We are happy to do this. We will be careful."

They watched as the packing case was opened, anxious as to why they had been forbidden to touch it themselves. It was the one with the gesso and paints. The senior officer took out a box, opened it, and peered inside.

"You take this to your mother?"

"Yes. She has asked for these painting materials."

The senior officer smiled slightly, then turned and barked a command to his assistants. Cave Thomas recognised it was a warning to repack the box carefully. So, there was nothing to read into the officer's abrupt manner.

"The frames?"

Cave Thomas indicated the packages holding frames. The officer selected one and it was brought it to the table. He took out a knife and carefully slit open the protective covering, revealing the carefully crafted frames within.

"Ah… beautiful work." He refastened the covers with deft but gentle hands. "Beautiful frames… for beautiful paintings."

Another command to his assistants and they were free to go.

"Enjoy your visit to our country," he said, then turned and went to talk to the other officials.

The driver and his mate were waiting outside. With no-one to help them, it took Cave Thomas and Robertson several minutes to load the luggage back into the carriage, but both driver and mate were needed to hold the horses steady, and the custom post did not provide porters.

Then they were off. It had all taken about two hours, but they were through the border, safely into Russia. Now they had five hundred miles of snow to cross before reaching St Petersburg.

Hour succeeded hour. At some of the post stations, they left the carriage to stretch cramped limbs and visit the latrine. A glimpse inside one of the buildings confirmed the wisdom of their decision not to stay in such a place. It was basic in the extreme, its shabby furnishing suggesting the strong possibility of dirt and bugs. On the move once more, they slept when they could and watched, through the dirty carriage windows, for dawn to break.

The day, when it came, promised snow. On they went, rushing towards their destination but seeming to make little progress through the unending waste of snow. The huge landscape was interrupted here and there by trees, farmhouses, villages, but set so far apart that to see a woman walking along with her children was an event.

"How do people live in such a place?" mused Robertson, as they passed a small huddle of peasants near a small wood.

"They endure the winter and live in the summer," Cave Thomas replied, adding, "those who survive the hardships of ice and snow." And a blinding squall of snow hit them, as if to underline his sentiments.

Evening came and still they travelled on. The driver and his mate swapped places every few hours. Presumably, one slept whilst the other drove, but their passengers didn't inquire into this. They were happy to be speeding in the right direction. Eventually, exhausted by the discomfort and tedium of the journey, they both slept, only waking when the carriage came to a sudden halt. They'd reached another post station, but this time they must climb down from the carriage and wait while it was placed on its sledge, or runners. The original driver came to explain what was happening. They would be there for an hour. There was time for a hot meal while the work was done. He promised to call them in good time. Robertson shot Cave Thomas a questioning look.

"You go first." Cave Thomas would stay and keep watch.

"I'll not be long." Robertson walked quickly over to the low building where food was being served.

The procedure required a lot of extra muscle and argument. Two teams of men heaved the carriage onto the sledge and bolted it into place, whilst bystanders offered unsolicited advice and criticism. It didn't take a Russian speaker to work out what was being said. Workmen were the same the world over.

Having eaten, Robertson returned, and it was Cave Thomas's turn to seek the warmth of the building. It was while he was eating a stew of vegetables and some unidentifiable meat, that another carriage arrived. It had come from Riga. Cave Thomas abandoned his meal and re-joined Robertson. The road ahead was blocked by snow, the driver warned. They must have the shovels ready. This sparked an animated discussion between the drivers and workmen. With so many men about, it was hard for Thomas and Robertson to watch their belongings, especially when a second carriage arrived, from Tilsit.

It swung into the yard and the horses were unhitched. Others were brought and for several minutes there was a melee of men around the two carriages. Cave Thomas and Robertson did their best to stay near their carriage. At one point, Cave Thomas noticed that the door on the far side hung ajar a little, but the driver's mate put up a hand and closed it as the final bolts were tightened.

As for the carriage heading towards St Petersburg, as soon as fresh horses were harnessed, it set off, flinging up icy snow and muck as it went. Cave Thomas looked up as it swung past them and caught sight of a face at the window. He'd barely time to register who it was, before the equipage was out of the yard and on its way, leaving the spent horses to the care of the handlers.

He beckoned to Robertson and the two climbed up into their carriage. They set off, at a modest pace, behind the one which had just left. It was still travelling on wheels. They might soon overtake it.

"Did you see who was on board the other carriage?" he asked Robertson.

"No, I was looking at our own. Who was it? Russell? Or Evans?"

"Neither." Cave Thomas declared. "It was our friend, Herr Finkel."

"Herr Finkel? What the devil is he doing here?"

"That's something I'd dearly like to know. And why he's followed us."

"Who do you think he's working for now?" Robertson mused.

"I can't say," was Cave Thomas's bleak reply, "but, in the meantime, until we know for certain, we must proceed with even greater caution and assume that he's possibly against us after all."

There was nothing more to be done until they arrived at the next post house, so Robertson shifted into the most comfortable position he could find and fell asleep. Cave Thomas remained awake as they raced on through the darkness, pondering the different scenarios running through his head. If Herr Finkel was who and what he purported to be, it could be that he was following them with an urgent message, hoping to intercept them before they reached Riga. But if that was the case, he could have handed it over at the post station – unless, of course, he'd failed to recognise them in all the upheaval.

On the other hand, if Finkel was working against them, his cover was not very convincing. And why would their enemies send someone he and Robertson might recognise? There were plenty of men not known to them, who would happily crack a head and steal a bag or two, putting an end to their journey. No, the more he considered the matter, the more it appeared to Cave Thomas that something had altered in their situation – something that had developed after the last telegraph sent from London - something big enough to set Herr Finkel chasing across Europe in their wake.

His thoughts were interrupted by the coach slowing down for the next change of horses. In the dim light before dawn Cave Thomas could see upwards of a hundred horses, tethered in long lines, drawn up under the shelter of a stand of firs, near to a three-sided hayloft. This must be one of the larger post houses, although not the largest. He'd heard tell of double that number of horses in some places.

Fresh horses were brought, and they were soon on their way. Robertson woke up.

"Any sign of Finkel?"

"No. He's still in front of us. Remember, there's deep snow ahead. We must brace ourselves for possible trouble."

Robertson thought this a good excuse to make tea, so he wedged the samovar in place, lit the flame and heated the water. The hot drink revived them and brought feeling back to numb fingers. Cave Thomas slid his hand inside his fur coat and pulled out his revolver. Having checked it carefully, he slipped it back into his pocket. It was a comfort to know it was there, even if he felt reluctant to use it.

Not much further along the road, and thankfully after the samovar had been returned to its basket, the carriage suddenly lurched sideways, tottered in the air and then slowly fell onto its side. Cave Thomas braced himself at the first lurch, and Robertson was only a split second behind him. Even so, as their world turned sideways, they were unable to prevent themselves falling into a tangled heap. Cave Thomas's first thoughts were for the packing cases and other parcels. They looked fine, being so wedged together that no harm had come to them. Now they must extricate themselves and help right the carriage. Strong arms assisted them up through the only door available to them. They stood for a moment on the side of the sledge structure which supported the carriage, and then jumped down into the thick snow. They were glad of their warm furs and stout boots. The driver pointed to the corner of the carriage and made it clear that he wished them to push from that point. Cave Thomas glanced towards the horses, anxious lest they had been injured, but they appeared to be unharmed and in good hands. Several people had appeared from nowhere and together they heaved and pushed until the carriage stood upright once more. The driver went slowly round the carriage checking all the fastenings, then finding nothing broken, joined his mate, who was holding the horses, steadying them with a soothing stream of Russian. They still quivered with shock but being accustomed to such occurrences, seemed ready to set off again soon. However, the driver turned to Cave Thomas and said, in a thick accent,

"We dig." He handed the two men a shovel each, took another himself, and strode to the drift in front of them.

"Dig!" he repeated, matching the action to the word. So, they set to and dug – even the rider whose job it was to guard them, who slid out of his saddle, flung the reins to the man holding the other horses, and took hold of a spade.

The reason for the drift was quickly revealed. An obstruction had created a wall against which the wind-whipped snow had quickly piled up and formed an impassable obstacle. The obstruction was uncovered. A wagon had overturned, shedding its load, and next to it lay an upturned handcart. It looked as if the two vehicles had collided. Cave Thomas bent to lift a corner of the cart, started to heave and then stopped. He called to Robertson.

"Quick! Take the weight, will you?"

He leaned down and scraped at the snow. The huddled heap of cloth he had spotted was revealed to be the figure of a young boy. He was so cold that it was hard to tell if he lived or not.

"How long can a child survive in this cold? He must have lain there for hours." Robertson touched Cave Thomas's arm.

"Can you help him?"

Cave Thomas took the boy in his arms and carried him to the carriage. The driver's mate opened the door and helped him lift the boy inside, where Cave Thomas covered him in a fur rug. Meanwhile, Robertson and the driver righted the handcart and tied it to the back of the sledge. The driver came to the carriage door.

"There is village near. We take boy to village."

Robertson climbed in and shut the door. Leaving the site of the accident, they set off at a steady pace towards the village. The gentle warmth of the furs might bring the boy back to life – it must be done slowly, or the shock would kill him, even if his time in the snow had not. Cave Thomas watched and prayed. He didn't know the boy, but he trusted in a God who did.

A mile or so on, his prayer was answered. The boy was breathing, and colour was beginning to return to his lips. Two miles more, and the driver slowed the horses to a walk. They'd arrived at the village.

It was a matter of moments before a door opened and a woman ran out of a building, followed by her husband and two or three little children. The driver called down to them in the local tongue but Cave Thomas didn't need their words translated – it was near enough to Russian for him to understand. The boy had been missed. A search party had gone out and returned empty handed. They'd been watching since dawn. They'd spotted the cart lashed to the carriage and knew it to be theirs. What news of the boy?

Cave Thomas opened the door of the carriage and stepped down.

"He is here," he said.

The woman ran to the carriage, where Robertson was tightening the furs around the boy, preparatory to handing him down to his mother.

"Thank you, thank you, God be praised!" she cried. In English! Then, as she saw her son, "*Mon Dieu, comme il est blanc*! So many hours in the snow!"

"*Maman*," the boy whispered, and a tear slipped down his cheek.

Wasting no time, Cave Thomas lifted the boy out, furs and all, and carried him to the house, where the door stood open. He looked back at the driver, who said, "Five minutes, no more."

Cave Thomas nodded. The driver returned to the carriage and someone closed the door, shutting out the cold. Cave Thomas still carrying the boy, walked towards the fire and set him down on a bench, covered with a rough blanket. His mother quickly took over his care.

"You are English?" he asked.

"*Non, pardon. Je peux parler en Anglais.* I was maid for a Russian lady. She speak to me in French and English." She turned to her husband and spoke quickly in the local tongue, which Cave Thomas recognised to be Lettish or Latvian. The man nodded and held out his hand to shake Cave Thomas's.

"There was an accident. We stopped to clear the way and found your son under the handcart. We don't know how long he'd been there."

"Sir, you are *comme un ange*!" The mother wiped her eye. "You have saved my son."

"I must return to my carriage," he said, slowly. The boy stirred and pushed the furs towards him.

"Thank you, sir," he said.

"He recovers. That's good. Where is this place?"

The mother told him the name. It meant nothing to Cave Thomas, but he would ask the driver where it was.

"Goodbye," He turned to leave.

The father seized his hand once more, speaking low and but too fast for Cave Thomas, who looked towards the mother for a translation.

"My husband say we owe you a life. One day we repay."

"You owe me nothing," he said. Then, attempting the local tongue, "*Tu man neko nav parādā.*"

As he turned towards the carriage, her voice followed him: "*Mille bénédictions!*"

As they set off once more into the white landscape, Cave Thomas described the scene in the house to Robertson.

"This journey is proving to be more of an adventure than I expected. I daren't conjecture what will happen next – but at least we've made friends along the way."

Robertson laughed, some of his earlier tension gone.

"We never know when we might need a friend," mused Cave Thomas, reaching for another rug to cover his knees.

11

Riga
Wednesday (evening) 25th – Thursday 26th January 1854

They reached Riga at 7 o'clock that evening - January 25th.
Drawing up before the posting station, they were invited to step
down and take a meal. There would be time enough to eat and even
to find a hotel where they could take proper rest and clean away
the dirt of travel, they were told. Cave Thomas and Richardson
were tempted to take advantage of the nearby hotel but decided to
stay with the carriage. They were soon joined by more officials
who checked their papers once more and counted the luggage.
They told them to go to Police Headquarters to register, pointed
out the way and then, appearing satisfied, moved on to the next
carriage, just arrived. At this point, their armed guard left them,
with no explanation. Their driver shrugged his shoulders. It was
nothing to do with him.

The posting house provided hot water for washing for a
moderately modest fee, so Cave Thomas stayed with the carriage
whilst Robertson bathed, changing places with him upon his
return. Glad of a change of shirt, Cave Thomas then walked over to
the hotel to see if any messages had been sent there. There were
none, but the man at the front desk suggested he try the post office
and gave him directions there.

"Could I make use of your writing facilities? I need to send a
letter to my family."

"Of course, sir," the man stepped out from behind the desk and
led Cave Thomas to a spacious room which was furnished in the
Prussian style. There were upholstered chairs, tables and in the
corner, a wide, heavily carved desk upon which stood ink and
writing materials.

"Would Monsieur like some coffee?"

Cave Thomas accepted gratefully, sat down and framed a letter
to Emily. He was just checking that the ink was dry, when the
coffee arrived, together with Robertson.

"Another cup, sir?" asked the attendant.

Robertson answered him, "Yes, please." And to Cave Thomas,
"We will be here for another hour or two. There's a problem with

the carriage. We didn't get off entirely without damage when it toppled over."

"Have you left the carriage un-…?"

"No," Robertson broke in. "Our friend Mr Russell arrived on the next coach. This is as far as he is travelling. He has business here and must then return to Munich. He offered to keep our bags company until we'd finished here."

"A happy coincidence," Cave Thomas said, musingly. "Very happy."

"Indeed, it is. We'll have time to call at the post office, in addition to the Police Headquarters, and see if anything has arrived from home. There'll not be another opportunity before the end of the journey."

The two men bent to the task of letter writing. Robertson to his brother and sisters, and Cave Thomas to his father and to his friend Madox Brown. He also scratched a note to Ellis, leaving it open until they'd visited the post office.

Once they had finished their letters, Robertson paid what they owed, and the two men set out in search of any mail. Cave Thomas checked his watch. They wouldn't be moving on for at least another hour, so he suggested extending their walk a little before confining themselves to the claustrophobic interior of the carriage once more. However, when Robertson pointed out that they might still be in danger, he abandoned the idea.

At the post office, they inquired whether any letters had arrived, poste restante. After a short wait, they were brought just two, made the requisite payments and took them to the carriage to read in private. Russell was sitting with his feet up on the seat, smoking a foul cigar. He swung his feet down when they flung open the door and moved to make room for them. It was a tight fit. Robertson left the door open, to clear the stale air, but Russell, apologising for his behaviour, insisted that it be shut.

"Never know who's around, sir."

"Well, we have a couple of letters here – no telegraphs of course, and somewhat out of date, but there may be something." Cave Thomas opened the first one, dated January 19th. It was a coded message from Ellis, telling them that Russell and Evans had been sent to assist them. Old news. The second was more interesting. It was signed by Herr Finkel and had been left at the post office when he'd passed through, the day before. So, Finkel was in Russia! Their eyes had not deceived them.

Cave Thomas worked on the code for several minutes, determined to do this himself, whilst Russell looked on with a wry smile. Then he sat back and exhaled slowly.

"This is news indeed. Finkel was followed all the way. He hid at one of the posting houses and managed to take another sledge carriage. He evaded his would-be captors for two stages, but they caught him at the next and spent some time interrogating him. He writes that he is battered but free – rescued from their clutches by none other than Evans! So, Mr Russell, what do you say to that?"

"I didn't know Evans would follow me – he said he'd wait in Königsberg for further instructions. Obviously, something happened to make him change his mind – and a good thing too, if you ask me!"

"I am asking you…" Cave Thomas went on. "I want to know what your orders are. What is going on here, actually? You clearly know more than you've admitted to so far."

Robertson grabbed the door strap to block Russell's exit, but Russell appeared to have no intention of leaving the carriage.

"Very well," he said after a pause. "I've watched you two and, for men who've had no training, you've done really well. You've stuck to the plan, made good time, kept the luggage safe and dealt with a few tight squeezes. Mr Ellis has confidence in you and so do I, but it was a different matter for Sir Henry. He wasn't sure and he wanted you watched. That's how we first became involved. He persuaded Mr Ellis to include us in his plan, on the understanding that you were to be kept in ignorance of our involvement. As you know, we followed you on the train and once we'd met you properly, decided to take you into our confidence – up to a point. Soon after you'd left Königsberg something happened to change everything. So, I came on and, as I said, Evans followed. I've been as close to you as I could manage, ever since Tauroggen and Evans has been five or six hours behind me."

"So, what happened to bring all this about?"

"The Quakers happened!"

"The Quakers? But we know about them – we were told in the telegraph."

"Yes, Mr Thomas, but no-one told you about Sir Henry. I can see now, that was wrong, very wrong."

"What about Sir Henry?" Cave Thomas's patience was wearing thin.

"He's dead, sir. Dead. Died of apoplexy because of the Quakers." This statement was met with a stunned silence.

"I'm sorry to hear that, Russell," said Cave Thomas, "but it sounds somewhat far-fetched. No-one dies of apoplexy these days."

"Well, maybe not, but he got very angry and then collapsed, so it amounts to the same thing, in my book."

Robertson spoke first. "Who's in charge now?"

"Mr Ellis, sir. We take all our orders from him now."

"Where does Herr Finkel fit into all this?" Cave Thomas was trying to see the wider implications.

"Herr Finkel works partly for Sir Henry – or *worked* I should say. Mr Ellis didn't know half the stuff he did, or who he was taking orders from – other than from Sir Henry."

"Are you suggesting that he's taking orders from someone else? If so, from whom? Is there anything in his behaviour to suggest he might be a traitor?"

"That's a difficult one to answer, Mr Thomas. I know what I think, but I don't have proof that I'm right. All I can say for certain is that Sir Henry was taking orders from someone near to the Queen, and that Herr Finkel was thick as thieves with some of the men who work for the Prince Consort."

"That's a strong accusation to make, Russell." Robertson was shocked.

"It is sir, it is. But when you've lain awake at night trying to work out a puzzle, and all the pathways you go down meet a dead end, then the only one that's left must be explored."

Cave Thomas took out his pipe, and with a rueful smile of apology, lit it. He pulled on it for a few minutes and when he spoke, it was quietly and reasonably, as if in his studio, mulling over the correct hue of a pigment.

"We have no proof of any of this. However, Russell, you've helped us thus far and we must trust your judgement. Our task is to get these packages safely to St Petersburg."

"I'll come with you," Russell broke in. "I'll not abandon you now. Munich will wait."

"Thank you for that, Russell," said Cave Thomas, "We'll be glad to have you. Now, we have bookings for a hotel in the city, and they are expecting us – we mustn't disappoint then, or anyone else involved in our mission. We must confound our enemies and act for our friends, and the best way we can do that is to do the opposite of what our enemies expect us to do. All this under military scrutiny, with a mounted soldier as escort and, if I'm not mistaken, troop movements in the countryside."

"So…?" Robertson looked at his friend, knowing he could trust him to take the wisest path.

"So, we will make a detour. They will expect us to go directly to Benson's Hotel in the English quarter, but we will call upon Mrs Robertson instead. We have some deliveries to make. And we will make them, with your help Russell. Will you smuggle yourself into Mrs Robertson's apartment and remain there to guard the luggage?"

"Of course."

"Robertson, you must stay there too – nothing could be more natural. With you both in residence, there will be a twenty-four-hour guard on the packages. We will do what we came to do, and no-one will stop us!"

They set off into the night, the armed rider tracking their carriage once more, but soon wished they'd stopped at an hotel and delayed travelling until morning. The snow, which had been threatening, closed in upon them an hour after they left Riga. The drivers. were used to such weather. They stoically tightened their scarves, pulled their hats down to protect their faces and carried on regardless. Their mounted escort came close to the carriage, keeping in line with it and spying out the marker trees along the way. They proceeded thus for two or three hours, before reaching a posting house sometime after midnight, where the exhausted horses could be rested. The driver approached the carriage. He made it clear that he was happy to go on, but that progress would be slow. A sledge arriving from the other direction brought news of heavy falls ahead, but that between where they were and Dorpat, the road was passable,

"Go on to Dorpat," Cave Thomas commanded, with a glance at his companions noting their agreement. "We'll break our journey there, if need be."

The driver nodded, and climbed back up to his seat, took the reins and away they went.

"A good decision, Mr Thomas," said Russell, who knew the country better than they did. "It should break soon. Then we'll make better progress."

"We have little choice," Cave Thomas replied. "We must fulfil our mission. We can't linger. Did you see the soldiers?"

"Yes," Robertson's reply was calm. "A troop, I think. Heading east. Horses and foot soldiers. I don't envy them."

"I've noticed that there's more traffic going west than towards the east," Russell commented. "It's war, isn't it?"

"Almost certainly." Cave Thomas thought about the letter he'd posted to Emily, full of quaint descriptions of their journey so far – things to entertain her, to be read out to George and to John and Jane. The samovar, the peasants, the food, the rustic dress, the wild animals on the horizon, the shipping locked in ice, the glitter of sun on snow, and the music of the sleigh bells. These were the things of which he had written – no mention of soldiers, of border guards, of bribes, of lost sleep, of anxiety and subterfuge. No, all that must remain in Russia when he returned to England, never a word to cross his lips.

They went on through the night, silent once more. With nothing to do except yield to the motion of the sledge and trust in the expertise of the drivers, weariness overcame them, and they slept. The shroud of snow through which they travelled was dark and impenetrable with no light to pierce it, yet still they went on. Some hours later, at a posting house, they became aware of a change in the air. Robertson opened the door and they peered out. Moonlight flooded the scene from a sky now clear of cloud. It silvered the buildings, casting long shadows, all colour reduced to black, grey and white. Figures moved about. A door opened and there was a glimpse of a fire within before it closed again. A solitary figure, bent with age, approached the carriage, carrying a lantern. He was dressed as a peasant - long beard, rough tunic and with a tattered blanket tied about his shoulders against the bitter cold.

"Russell?" he inquired, in a deep voice. The lantern light shone on a face, upon which the hardships of life were deeply etched, but the eyes searching their faces, seeking a response, were full of intelligence.

'What a face!' thought Cave Thomas, wishing he had his sketch book to hand.

"Here," said Russell. "I am Russell."

"Take," said the old man. He held out a letter with shaking hand.

'Perhaps he was a soldier once, but enfeebled by age, reduced to the level of a general servant,' thought Cave Thomas, 'to work until he can no longer stand. It's the way in this harsh country.'

The man remained standing, hand outstretched, awaiting his reward.

Russell took the letter and handed the man a few coins. The old soldier bowed his head, turned, and walked slowly back to the shelter of the wooden shack.

"This is a thing," said Russell, "It appears to be a note from Evans." He opened the folded sheet. The message was short.

'I have overtaken you. Will await you at Dorpat. Finkel has gone on to St Petersburg.

Look for the Eagle with the Broken Wing. A.E.'

"No code?" Cave Thomas was quick to see this.

"It may not signify – he left it with a man who cannot read English - or Russian, come to that. Perhaps he was in haste." Russell seemed unperturbed.

"What does he mean by the eagle with the broken wing?" asked Robertson.

"An inn, I imagine – and probably not very savoury. He'll be keeping away from the obvious places." Russell reassured them. "He's good at mingling with the crowd."

"Well, Dorpat it is, then." Cave Thomas took command. "I have a mind to stay there overnight. The drivers need a rest and we could all do with a few decent hours' sleep."

"Have we time, Cave Thomas?" Robertson was thinking of his previous imprecation to hurry on to St Petersburg.

"We must bend to the climate. We ignore advice at our peril. Better to arrive a day late than to fail in our mission."

The sledge set off once more, this time gliding effortlessly over the frosty ground. The wind had taken what snow had fallen and dumped it in drifts at some distance from the route they intended to take. They were travelling east, ever further from the Gulf of Riga, and the air was biting cold, but less damp now they were away from the coast. Stretches of woodland etched their way along the horizon, visible in the growing light. Figures on horseback could be seen from time to time, moving along at a distance from the road: more troops. Then, at last, they pulled into a posting station to be told that their next stop would be Dorpat. After Dorpat, they would skirt the massive Lake Peipus and then make the final run towards St Petersburg. The end, if not in sight, was now, at least, within reach.

12

Dorpat, to St Petersburg
Thursday (evening) 26th – Sunday 29th January 1854

Dorpat, an old university town, was to be their last stop before the final approach to St Petersburg. The sledge drew up in the town square towards evening on Thursday 26th. At the driver's recommendation, they took rooms in a small hotel, tucked behind the main street. They unloaded their bags and left Russell in the carriage with the remaining luggage whilst they negotiated its transfer to their room. The whole business took upwards of an hour. Their guard watched proceedings, had a brief word with the driver and then left them. It would be the last they saw of him.

The driver had kin in the town, so disappeared with the carriage, promising to return at six the following morning. Russell kept a little apart from Cave Thomas and Robertson, acting the part of a casual acquaintance, made on the journey. The two artists signed the hotel register together and then went to present themselves to the police, leaving Russell to keep an eye on their belongings. Upon their return, he went in turn to register. They all found the Russian bureaucracy lengthy and tedious but not hostile. Their two countries might be on the verge of war, but day to day routines appeared unchanged.

After a welcome meal, Robertson was keen to take some exercise, so he and Russell stepped out into the cold night to explore the centre of the town. A bright moon lit the streets, augmented by lights set outside the main buildings. Despite the intense cold, the streets were busy with townsfolk and students, many shopping in an evening market. Russell and Robertson returned after half an hour or so, keen to drag Cave Thomas away from his letter writing and show him the town.

"I'll stay here," said Robertson. I have letters of my own to write. Russell, take him to the market and buy some food for tomorrow."

Cave Thomas was more than willing to abandon his task. He donned his fur coat, dragged on his boots, and went with Russell. At the market, they selected provisions for the last part of the journey, then found a quiet corner in a nearby inn. Russell ordered them drinks and steaming beakers of the local winter brew arrived at their table.

"Allow me," Russell handed the barman a handful of coins. They exchanged words in Russian. Russell asked a question and the man's reply was lengthy. Cave Thomas looked on with interest. Russell's Russian was as good as his own. At last, the man went back to the other room.

"I was asking him about the state of the roads," said Russell. "He spoke quickly and my Russian is far from perfect. Did you catch what he said? I think he told me that they're clear towards St Petersburg, although clogged with soldiers. I'm not sure about the rest."

"He said that his son's in the army. He passed through here yesterday and managed to get a message to his father. It's as we thought. They're mobilising the troops in readiness for war."

"I caught the bit about war – but wasn't he suggesting it might be weeks or even months before anything happens?"

"He said he doesn't want war – it's not good for business! As to when – who knows? Our business should be swiftly concluded, I think." Cave Thomas finished his drink and stood up. "I must return to Robertson. I don't like to leave him for too long. He's worried about his mother and needs company."

"I'll come with you," Russell emptied his cup and set it down. "Best not to walk alone in a strange place."

With this reminder of their need for continual vigilance, they set off back to the hotel. Robertson had finished his letters, but he was alone. There was no sign of Evans.

"Something may have delayed him," said Russell. "If in doubt, press on. No need to change our plans."

The driver was prompt the next morning. The coach, still bolted to its sledge, was drawn up outside the hotel at a little before six. The morning was cold but there was no more snow. The travellers were ready, so the repacking of the coach went ahead without any problems and they were on their way once more by a quarter past the hour. There was no sign of the guard. Perhaps he'd joined the troops mustering nearby. The driver made no comment about this and was seemingly unconcerned.

They caught tantalising glimpses of the old town as they headed towards the frozen Lake Peipus. Cave Thomas wished there'd been more time to explore the town. Perhaps he'd come back that way on the way home. But as they swept north-east towards the lake, such thoughts were banished. There was still much to achieve before he could begin to think of returning to England and meanwhile, he must keep his wits about him. He didn't like the fact that Evans had failed to keep his rendezvous, no matter how calmly Russell appeared to take it.

Lake Peipus was a huge obstacle across their path. There was a choice of routes around it – crossing it on the ice or going up along its western edge. The driver had already negotiated this with his passengers. The western route had been selected, as more likely to be free from obstructions. The road was busy, and they were held up for a while by a long line of carts blocking their way. Unwilling to endanger the carriage by leaving the road, the driver had no choice but to travel at the pace of the slowest vehicle. Eventually the land opened out and he was able to give the horses their heads. The sledge swept past the carts and wagons – mostly driven by farmers, although were some carrying men in army uniforms. Cave Thomas watched it all, wondering if it explained Evans's failure to arrive in Dorpat. If he'd been caught up in the troop movements, he might have abandoned his plans and would meet them in St Petersburg instead.

The Lake lay to their right, a seemingly never-ending expanse of ice, frozen in ripples as the wind had whipped up the surface at the very moment the water froze. It was bleak but exceptionally beautiful in the weak winter sunshine. Slowed by the depth of recently fallen snow, they went on beside it for many miles until, leaving it at last, they turned north-east and struck out towards the coast and the Gulf of Finland. They were heading for Narva, where they would find food. Then they'd turn east once more and travel the last hundred miles to St Petersburg.

They reached Narva just before dawn on the 29th. There was light enough to gain some idea of its age and size. The old defences stood towering above the town, solid and forbidding. The river Narva, which drained Lake Peipus, lay frozen within its banks, making the bridges redundant. But when the spring thaw eventually came, the river would surge against the bridge supports and the townsfolk would keep well away until it settled down once more. However, on this morning, they were glad to cross to the old town on the ice and seek somewhere to stable the horses, whilst they found food for the rest of the journey.

Once more, they went through the rigmarole of reporting to the police. Again, there were no problems with their papers. Cave Thomas thanked Ellis for his diligence regarding the formalities.

102

Nowhere had they been challenged. In that respect, all had gone as smoothly as possible. Free to go, they completed their purchases and went back to join Russell near the carriage, not wishing to prolong their stop beyond the consumption of a meal and an opportunity to wash and, in Robertson's case, shave. They left around midday, a hundred miles still to travel. They hoped to arrive in St Petersburg the following afternoon if all went well.

During the afternoon they fleshed out their plans for delivering the gold to the merchants in St Petersburg. They would need time to establish the right method of delivery and to the right people. The plan – to go first to Robertson's mother, and only then contact the authorities, seemed a good one. They'd every reason to visit her as soon as they arrived. It would hold them up only an hour. Their luggage had been checked so many times that they felt they could justify its immediate delivery. Any queries could be dealt with once it was safely with Mrs Robertson. They would have to abandon it there with Russell to guard it, whilst they went to register at the police headquarters. Russell would only go to register himself once Robertson had returned.

Cave Thomas would leave them. He'd go to Mrs Benson's Hotel, in the English Quarter. Once there, he'd contact the people whose names he'd been given at the outset, using the letters of introduction, kept safe throughout the journey. Robertson could stay at a distance, claiming a need to be with his mother. His presence wasn't necessary at these meetings. Russell would stay in the background. As for Evans, there'd been nothing further from him since Dorpat. It was possible that he'd arrive in St Petersburg in front of them, or he could be a few hours behind, or…? Russell hoped to hear something in St Petersburg. If anything had happened to Evans en route, they may never hear of it. It was a sobering thought, and each man reflected that although the journey had been, at times, uncomfortable – or even dangerous - so far nothing serious had happened to them. This was something they could not have guaranteed before setting out.

The night passed, the movement of the sledge lulling them to sleep. Then, halfway through the morning of the 29th, they came to a halt, near to a small wood. The driver climbed down from his perch, knocked on the door softly and then opened it a crack.

"Trouble ahead, I think. There are men. Horses. Fires. I hear a gun. Stay inside. Let me do talking."

He climbed back up and took the reins from his partner. They moved on at a slower pace than before. As they neared the edge of the wood, the road narrowed between trees and a rocky outcrop. Two men stepped out in front of them and the driver stopped the sledge. There was an exchange of greetings, not unfriendly in tone but, inside the carriage, the three men were unable to distinguish what was said. Through the smeared window, they could see figures taking hold of the horses' heads. The driver and his mate were then forced down from their seat and led away to one side.

"Keep quiet," whispered Russell. "Let the drivers do the talking."

More men approached and the door was pulled open. Several pairs of eyes flicked over Cave Thomas and his companions. One man leaned in and prodded the bags and packages with a rough stick. He lifted the fur rug and, with a flick, pulled it towards him and hauled it out. He turned to his mates and said something which made them laugh.

Cave Thomas looked at the group, committing their faces to memory, noting their torn clothing and ill-kempt appearance. It appeared that he and his friends had fallen amongst thieves. It was a pity they no longer had their military guard. His next thoughts were for their cargo. How could these vagabonds be prevented from stealing the gold and doing away with them all? His mouth felt dry. He swallowed, trying to master his fear. Pressed close together in the carriage, as they were, he was aware of his friends' shallow breathing, the tension in their bodies as they recognised the danger, they were in. He breathed a brief prayer and waited.

The leader of the group by the door walked away with the fur rug and went to talk to the drivers, who were still detained near one of the fires. The conversation went on for some time, looking, for all the world, like a bargain being struck in a marketplace. Russell shifted uneasily in his seat and muttered to Cave Thomas, in an undertone,

"Looks like we're for sale."

"I don't think it's a plot." Cave Thomas had seen the lack of recognition between drivers and ruffians.

"Do you have guns ready?" Russell slowly eased his hand into his pocket to access his.

"Against so many? And without a driver?" Robertson knew it was hopeless.

"Stay calm," said Cave Thomas. "Don't look at the bags and don't let them know that we understand Russian."

The man with the stick returned to the carriage, the driver in tow. He pushed the driver forwards and indicated that he should speak to the passengers.

"These men are cold," said the driver. "They see that we have furs. They want furs. Then they let us go." The man lifted one eyebrow a fraction. The message was clear: give them what they want. Give us a chance to get going. Don't trust them. Don't object.

'What an expressive face,' Cave Thomas thought. Another image for his mental sketchbook. Suddenly, he felt a glow of courage. Words came unbidden to his lips.

"Tell the men that we are sorry for their plight, but that we cannot spare all our furs. Please will they allow us one to share between us until we come to our journey's end?"

Robertson tensed. Russell's hand tightened on his gun. This was the critical moment. The driver nodded slightly and translated the request word for word. The leader of the men paused for a few seconds, then grinned, showing broken teeth. He clapped the driver on the shoulder, said something clearly crude, and the men about him laughed. With the laughter, came a relaxation in the tension. The driver spoke again.

"He say - he can leave you naked, but he think you weak so do not wish you to suffer. He thank you for your gift. Please to throw all furs out of door. You can keep rug."

Robertson shrugged off his fur coat, surreptitiously emptying the pockets of all but a few roubles. Russell and Cave Thomas followed suit, the confined space helping to conceal their actions. They dropped the furs out of the door. Two of the men stepped forward and quickly removed them. The man with the stick, pointed at their feet. Fur boots followed the coats. Two more rugs followed. The leader of the gang then peered in and looked the luggage over. He ripped the corner of the nearest parcel. Luck was with them: it was the parcel of pastel boxes. The man pulled one out and opened it. Then flung them a question. The driver translated.

"What is this?"

"Crayons for a painter." Robertson used simple words. These men knew nothing of art.

The driver passed on the information and the man threw the box carelessly back. Another question.

"All like this?" asked the driver.

Cave Thomas nodded. "Yes."

"Artists," he went on, pointing to himself and his companions. Then he slowly reached for his small sketchbook, which was lodged in a pocket at the side of the carriage. He opened it and showed the leader some of his drawings. The men about him crowded closer to look.

Suddenly there was more laughter. The drivers, who'd been allowed to keep their coats and boots, climbed back onto their seat. 'So,' thought Cave Thomas, 'these thieves are not altogether without honour.' The carriage door was slammed shut and the horses released. There was a shout and they were once more on their way. A couple of gunshots punctuated their departure, making the horses shy and skitter, before pulling hard once more. The thieves rapidly became distant dots. The three passengers relaxed, teeth chattering, and thanked God from their hearts that they had been spared worse treatment and that the gold was safe.

They quickly pulled out the bags that held their spare clothing. Cave Thomas located the spare boots in which he'd hidden some of the gold. He tipped the coins into a pair of socks and eased his feet into the boots. Dressed in thick coats, hats and gloves, they unpacked the samovar and lit it. Hot drinks would bring back the circulation to their cold hands and feet. They'd paid a small price for survival.

The final staging post was reached at last. The driver made a point of checking to see that his passengers were well. Once the horses were changed, he returned and spoke briefly to Cave Thomas.

"Those men. They run from army. They not wish to fight." He spat in the snow. "Not true Russians." Then he climbed back up and they were on their way to the city.

They reached the outskirts in a burst of sunshine, which sparkled on the fresh snow and hid some of the squalor of the rough wooden houses. This was not the St Petersburg of western imagination but was reality for the masses of working people who maintained the place. They built and mended and cleaned and serviced the gleaming buildings in the centre, but lived like their ancestors, in abject poverty. The rough corrugated wooden track jarred every muscle and joint as they proceeded towards the centre of the city. The logs were necessary to prevent vehicles becoming mired in the mud but made travel across them far from comfortable. As they neared the river, they entered the stone-built district. Here the streets were wide and well paved, with a coating of compacted ice upon them, making troikas the preferred mode of transport. The streets thronged with these, which raced along at impossible speeds, putting pedestrians at risk. As they came closer to the frozen river and canals, a biting wind made the temperature drop a degree or so lower, and the men felt the lack of their warm furs and winter boots.

Robertson had given the driver directions to his mother's apartment, so it was there that they made their first stop. Robertson jumped down from the carriage and knocked on the outer door of the building, to be admitted by a concierge. He raced up the long staircase to the first floor, where his mother had rooms, whilst the others waited for permission to unload the luggage.

After several minutes, Robertson reappeared.

"Yes," he said, "My mother is asleep, but her maid – the one who wrote to us - tells me we are expected and can leave our luggage here."

They unloaded the carriage together and carried the precious parcels up to his mother's studio.

So far, so good, but much more must be achieved before the day was out.

13

A Mystery
Sunday 29th January 1854 (evening)

The afternoon light was already beginning to fade. Cave Thomas was eager to press on, so Robertson left messages for his mother, who was in bed, asleep, and went with Cave Thomas to register. Russell remained at the apartment, getting to know the concierge and spinning a yarn to her and to Robertson's mother's maid, Marie-Claire, about his adventures in Europe as a travelling salesman. By the end of half an hour, he'd been prepared a meal by the maid and learnt much of the local scandal from the concierge.

Robertson and Cave Thomas joined a queue at the police headquarters – people like them, registering their presence, others with complaints against neighbours, fines to be paid, lost property to declare and so on. However, their conversation, in English, helped move them forward in the queue, and their ability to speak Russian meant that the procedure was completed in under an hour. Robertson then disappeared on foot to find his way back to his mother, and Cave Thomas took the carriage to Benson's Hotel. Here, the remaining bags were unloaded and taken in, whilst he worked out what was still owed to the driver. As he scribbled in his notebook, he heard a voice he recognised.

"Cave Thomas! You're here at last! I've been looking for you for a day and a half. What kept you?" It was Evans. "No, don't shake hands... we might be being watched."

"We were held up on the way, I'm afraid, but we're here now." Cave Thomas kept his voice low. "I'm sorry we missed you at Dorpat. What happened to you?"

"I'll tell you all about it in the hotel," Evans replied. "Too cold to talk out here. Can I help you with your luggage?"

"It's all in the hotel," said Cave Thomas, suddenly alert.

"I'll take a bet on you having missed something," Evans went on. "Let's just take a look."

He walked around to the opposite side of the carriage and opened the door. Cave Thomas reopened the door on his side and the two leaned in, heads close together.

"I've reason to believe there's something in here you'll have missed," he whispered.

"Where? We've emptied it."

"Let's just take a look …here." Evans had whipped a spanner out of his pocket and was attacking the bolts that secured a panel underneath the rear facing seat. Cave Thomas watched in amazement as it came away to reveal a battered box. Evans pulled it out and tested its weight.

"Heavy," he said quietly. "Do you think you could manage its weight without its seeming obvious how heavy it is?"

Cave Thomas was strong. He lifted a corner and flexed his hand.

"I think I can – as far as the hotel, anyway."

"Let's go then. I'll cover you with a plausible story. Here, take my scarf and ease it under the box. It may help."

As Cave Thomas took the weight of the box, Evans swiftly replaced the panel and the bolts and backed out of the carriage. He jumped down from the sledge and slammed the door. Joining Cave Thomas, he cuffed him on the shoulder.

"Always worth checking," he laughed, in a voice that carried. "You'd have been totally lost without your paints."

Together, they entered the hotel and Evans shut the door behind them. He inclined his head a fraction and Cave Thomas left the hallway and climbed the stairs to his room. He checked both ways along the corridor before unlocking the door, then took the box inside. He kicked the door shut behind him and carried his heavy load to the bed, where he set it down and took a good look at it.

Meanwhile, Evans had ordered drinks to be brought up to the room. He followed Cave Thomas upstairs and tapped on the door. Cave Thomas opened it gingerly, then let Evans slip by him and shut and locked it. The two men stood for a moment before allowing themselves to breathe easily again.

"A waiter is on his way. Say nothing for a moment." Evans shrugged his coat off and laid it on the bed, concealing the box. Cave Thomas removed his own coat and did likewise.

Another tap on the door and Evans opened it to the waiter. The man came in and set a tray of drinks on the table.

Evans thanked him and gave him a tip. The waiter left without looking towards the bed.

"So," said Cave Thomas. "Tell me what you know."

Evans went over to the bed and pulled back the coats, revealing a strong box – identical to those used in banks. Dipping his hand into an inner pocket in his overcoat, he brought out a small bundle of tools, wrapped in a leather cloth. He selected a strip of metal and used it to pick the locks. He found the secret bolt in seconds, slid it back and lifted the lid to reveal the interior. It was unusual in style - wood, lined with thin metal. A chamois leather cloth concealed the contents. Evans pulled this aside and the two gasped. There, packed in stacks, pressed closely together and divided by what looked like paper, were gold sovereigns - clearly a fortune. Cave Thomas went to the door and checked that it was locked. He returned to stand and stare at the gold.

"Now, Mr Evans, I think you'd better tell me all you know," he said, with quiet calm.

The story was soon told. Evans had become separated from them when he went after Herr Finkel. He'd chanced to see Finkel place the box in the carriage at the staging post, where Robertson had spotted the man's face in the departing carriage. With the Englishmen's carriage being bolted onto the sledge and the number of men competing to help, it had been easy for Finkel to stage a distraction. Evans had later discovered how desperate Herr Finkel had been. Evans had been concealed in the post house, waiting for a chance to join another coach party. Seeing what had happened, he'd seized the slimmest of all opportunities and managed to follow Finkel on the next coach travelling east. He'd gradually caught up with him, and finally managed to change carriage and travel on with Finkel. The story of the box was eventually revealed when the pair found themselves alone for half an hour at a staging post. Finkel, relieved to have an ally who had faith in him, had explained it all.

"The box came into his keeping after your meeting with him," Evans continued. "Finkel was forced to bring it into Russia, himself. Realising he was being followed, he knew that he was likely to fail. When he spotted you, he seized the opportunity to pass it on, trusting you'd be successful."

It was all getting incredibly involved, and Evans's story had raised as many questions as answers, but put plainly, the box had come from another source – separate from the money carried by Cave Thomas and Robertson. Having painstakingly concealed the British Factory money, they'd had this unconcealed gold thrust upon them, potentially endangering their mission and even their lives. Cave Thomas thought of their encounter with the army deserters. If the box had been discovered, he and his friends might never have reached St Petersburg alive. It was a sobering thought.

"What do you know of the origin of this box?" Cave Thomas asked.

Evans sighed. "I thought you'd ask that. I can't tell you because I don't know, myself. But what I do know is that it didn't come from the Government, or from the coffers of the British Factory's London account. However, I've an idea who might be behind it..." he paused, choosing his words carefully. "Her Majesty, the Queen, has been zealous in maintaining good relations with her cousin, the Czar. Letters have continued to flow between them despite the worsening relationship between the Emperor and the British Government. I understand that Prince Albert also has strong interests in the matter. He is Prussian, and Prussia is heavily involved in anything to do with Russia and the west – after all, it lies directly in the way of any troop movements."

"You really think that the royal family is behind this?" Cave Thomas was stunned. He'd had his own thoughts on the matter but had scarcely dared to speak them.

"I can't say for certain," Evans admitted. "But, even if they're not directly involved, there are many who might do something like this in order to curry favour."

"To further their own interests, do you mean?"

"Perhaps. Or maybe they are patriots, seeking to support their friends over here."

Cave Thomas pulled out his pipe and lit it. He needed to think.

"So," he said slowly, "what do you suggest we do now?"

Evans rubbed his hands over his eyes. He was exhausted from the chase across Russia.

"I've received a note from Herr Finkel. It doesn't say much but..." he took it from his pocket-book and handed it to Cave Thomas "...see what you can make of it."

Cave Thomas took the note. It was certainly short and, judging by the writing, written in the coach as Finkel travelled. He read it aloud.

"Take the box to the English Church. Leave it with... the name is tricky to decipher. Who is this person?"

"I believe he works within the church to provide succour to the hungry. He also advises our secret service here in St Petersburg and has links with Prussia."

"My word! This is deep, Evans."

Evans grimaced. "Deeper than we know, I suspect. But we must do as we agreed and try to complete the mission. When do you see your connections here about the other payments?"

111

"Tomorrow," Cave Thomas reached for his bag. He opened it and found the sheaf of letters of introduction. "Run your eye down the list of names," he said. "Do you recognise any?"

Evans took his time.

"There's one here whose name could be that on the note – take a look." Evans held out the letter. Cave Thomas compared it with the scrawled signature.

"I see what you mean. Do you think I should try to see him first?"

"I'm not sure. Maybe see the man in charge at the English Church – Cattley, I believe. If this man is there, you might be able to spot him and work out the best way to contact him. Take someone with you maybe – me or Russell. Not Robertson – he'll be busy with his mother."

"The rest of the money is there and must be recovered and cleaned before it can be passed on. I'd like to get all this done as soon as possible and then head for home whilst I can get out."

"A good enough plan," Evans agreed. "I wish we still had Sir Henry at the helm. He may have been a bit difficult to deal with at times, but his knowledge and scope were second to none. Ellis is good, but he's not been in the job that long. There'll be subtleties that pass him by, I fear."

"You forget, Evans. You have experience, yourself, and Russell is a wise man. As for me, I've learnt a lot over the past couple of weeks."

"Aye, and I venture that your father's work must have had some effect too."

So, Evans knew about his father. What more was there to be discovered?

Another tap on the door sent them scurrying to conceal the gold. When the room was tidy, Cave Thomas opened the door. It was the hotel manager to ask whether he and his guest intended to dine in the hotel. Cave Thomas turned to Evans.

"Would you like to be my guest?" he asked.

"With regret, I cannot stay tonight. Perhaps another time."

"It will be just me, then," said Cave Thomas, and closed and locked the door once more.

"What shall we do with the box?" asked Cave Thomas. "I'm here alone, but it must be watched."

"That's not a problem," said Evans. "I'll leave in a few minutes and return via the back stairs. I'll keep guard whilst you eat. You can make good use of your time in the dining room and see if there are any faces you recognise."

"But first," said Cave Thomas, firmly, we'll count the money and make a note of how much there is."

They lifted the box onto the table and sat down, one either side. Cave Thomas began to count.

14

Promise of Payment
Sunday 29th (evening) – Monday 30th January 1854

William Cave Thomas went down to the dining room, ready to observe and be observed by, the other guests. He'd taken some trouble over his dress, wishing to conceal the rigours of his journey, so it was a quietly dressed man who entered the room to face the mild interest of the diners, already at their tables. Evans, true to his word, had left through the front door, returned unseen, and was guarding the box of gold. They'd counted £1,250 in gold sovereigns, bringing the total value of gold in their possession (including the gold they'd brought with them from London) to in excess of £3,300. The original cargo had been painstakingly concealed, but this other fortune had been tossed under a seat as if it were nothing more than an old blanket, albeit locked and bolted. It had massively complicated their mission. It was one thing to trust one's life to a venture under the steady hand of Sir Henry Loughton, but quite another to be used as a carrier by person or persons unknown; all this whilst simultaneously being robbed of Sir Henry's oversight and left to complete the mission under inexpert management, and in a country about to become Britain's enemy. Small wonder Cave Thomas took time to adjust his necktie, brush his coat and pare his nails. He crossed to his table with an air of intellectual preoccupation, sat down, and placed a copy of Bradshaw beside his plate. The menu was limited but the food smelt good. He ordered his meal, accepted a glass of water and opened his book.

"Monsieur?" The waiter had brought his soup. Cave Thomas thanked him and unfolded his napkin. The soup was delicious, and Cave Thomas took a moment to savour it, taken from a silver spoon, surrounded by the trappings of civilised society, in a warm room and dressed in clean clothes. Had the past ten days really happened?

As he ate his meal, Cave Thomas seized the opportunity to observe his fellow guests. There were a few family groups and couples, but most were men, like himself, eating alone. No-one stood out particularly. If he, in turn, were being watched, he was unaware of it. His main course was brought, and he tucked into it with a relish born of ten days' worth of skimped meals and irregular hours. It was well cooked: cutlets, potatoes and vegetables. He could have been dining in London. The steamed pudding which followed, did nothing to dispel that feeling. For the time being, the English Quarter was going on as normal.

At the end of the meal, he opened his Bradshaw and turned to the page about St Petersburg. Reading what was written about the city, he longed to go out and explore, but he had other matters to sort out first. He must visit the headquarters of the British Factory, and that could not be delayed. He glanced at the paragraph at the top of the page: 'Every Foreigner who wishes to leave Russia ought to present a petition to that effect to the Military Governor-general, or Civil Governor, accompanied with a certificate from the police that there is no legal impediment to his leaving the Empire.'[3] He would need to move quickly and be discreet. He could not afford to blot his copybook if he hoped to be home before Easter.

He left the dining room. Nobody had bothered him, and no-one followed him. Back in his hotel room, he found Evans writing a report.

"Just one moment," he said, returning to his task. "There. Done. I'll get it into tomorrow's post. How was dinner?"

"Very English. But, for all that, a good solid meal was what I needed. Do you intend to eat?"

"I had something earlier. If you have letters to write, I'll happily take them with mine."

"I need to arrange to see someone at the British Factory." Cave Thomas took out his pocketbook and withdrew a slip of paper, closely written with names and addresses.

"The man to see is the Treasurer, Mr Cattley – the man you spoke of. Where will I find him, do you think?"

"I'd look for him at the English Church. He's senior Churchwarden and I believe he spend much of his time in his office there. I gather the church is worth a visit – quite a building."

"Will you come with me?"

"Yes, and no," Evans replied. "On reflection, I think that you'd do better to take Robertson, if he's free – it would be more natural, since you travelled together. If anyone is watching you, it would be

---

[3] Bradshaw's Continental Railway Guide 1853, page 289.
HarperCollins, 2016

better for them not to see you and me together from now on. I'll be around though, in the background, watching your back."

"I value your dedication to duty, and I'd rather not receive a bullet in the back, so be careful how you guard me!" Cave Thomas's smile was rueful. "It's easy to make mistakes in a crowd."

"I'll do my best to miss you," Evans returned, "but seriously, if you are being followed, I should be able to spot them and maybe work out who they represent. And, at a distance, I might be able to spot our man there and let you know who he is."

"Good points," said Cave Thomas, and the subject dropped.

"I'll take my sleep now, if that's alright with you," Evans said.

"Use the bed," Cave Thomas gathered the few items he'd need for the night vigil. "I'll remain near the window for first watch. I'll wake you at three."

Evans slipped under the covers and turned the oil lamp down to a low glow. Another watchful night lay ahead. Soon, very soon, they would be free of their tempting cargo. Until then, no-one would sleep well.

The next morning, Monday, having exchanged places with Evans at three, Cave Thomas woke to Evans's hand on his shoulder. He was leaning over the bed, finger to his lips. Cave Thomas was awake in an instant.

"Someone at the door," whispered Evans. "Answer the knock but keep them out. I'll hide under the bed."

He ducked down and disappeared as Cave Thomas reached for his dressing gown.

"Just a moment," he called, sounding as if he were still half asleep.

He approached the door and unlocked it, then opened it a crack, his foot firmly behind it in case he was rushed. It was Robertson.

"Come in man," Cave Thomas said in a low voice. "Are you alone?"

"Of course. Who do think I'd bring with me? I've left Russell with my mother and I've come to see what we're doing this morning."

Evans emerged from his hiding place, making Robertson jumped a little. Cave Thomas realised that there was a lot to explain, but aware that time was of the essence, he said,

"I'll explain it all later, Robertson. Now he's here, we can make good use of him."

116

Robertson nodded. His trust in Cave Thomas was absolute. He could wait for explanations.

"Well, it's good to see you, Evans. We'll be glad of your presence here in St Petersburg – being just the three of us, we were feeling somewhat exposed."

Cave Thomas was grateful for his trust. However, Russell must also be put into the picture as soon as possible, so they must press on with their morning's business. He turned to Robertson. "How is your mother today?" he asked.

"Not well. She's keeping to her bed. The doctor will call at noon."

"Then we must hurry. You'll wish to be there when he comes. Evans," Cave Thomas took command, "you go and find some breakfast and then follow us when we leave, say, in half an hour? That should get us to the Church at about ten. He should be free to see me by then."

Evans nodded.

"I'll be there, but you won't see me."

He left. Robertson turned to Cave Thomas as soon as the door was locked.

"When did he arrive?"

"Yesterday. He was outside the hotel. He's going to follow us and make sure we don't get into trouble. He beat us to St Petersburg by a day or so. It's a long story, but I'll tell it later, if you don't mind. How's Russell?"

"He's fine," Robertson replied. "He intends to guard the luggage until we can get there to sort it out. The sooner we head to the Church, the better. I suppose that's where we'll find our man?"

"Yes. Mr Cattley. Do you have your gun?"

"Of course, but I don't want to have to use it, so let's be careful."

Cave Thomas quickly combed his hair and beard, brushed his jacket and put on his overcoat. Then he unlocked the door and the two men left the room. As Cave Thomas inserted the key to secure the room, he paused. The gold! He couldn't leave the gold! He turned to Robertson with a look of dismay. The plan was flawed.

"Just a moment, Robertson, there's something I've forgotten." He unlocked the door again and they returned to the room.

"There's something you need to know," he began, and set about giving Robertson a rapid explanation about the box hidden under the seat in the carriage, and now concealed in the hotel room.

Astonished and shocked, Robertson immediately perceived their current difficulty.

"One of us must stay and guard the gold," Robertson shook his head. "We're both tired – let's think this out clearly. I'll stay. It must be you who sees Mr Cattley."

Cave Thomas agreed. "I'll be back as soon as I can. If questioned, you're my cousin and I've gone out to post a letter."

He checked that the way was clear and then set out for the English Church. Robertson closed the door, locked it and sat down to wait.

The sky was leaden. Small flecks of snow fell intermittently, promising more later. Cave Thomas's route led down to the Neva and along its bank to the English Church. It was less than half a mile, but the cold wind made it unpleasant. He added 'purchase furs' to his day's tasks.

There were a lot of people moving about. Most were on foot, but troikas whipped along the streets at such speed as to make crossing risky. He was glad to reach the shelter of the buildings along the English Quay. The church, an imposing building, stood close to the quay. Cave Thomas paused, to take in its proportions, which spoke of wealth and grandeur. He looked around at the throng which passed up and down the quay. As Evans had promised, there was no sign of him. However, knowing that he was there, was a comfort.

The door to the church was to the right. He approached it with confident step. The door opened, forcing him to step aside to let others leave. Once inside, he knocked the snow from his boots and looked about him. The entrance was unimposing for such a fine building but seeing a broad staircase ahead, it struck him that the church itself would be upstairs. This floor, and possibly that below and the another above, were devoted to offices, classrooms and accommodation.

A man, who'd been in the shadow near the stairs, walked towards him to inquire his business.

"I would like to see Mr Cattley if that's possible. I don't have an appointment, but he may be expecting me." He handed the man his card. The man bowed and indicated that he should wait. He walked off down the corridor and disappeared. Cave Thomas wondered if he could be the man referred to by Evans – the man who 'advised the secret service' in St Petersburg. If so, he was well camouflaged, blending into the background in his dull clothing.

118

Cave Thomas schooled himself to patience, but the man returned almost immediately and indicated he should follow him. They walked some way down the corridor, stopping at a solid-looking door. The man knocked and opened it.

"Mr Cave Thomas," he announced. Cave Thomas went in and the door closed behind him.

"Mr Cattley?" he inquired. "I'm William Cave Thomas and I've come all the way from London to see you. I have news of your aunt."

"Mr Thomas," Mr Cattley stepped forward with outstretched arm, and shook him warmly by the hand. "My aunt, you say? The one in Rochester Square?"

Cave Thomas nodded. "The very one. She's in the best of health."

"That's good to hear." The coded preliminaries over, the two men relaxed.

"Mr Thomas, I'm pleased to meet you. You must have had an arduous journey."

There were armchairs near the window. Mr Cattley indicated to Cave Thomas to remove his coat and hat and be seated. "A drink?"

"No thank you, I've not long breakfasted." Cave Thomas took the seat he'd been offered. "The journey from England has been… interesting," he added, with wry understatement.

"I imagine so, at such a time as this. We have been most concerned. With matters as they are…"

"It's not the best of times to be outsiders in a foreign land." Cave Thomas wished he could take out his pipe.

"We have not been inactive. A letter – more than one – has been sent to the Czar himself. He answered the last with his own hand, but we are still uncertain regarding our future. War changes things in an instant."

"Your position is perilous. But I hope I bring you good news."

"Mr Thomas, if you bring me what I hope you do, you bring the hope of life!"

"I've managed to get the cargo as far as St Petersburg and have it under lock and key. I expect you'd like to see it."

"This is good news indeed." Mr Cattley reached for two glasses. "Perhaps, we should have that drink and raise a toast to life!"

Cave Thomas, moderate in his ways, agreed that this was perhaps a time to celebrate.

Then they could work out how to move the gold.

119

15

A Significant Purchase
Monday 30th January 1854

The discussion with Mr Cattley was soon concluded. Once Cave Thomas had made clear where the money was to be found, a plan was made for it to be collected from Robertson's mother early the next morning. Cattley would oversee the transfer and once that had been satisfactorily concluded, Cave Thomas's part in the business would be over. Without going into detail, Cave Thomas gave Cattley to understand that there were some preliminaries that required his attention. He was eager to be gone, but when Cattley pressed him to stay so that he could show him the church, he felt duty bound to agree.

They left Cattley's room and began a tour, looking at the office facilities first, and then descending to the basement to inspect the strong room.

"The gold will rest here, safely enough. This room is strongly fortified." Cattley's voice shook a little as he went on; "We have the Emperor's assurances that we will remain unmolested, but it's been hard to reassure our people. Many have lived here for generations – married into local families. Their roots are here. But others, with families still in England, have been queueing up to apply for repatriation."

"A costly business," said Cave Thomas. "Who pays?"

"They have every right to apply to us for money, but when they come in great numbers, our finances cannot stretch to meet every request. We intend to discuss it at our next meeting."

"Haven't they left it too late?" Cave Thomas, aware of troop movements and the possibility of danger on the road, had difficulty in imagining a mass migration of merchant families.

"You're right," said Mr Cattley. "Far too late. But, as I say, we'll discuss it at the meeting."

"I'd like to meet some of the merchants," Cave Thomas was keen to turn the conversation. "Could that be arranged – once our business is concluded? I should have a few days to spare before setting off back to England."

"I'm sure that something could be arranged. If you are seeking to buy furs, I can recommend a furrier. I see you came ill-equipped for our weather, today."

"Ah, yes. A misfortune upon my journey. I mislaid my furs."

Cattley shot him a piercing look. He understood immediately. Taking a slip of paper from his pocket, he jotted down the name of the merchant: Kobyzev and handed it to Cave Thomas.

"Try this man and tell him I sent you."

Cave Thomas took the note and thanked him.

"Perhaps you will worship with us on Sunday?" Cattley spoke as if their previous exchange had not taken place.

"If I'm still in St Petersburg, I shall certainly hope to be here."

"Good, good," Mr Cattley was pleased. "And now I must show you what a jewel we are blessed with."

He led the way out of the strong room and locked the door. Leaving the basement, they returned to the ground floor, where Cave Thomas had been welcomed. Then, passing through an archway, they came upon the wide staircase which led up to the church. Reaching the top, they stepped into a vast room, with seating for hundreds. The pillars and ornamentation added to the sense of space and grandeur. Deep mahogany tones worked wonderfully with the colouring on the pillars and strikingly decorated ceiling. It was remarkable, after the white world through which Cave Thomas had walked that morning.

"Magnificent," he breathed, turning slowly to examine the high friezes and patterning. "Marvellous."

"We have devoted much time and money to the decoration, and the organ has made a huge difference to our worship."

"I can see that it means a great deal to you," said Cave Thomas.

"To me and to our congregation. But I must not delay you further. You said that you have much to do before tonight."

"I should be on my way. I'll await your men at…" and Cave Thomas gave Cattley the address once more.

"Christina Robertson is well known to me. She has been ill for some time, I believe. I hope she recovers so that her son can take her home to England."

"We all hope so, Mr Cattley," said Cave Thomas, and the two men parted.

Outside, Cave Thomas was immediately aware of the thinness of his coat. He took out Cattley's note. The address was in the merchant quarter. He could go there on his way to Mrs Robertson's studio, later that day. He strode away from the church and made

121

his way along the quay, to the north-east, turning down a side street just before the Admiralty buildings. If he walked quickly, he'd reach his hotel in time for lunch. Robertson would have to take an active part in the next stage of the transfer of gold - and Evans, if he returned. Russell should be waiting for them at the studio. They'd have to get the other box across there, directly after lunch. Robertson would be the best person to do this.

He reached the hotel just as snow began to fall more thickly. This was useful as it shrouded his arrival and he slipped in unnoticed. He reached his room and tapped on the door. It was opened by Evans – whose coat also dripped with melting snow. He'd preceded Cave Thomas by only a few moments, having slipped up the back stairway. Robertson greeted them eagerly, wanting to know what had happened.

"A waiter is on his way," he said. "I was hungry and thought it a good idea to order something – enough for us all. We'll act like traders holding a meeting."

He'd set chairs around the table, so the two men shed their dripping coats and sat down in readiness. Coffee would be welcome.

Cave Thomas gave a brief outline of his visit to the English church and his encounter with Mr Cattley, whom he described as 'earnest and anxious, but holding his own'. He was keen to know whether Evans had spotted anything suspicious.

"I never saw you, but I'm guessing you were there."

Evans smiled. "Yes, I was there, and I saw nothing suspicious. No-one followed you, apart from me, of course."

There was a pause whilst the waiter brought the ordered refreshments.

"Did you spot anyone matching the description of the man I mentioned?" Evans asked, once the waiter gone.

"Not really. I can't imagine it was Cattley. It could have been the man who led me to him, but he hardly spoke. My meeting with Cattley was productive. I've arranged for the transfer to go ahead early tomorrow so we've a busy night ahead of us. We must have the gold ready by five tomorrow morning."

"Will it take long?" Evans wanted to know.

"About an hour or hour and a half to cut it all out, didn't you say, Cave Thomas?" said Robertson.

"Yes, and another to wash and dry the gold and pack it in a box, or boxes," Cave Thomas explained. "Then we'll need to tidy everything so that suspicions aren't aroused by the broken plaster."

He'd had had plenty of time to think it all through. "And we must smuggle the gold out of here as soon as possible," he added, aware that time was passing.

"With the weather as it is, we stand a good chance of doing this without drawing attention to ourselves. You lead, Robertson. You can make up a story about your mother being taken worse." Evans missed the tremor in Robertson's face as he considered this. It was all too possible to be a comfortable thought.

"Very well," said Robertson. "My mother is unable to leave her room. She'll know nothing of our activities, but her maid has sharp eyes. We'll need to see that she's kept busy, away from us. I'll do that."

"I'm conscious that we've imposed on you a great deal, Robertson," said Cave Thomas. "Your plan to come here was always in order to take your mother home. We'll make sure that that remains possible. We'll protect both her and you."

Evans's thinking diverged in several ways from Sir Henry's and even Ellis's regarding the two 'meddlers', but he realised that their personal reasons for travelling so far must be respected. They could not be treated like agents of the crown. Robertson and Cave Thomas had given up much to help. They deserved the chance of a good outcome regarding Mrs Robertson.

"I'll help in any way I can," said Evans. He stood up. "Might as well get started."

He pulled the box out of its hiding place and dragged Cave Thomas's portmanteaux over to the bed, emptying their contents on the coverlet.

"Best use these for the journey. You can have them back once we've safely reached Mrs Robertson's studio."

With Cave Thomas's help, he began the painstaking task of concealing the gold sovereigns in the two bags. The process took a while, but at last they were satisfied. Then Evans took hold of the empty box and turned and inquiring eye to Cave Thomas.

"Do you have some art materials I can put in here? Any checks would first be made on this box. If it proves innocent, the bags are likely to be ignored."

Cave Thomas rooted about and found some things for the box: paints, brushes, pastels, rags.

"That'll do," said Evans. "Perfect."

"Time to put it to the test," said Robertson. He took his coat off the bed.

Cave Thomas accompanied him down to the lobby, carrying one of the bags. Robertson held the other bag and the box. The doorman ran out to hail a cab. A small fast-moving troika pulled up on the ice outside the door, and Cave Thomas helped Robertson in with his luggage. Evans emerged from the hotel and jumped in after him.

"Tell your mother I'll attend her directly," said Cave Thomas. Then Robertson and Evans set off across the city to the studio.

Cave Thomas went back up to his room. He looked at his watch and was pleased to see that there would be time to visit Cattley's merchant before he joined the others. He picked up his satchel and left in search of furs and 'faces'. He hoped he might meet some 'characters,' to add to his sketchbook.

Having sought directions from the man at the hotel desk, Cave Thomas set out through falling snow, to find the marketplace. It was a little distance, and he was glad to reach the street where the fur merchants had their premises. He looked for the name he'd been given and arrived at a shop, *Mikhail & Pyotr Kobyzev: Furriers* inscribed in English and Cyrillic above its doors, which were shut tight against the weather. He tried the handle; the door opened with a creak. He entered the dark room, blinking snow from his eyes, and tried to focus on what lay within. A man stepped forward and greeted him in Russian. Cave Thomas replied in the same tongue and the merchant broke into a smile. He'd noticed the foreign cut of Cave Thomas's coat.

"How do you do?" he asked, in good English. "How can I be of help?"

"Good day," said Cave Thomas, somewhat taken aback. "You speak English."

"Yes, I have an English wife, but I was born here in Petersburg. My family is Russian. I am Pyotr Kobyzev. My brother, Mikhail owns the business, but I work as manager here."

The man's face and costume had made his nationality clear. Long brown hair framed his face, and a beard flowed down over his linen tunic. A fascinating face.

"I am in need of furs," said Cave Thomas, having introduced himself. "Mr Cattley recommended you. I was robbed, out in the country. Can you show me a coat, and boots?"

"A coat, yes, but for boots you must see my younger brother, Leo. Come this way."

124

He led Cave Thomas through a door at the back of the shop. It opened upon a workroom where three or four family members were busily engaged in a variety of tasks. Some were sewing fur garments, others stitching boots. Stock was piled high on the tables, and one woman was wrapping parcels ready for delivery. Shelving along one side of the workshop was loaded with finished furs - coats lying one upon another.

"I will show you what I have in your size." He went to a shelf, pulled out a couple of coats and brought them over to a table. "Try them on," he said.

Cave Thomas selected one and, removing his coat, slipped it on. It was heavier than the fur he'd bought in Germany. He wondered if that would be reflected in the price. The merchant held up the other coat.

"This, I think. It's made for your height." He took the first coat and handed Cave Thomas the second. It was a better weight and fitted well.

"How much?" asked Cave Thomas.

The price was fair, so he nodded. "And boots?"

A man – Leo - brought two pairs for him to try. Cave Thomas sat down on the proffered stool and removed his leather boots, now sadly snow damaged. He put on the first pair of fur-lined boots. They were fine. Again, the price was modest. He asked if he could keep them on, not wishing to expose his leather boots further rough treatment.

"Of course," Kobyzev agreed. "But leave your other boots here. My son, Iosif, will repair them for you and return them to your hotel."

Business concluded, Cave Thomas asked for his overcoat to be wrapped so that he could wear the fur coat.

"Will you not wear a fur hat, too, sir," said the merchant. "It is good to keep away the cold."

Cave Thomas had forgotten his stolen hat. He would certainly need a fur hat for the long sleigh ride back across Russia.

"Yes please."

A hat was brought: a perfect fit. Cave Thomas paid with the money he'd brought from London. Leaving directions to his hotel, but insisting on taking his parcelled coat with him, he bade the merchant goodbye and set off for Mrs Robertson's studio. Little did he know that his preoccupation with the artistic potential of the merchant's expressive face would one day bring him recognition and respect as a painter.

125

16

Midnight Disagreement
Monday 30th – Tuesday 31st January 1854

Robertson, Evans and Russell were together in the studio when Cave Thomas was shown up by the servant. Mrs Robertson, still unwell, remained confined to bed. They emerged from the studio and greeted Cave Thomas with relief. He'd been expected for the past hour and they'd begun to worry about him. Robertson led the way into a dining room where a stove had been burning all day. Cave Thomas set down his parcelled coat and explained where he'd been, removing his new furs and holding them out for inspection.

"Excellent quality," he said, "and at a sensible price. You should go there Robertson. The merchant has even promised to mend my leather boots and deliver them to the hotel tomorrow. I kept my coat though – I remembered that my notebook was in the pocket. Didn't want him to see that!" He hung the coat over the back of a chair and then inquired about the luggage and packing cases. "Have there been any problems?" he asked.

"No, all seems well. Your portmanteaux arrived safely. They're tucked out of sight at present, with our other luggage. The servant, Marie-Claire, will be at large until supper has been served, so we've decided to eat first, and then sort everything out once the house is quiet." Russell had taken charge, it would seem.

"It makes sense, Cave Thomas," said Robertson. "And I must sit with my mother for a while."

"May I see her?" Cave Thomas asked, wishing to do his duty.

"Not tonight, my friend. She is extremely low."

"Very well. Take her my best wishes. I'll hope to see her tomorrow." Then, with a change of tone, "What shall we do next?"

Marie-Claire knocked and entered, bringing food for the table.

"Shall we sit down?" Robertson slipped into the role of host, leading the conversation and keeping their minds away from the forthcoming task.

The meal passed with trivial remarks about the weather, the depth of the ice on the Neva, and the price of furs, whilst Marie-

Claire was present. However, once the dishes had been removed and they were left to their own devices, the planning began in earnest.

"I'll take you to my mother's studio as soon as the house is quiet, then leave you to it," said Robertson. "Marie-Claire will stay near her. I'll keep an eye on her and make sure she doesn't wander. You must release the gold and conceal the evidence. We must act quickly. The apartment is easily accessed from the street, and the small door in the courtyard would probably yield to a determined attack. It opens onto a secret staircase leading up to the studio, so remain alert. There may be watchers, and we cannot rule out the possibility of unwanted visitors."

Russell took over from Robertson. "Cave Thomas knows how the gold was concealed. He must take charge of that process. I'll help him. Evans, you can stand guard."

"Very well." Evans took out his gun and checked it.

"Let me go ahead and sort out the tools in the studio. If there's anything amiss, I'll return here straight away." Cave Thomas was eager to proceed.

"I'll come with you and cover your back," said Evans, and the two men pushed back their chairs and walked over to the door.

"I'll show you the way," said Robertson. "What could be more natural?"

"We may as well all go then," said Russell, joining them.

Robertson opened the door carefully. He paused briefly, to listen, then led them along the passage and opened a door at the end.

"Much of my mother's work is here – the paintings I was telling you about. I'd be glad of your opinion, Mr Thomas," he said, for the benefit of any eavesdroppers. Then he led them in, and Evans shut the door.

The studio was spacious, with three large windows facing the street, now shuttered against the night and with heavy curtains looped up beside them. Russell swiftly crossed the room, loosed the curtains and dragged them across the shutters to ensure no light escaped. They must conceal their clandestine activity in every way possible. Cave Thomas glanced around the room. There were cupboards and shelves along two walls, space for hanging completed works, and two easels in the centre of the room, each bearing a portrait, almost finished. A large chair and an arrangement of drapes in one corner were replicated in one of the

127

portraits. Paints, brushes, palettes, canvasses and wood panels were arranged along the short wall to their right. Opposite the door, a huge cupboard stood, doors open, its shelves crammed with sketchbooks, pigment pots, bottles of oil and turpentine, linseed oil and varnish crystals. The whole appearance was of activity and of jobs not quite completed. Another curtain hid a section of the wall to their left. Robertson went over to it and drew it back. On the wall, properly hung, were three beautiful portraits. Cave Thomas recognised two immediately, as being the works described by Robertson – the ones returned by the Czar – the portraits of his children, with which he'd found fault. Cave Thomas went over to them and gazed intently at the composition, colour and brushwork. They were not perfect. There were a few signs of Mrs Robertson's failing powers – perhaps coinciding with the onset of her illness. Here and there were clumsy touches, where the brush had skittered on the canvas. The work on the faces was immaculate, but a hand here, and the turn of a drape there, could have been done a little – but only a little - better. It was not enough to excuse the Czar's casual rejection of the portraits. Cave Thomas wondered what other purposes had been at work when he'd returned them out of hand, and with such cruel and scathing criticism. The Czar's actions had cost Christina Robertson her livelihood.

"Beautiful work," he said, seeking to bring solace to his friend.

"She didn't deserve the treatment she received. She could have come home at any moment but stayed out of loyalty. My father…" But Robertson broke off, unable to describe his father's grief as he neared the end of his life, and his wife failed to return to nurse him.

"Come, Robertson. Another time. Now, we must begin our work. Where are the parcels and packing cases?"

"Here." Robertson stepped past him into the corner of the room, beside the open cupboard. He pulled aside another curtain and revealed a hidden door. "This is the second exit I was speaking of, built years ago for some purpose long forgotten. It opens into a small room and then there's a locked door leading down to the courtyard behind the building."

He drew a key from his pocket and unlocked the door, then he and Cave Thomas ducked down under its low lintel and found themselves in a room not much bigger than a pantry. The packing cases and packages they'd brought from England were all there, and the bags containing Herr Finkel's gold. Between them, they carried the first cases out, then returned for the packed frames, leaving the bags for later. Once they were in the studio, Robertson

128

produced a box of tools. Cave Thomas selected those most suited to the task and put them on the worktable. Robertson found dust sheets, cloths, a broom and other materials for clearing up any mess they might make. They must leave no evidence of their work.

"Any neighbours to disturb downstairs?" asked Russell.

"No. The family has gone to the country. The apartment is empty."

"I checked it earlier," said Russell. "There's no-one using it."

"Good luck to you, then," said Robertson, and went to sit with his mother.

Evans locked the door after him and stood beside it, his ear to the wood, listening as the footsteps grew fainter. Then he pulled the heavy curtain across, to keep out draughts and to keep in any noise.

Cave Thomas took charge. He began with the frames – they would be the messiest part of the job. He picked up one of the dust sheets Robertson had provided. Russell stepped forward and the pair spread it out on the floor. Then, taking the first frame, Cave Thomas placed it face down in the centre of the sheet.

"The gold is concealed here and here," he said, pointing to the corners and sides of the frame. "Watch as I start on this one, then do as I do."

He took a sharp knife and began to slice carefully along the edges of the moulding. Then, with a chisel, he prised away the protective layer that William Thomas had introduced. He gently pulled at fibres in the filler, and gradually teased it out, revealing the packed gold. With a few deft actions, the gold was out, still stuck together with the filler. Cave Thomas placed it on the table. "We'll get it all out, then clear a space to work on separating the gold."

The pair worked methodically together. Each frame was stripped of its concealed gold, cleaned and placed against the wall. The debris was collected after each frame was done and heaped on a separate dust sheet. They'd decide what to do with it later.

Once all the frames were empty, they returned them to the storeroom and collected the other items in which the gold was concealed. Cave Thomas explained the hiding places, one by one, and how to deal with them. The two men carefully began to release the gold, conscious all the time of the noise they were making and seeking to reduce it to a minimum. After two hours' hard work, the table was full, and the last box had been cleaned. Evans looked at his watch.

"Midnight," he said. When are they due to come for it?"

"Early morning – Cattley suggested five, but I'd like us to have everything ready by four, in case they arrive early." Cave Thomas knew that in this fast-moving situation, all plans must be flexible.

"We'll be ready if we work steadily." Russell was optimistic. "Come on."

"Wait," Cave Thomas checked him. "What about the other gold – Herr Finkel's gold? What are we going to do with that? Hand it over with the rest?"

Russell put down the cloth he was holding and straightened his sore back.

"We have no dispensation to do that," he said.

"But if it stays here, it will put Robertson and his mother at risk." Cave Thomas was anxious for his friend. "If we pass it to Cattley, we'll know it's in safe hands."

"But, as things stand, we have no instructions. We can't just pass that amount of money to Cattley. We have to know the sender's intentions," Russell replied, doggedly adhering to protocol.

"And how do you think a message will arrive? Who will bring it? Will it come at all? In these times, messengers can fail to reach their destinations – look at what happened to us!"

Evans, who'd remained silent, broke in with a harsh whisper: "Quiet! I hear footsteps."

All three men froze. The steps approached the door then stopped. A quiet triple tap announced that it was Robertson, but nevertheless Evans was cautious in opening the door; ready, with gun in hand. Robertson slipped through the narrow gap and Evans swiftly closed and locked the door once more, returning the curtain to its place.

"How are you getting on?" he asked.

"We're well on the way. We have all the gold ready to be chipped away from the last bits of filler, and then washed." Cave Thomas explained. "But we were just taking a few minutes to discuss the other gold."

"The gold I brought here today – or rather, yesterday?"

"Yes," Russell replied. "Cave Thomas thinks it should go with the rest, to Cattley and the British Factory, but I think it should stay here until we have further instructions."

"As for me, I tend to be with Russell. We should wait," Evans added.

130

"Well? It's your mother's apartment. What do you say, Robertson?" asked Russell. "After all, you and your mother bear the risk."

"Yes, what are your thoughts, James?" asked Cave Thomas.

Robertson looked from one to another, his mind racing over all the possibilities.

"My mother's illness is such that I don't think she'll be fit to travel for some time – or perhaps, ever. It's clear to me that my place is with her. I shall remain here. If you all agree that the gold should stay here too, then so be it. I'll accept the risk. A few more days may clarify what should be done. Will you all stay in St Petersburg too, until this is done?"

"Of course, my friend," said Cave Thomas. "I will go nowhere until the time is right."

"Then I say 'wait'," said Russell.

"And I," Evans agreed.

"Very well. So be it," said Cave Thomas, and bent once more to his task.

The work of releasing the money continued for another hour. Cave Thomas re-examined the gold, still locked in filler. The job would require care if they were to avoid damaging the gold. Once free, the coins would need to be washed, so Robertson, who had best knowledge of the apartment, was sent in search of water. He returned about fifteen minutes later and they began the task. Once the worst of the filler had been prised off, the gold was dipped in the bucket and dried with the cloths Robertson had provided. No traces of filler could be left, for fear of betraying its temporary hiding place and throwing suspicion on Cave Thomas and Robertson. No-one must ever guess how the gold came to Russia.

They stacked the coins on the table in piles of five, so that they wouldn't topple. Each time they reached fifty coins Cave Thomas tipped them into one of the bags they'd brought with them from England. Evans, from his station by the door, watched with fascination as the table filled. At last they were done. £2,055. Cave Thomas was grateful for the money bags, which hid the gold from sight. So much gold had power in it – power which impressed and dismayed him. It crossed his mind that many might kill for such a fortune, and his thoughts went back to the gang of deserters they'd encountered by the wood. Had they known of the fortune hidden in the carriage, the lives of all three of them would have been expendable. They'd been lucky to lose only their furs.

131

17

Collection
Tuesday 31st January 1854 (early)

Final concealment of the night's activities was soon completed. Russell and Evans cast an eye over the room and declared it safe.

"Time to catch some sleep. I'll stay on guard," said Evans, conscious that he was the younger of the two agents.

"We can lie down by the stove," said Robertson, producing thick Scotch rugs from a cupboard. "My mother brought these with her. She never trusted anything foreign."

Cave Thomas took the one offered him, noting the past tense. How ill was Mrs Robertson? A question for another day. He pulled a drape from the portrait dais, lay down on it and curled up under the woollen blanket. Within seconds he was asleep. Robertson took a little longer to yield to fatigue; his thoughts were too clouded by concern for his mother and the huge responsibility of having brought the gold, and all the dangers it held, into her apartment. When they'd arrived with the concealed gold, he'd told his mother and sought her blessing. He knew that he'd placed her in danger, but knew, too, that she would regard such risk as worth taking, for the good of the British Factory. He'd now brought more gold into the apartment, doubling her danger. But she'd been adamant. She'd even provided its hiding place. He was filled with respect for his mother and concern for the risks they were all taking. His last waking thought was of the morning, and what the new day might bring.

Russell remained awake for a few minutes, scribbling notes in a pocketbook; then, with an encouraging nod to Evans, he, too, fell asleep. The sounds of the night, muffled by an unseen and steady fall of snow, kept Evans vigilant. He'd schooled himself well. Knowing that, when the task was completed, he could sleep for as long as he chose, he remained wide awake, alert to every creak, scratch, yowl of a cat, squeak of a rat. Once, he heard footsteps from another room, and the low exchange of words. The voices were female – Mrs Robertson and her maid, Marie-Claire. Clearly, the long night watch was shared by the sick woman along the corridor. As for Marie-Claire – Evans wondered what he should

132

do. He'd managed to conceal his surprise when she first entered the room, and she'd been discreet, but it could only be a matter of time before their secret would come out.

Around four, Russell stirred and got up quietly, to join Evans at his post.

"Which way will they come?" whispered Evans.

"Robertson said the back stair. I'll go through to the locked door and listen. I'll warn you if I hear anything."

The sound of the lock being turned on the door to the hidden room, woke Robertson. He slipped out from under his blanket, rubbing the sleep from his eyes. Cave Thomas rolled over and sat up.

"What time is it?" he asked.

"Just after four," Evans replied, in a low voice.

"Are they here?" asked Robertson.

"Not yet. Russell is by the locked door."

"I'll take him the other key," said Robertson. "The outer door will need unlocking too."

"Then stay with him," said Evans. "Cave Thomas, will you guard the door at the top of the stairs, please? I'll take the door to the corridor."

They each went to their places and stood in readiness. There was no sound from Mrs Robertson's room, where Marie-Claire slept at the foot of her mistress's bed.

At around four-thirty, a pre-arranged pattern of tapping on the courtyard door, accessed by the hidden stair, announced the arrival of their expected visitors. Cave Thomas caught voices exchanging the password as they entered the building. The door opened and closed swiftly. Cattley's men had arrived. Another mumbled exchange, followed by the sound of men cautiously climbing the stairs, and then they were in the room.

Mr Cattley had come himself, and had not one, but two powerfully built men with him, dressed in thick Russian overcoats. Robertson invited them into the studio, as if hosting a social occasion. He spoke in Russian. Cattley addressed Cave Thomas in English.

"These men are to be trusted completely. They will help remove the gold and we'll take it directly to the church and place it in the strong room safe. We weren't followed but we must make haste to complete the transfer in the dark. The weather is with us; the streets are empty, and the snow is heavy. We're unlikely to be seen."

"We have the money ready. We've written down the amount and would appreciate it if you'd sign a receipt for it. You know what they're like in London."

"Of course. I'll sign immediately. No need to count it; I have every confidence in your probity," said Cattley. Then he turned to his companions and explained what was going to happen. Robertson and Russell went to retrieve the gold, whilst Cave Thomas and Evans stayed to witness the signing of the receipt.

Once this was done, they helped their visitors unpack the bags of gold and transfer them to the satchels they'd brought for the purpose. These stout leather bags fitted under the folds of the Russians' capacious winter coats, completely concealed from view. When Cave Thomas saw the men thus loaded, he realised the sense in Cattley's choice of assistants. Each carried two satchels, slung criss-cross across his chest, the weight evenly distributed. There would be no danger of the men slipping, off balanced, in the snow.

"Mr Thomas," said Cattley when all was done. "And you, too, Mr Robertson..." He turned to Robertson with an eye of gratitude mixed with sympathy, knowing his mother was sick, "We, the people of the British Factory thank you for your courage and willingness, in making such a perilous journey to bring us this gold. Once it is safely in the church, it will be used to maintain and relieve the English community here in St Petersburg. We do not know what lies ahead, but I believe that in all likelihood your brave and stalwart service will be the key to our safety over the coming months." He turned to Evans and Russell. "You, sirs, I know to be agents of the British Government. This journey has been a part of your work. But, nevertheless, I thank you too, for without your commitment to duty, Mr Robertson and Mr Thomas might not have been successful in their endeavour."

The two men nodded politely.

"I will not tarry. We must be on our way. I trust we will meet again before you leave for England, Mr Thomas and Mr Robertson?"

"If we can," said Robertson.

"It would give us great pleasure," added Cave Thomas.

"We'll see you out," said Russell, and follow you to the street's end, to be sure you go unmolested."

"Thank you." Cattley turned to his men and spoke again in Russian. The two men saluted the Englishmen with customary politeness and turned to go. Evans preceded them down the stair and Russell followed.

"Come after me, Cave Thomas and lock the outer door. I'll give the usual knock when we return."

As quietly as they had arrived, the party left. Cave Thomas followed them down and stood waiting for Russell and Evans to return, which they did about ten minutes later. Then they all returned to the studio, locking the doors behind them. Robertson, left alone, had boiled a kettle of water on the stove. He handed them all coffee and they sat to drink it, feet to the hearth. A clock struck five as they sat there. The last day of January and their mission was half complete.

"This may not be a good time to ask," said Cave Thomas, "but what exactly are we going to do about the rest of the gold?"

"I know I agreed to it coming here but considering the danger to my mother, I'd much rather it wasn't left here," said Robertson. "Any ideas?"

"We agreed last night that the hotel was too vulnerable," said Cave Thomas. "That's why it was moved here."

"Can we leave it where it is, today?" asked Evans. "We might well receive instructions in the post."

"I thought we'd settled this last night," said Russell. "You said the apartment was safe."

"In principle, yes, but we didn't consider its precise location." Cave Thomas was scratching at a thought which had irritated the back of his mind on waking. "Imagine that Cattley and his men were being watched this morning. This would be the first place to be searched."

"If they were seen coming out of the building, then the back stairway would certainly attract attention, but I imagine that a second man might come to the front door, to cut off any escape." Robertson had already perceived the possibilities.

"You're right," said Russell, appreciating their skill. "We need to find a new hiding place. Robertson, is there somewhere safer in the apartment?"

Robertson stood up and paced the floor. He walked over to the portrait wall and gently tapped it, without success. Then he went over to the dais, with the chair and drapes upon it. He lifted the rug and felt the boards underneath, with sensitive fingers. Cave Thomas joined him.

"Another secret way?" he asked.

"I'm not sure," Robertson replied. "I seem to remember something, but I can't quite recall…"

The pair continued the search and Russell and Evans joined in. They gently tapped, probed and peered at every conceivable place where an opening might be concealed. Eventually, they gave up. There was nothing.

A knock at the studio door alerted them to the arrival of the servant. They quietly moved to the table and sat down. Robertson went to open the door.

"Good morning, Marie-Claire," he greeted the maid. "My friends stayed the night because of the snow. Ah, I see you've brought breakfast for us all."

Evans, seeing Marie-Claire struggling with a heavy tray, jumped up to help her. There was something in his manner that caught Cave Thomas's eye. Had he missed something? Evans carried the tray across the room and the maid unloaded four bowls of salt porridge, placing them on the table. She left, to return a moment later with coffee and rolls, then she curtsied and withdrew from the room. Cave Thomas, watching them, noticed Evans's hand touch Marie-Claire's. Their eyes met, momentarily, and then Marie-Claire left the room.

"Scotch porridge!" cried Evans, with enthusiasm, "I've not tasted salt porridge since I last visited my old aunt in Perthshire, as a lad."

Cave Thomas turned his attention to his breakfast. Salt porridge was not his favourite dish, but all four men discovered that they were hungry and did justice to the meal.

"I'll leave you while I go to my mother," said Robertson. "Will you all wait for me? I think we should talk some more, before you depart."

"Of course." Cave Thomas had no intention of leaving until he was sure Robertson was satisfied with the storage of the gold. Evans had agreed to stay with him, in any case, and Russell planned to accompany Cave Thomas, in due course, to check for post.

Marie-Claire returned and announced that there was hot water in Mr Robertson's bedroom, for the men to wash and shave. Glad to accept this act of hospitality, they took turns to leave the room. Cave Thomas went first, looking around as he went, to get his bearings in the apartment. He'd need to know where everything was, if they had to leave in a hurry; his movement had been restricted to the studio, the dining room and the secret stairway ever since he'd arrived the previous day.

Russell and Evans, left to themselves, had a quick council of war and planned what to do if there were no message about the gold. Cave Thomas returned just as they were finishing, and caught the words, 'get out of Petersburg' before the two men stopped talking. He waited for them to return from their ablutions before pursuing the issue.

"I realise that we must have a plan which covers every possible scenario," he began. "Not one of us is sanguine about this extra gold. I suggest that we give it today, meet again tonight, and take matters from there. What do you say?"

"We agree Cave Thomas. We must set a time limit on this. I'll go to look for post this morning," said Russell. "Evans will do his own investigations once I've returned. We'll not leave Robertson here, alone."

"Thank you," said Cave Thomas. "Shall I go back to the hotel this morning? I could lunch and dine there and make it clear that I've been trapped by the weather."

"A good plan. And, you never know, someone might come looking for you, and that's the first place they'd look."

"True, Evans. I wonder whether Mrs Robertson is up to visitors this morning; I'd like to see her if I can. Then I'll be on my way. A pity about the hiding place, though. I wish we could have found somewhere different."

At that moment, Robertson returned. "My mother is feeling stronger this morning Cave Thomas. She has sent me to bring you to her. She is anxious to meet you."

Cave Thomas stood up, "Now?"

"Yes, while she is awake."

The two men left the room and made their way down the corridor to Mrs Robertson's room. Her son knocked gently on the door, and they entered. The room was pleasant. The maid had opened the shutters and the white world beyond threw a sharp light across the bed where Mrs Robertson was propped up on pillows and wrapped in a warm shawl. A good fire was burning in the grate and its light and that of the oil lamp by the bed, softened the sick woman's complexion. There was a pleasing hint of perfume in the atmosphere. It didn't smell at all like a sick room, although the figure in the bed was clearly wasted by long illness. Her hair, half hidden under a cap, was neat, but thin; her eyes, though sunken, were full of character. She was an artist still, not merely an invalid.

137

Cave Thomas approached and bowed.

"Mrs Robertson," he said, gently, the Welsh lilt sounding in his greeting, "It is an honour to meet you. I'm sorry that you have been so ill."

"Mr Thomas," Mrs Robertson replied, "I am delighted to meet a friend of my son. I have heard much about you. James tells me that you paint in the fashion of the German Nazarines, but I hope you enliven the colours somewhat; I always find their work quite bleak."

Cave Thomas smiled. "I do my best," he replied. "My dear friend Madox Brown tells me the same – but in more forceful language!"

Mrs Robertson returned his smile. "Then listen to him, Mr Thomas. Listen to him."

"Cave Thomas paints masterfully," Robertson broke in. "He is too modest."

"No, not modest. I know my faults, that is all," said Cave Thomas.

"We all have those," Mrs Robertson said in her soft voice. "Honesty is an artist's guardian." She paused, then she said. "Come and sit with me. Perhaps you will tell me why you are here. My son has been suspiciously reticent on the subject." She indicated a chair, and then communicated with her son that he too, should sit. They each obeyed.

"Well," she said. "No lies. Tell me the truth about your visit…at a time like this."

18

A Revelation
Tuesday 31st January 1854 (morning)

Robertson and Cave Thomas left Mrs Robertson to sleep. The interview had taken all her powers, so they went back to the studio, promising to return later in the day. Cave Thomas looked at his watch and saw that he must soon leave if he were to arrive at the hotel in time for lunch. But first, they had something to do. Robertson put Russell and Evans in the picture.

"There's a small hiding place, in my mother's room, large enough for the gold. My mother is resting and has sent her maid away. The room is accessible to us if we are quiet. Cave Thomas knows where the secret panel is. I'll go to the kitchen and make sure Marie-Claire is detained there." He handed Russell the key to the room where the gold lay and, with a nod to Cave Thomas, left them to their task.

Russell quickly retrieved the gold, in its bags. He relocked the door and placed the bags on the table.

"We'll need to put it into something smaller. Do we still have the box?"

"Over here," said Evans, taking it from the shelf where it had been discarded. He turned out its contents and Cave Thomas opened the first portmanteau. The gold was hidden under its leather floor. Soon it was back in the box in which it had originally travelled. Another minute or so and the contents of the second bag were also in the box. He closed the lid and examined the locks. Useless, without a key. Taking a piece of unstretched canvas, he wrapped it round the box, like a parcel. Evans passed him a length of twine and he used it to tie the canvas in place. It would have to do.

"Let's go," he said to Russell.

"Watch our backs, Evans," said Russell, and joined Cave Thomas at the door to the corridor.

They crept along it silently, Cave Thomas holding the gold to his chest. At Mrs Robertson's bedroom, he passed it to Russell and tapped quietly at the door. They entered and closed it silently behind them. Mrs Robertson appeared to be asleep. With a finger to his lips, Cave Thomas pulled the rug away from the side of the bed, knelt, and fumbled with a board somewhere out of Russell's sight. He eased it up to reveal a shallow compartment. Russell stepped forward and passed him the parcelled box of gold. Cave Thomas slid it under the bed and guided it down into the hiding place. He fixed the board back in place and turned the hidden mechanism, designed to keep out thieves. Then he took out his handkerchief and wafted dust over the board. He rose to his feet and slid the rug back into place, checking that all looked untouched. Then, with a signal to Russell, he returned to the corridor. Russell closed the door carefully and they retraced their steps to the studio. When Robertson joined them a few minutes later, they were pleased to report that all had gone according to plan.

"Did my mother wake up?" asked Robertson.

"No," replied Cave Thomas. How could she? He was certain that she'd not been asleep when they entered the room and had been awake throughout the process.

"Good," said Robertson, "I don't like to think of her being in any danger."

They were all in danger Cave Thomas thought, but had the sense to remain silent.

The journey back to the hotel passed without incident. Cave Thomas checked to see if there were any messages for him, collected a letter and his mended boots from the desk, and retired to his room. Placing his furs to dry before the stove, he sat down beside them to read the letter. It was from his sister, Emily.

'So,' he thought, 'the postal service from England is still functioning.'

To read Emily's letter was to travel back to that other life in England – the life of fireside chats, of family and friends, of the certainty of meals and clean clothes and a safe place to lie down at night. It was a place of familiarity, with no hidden corners where a man with a gun or a knife might lie in wait, no armed ruffians ready to steal your clothes.

He read on. They were well. George was busy and she was joyfully expecting their first child later that year. Cave Thomas smiled. So, he was to be an uncle.

'Hurry home so that I can see you. Do not tarry in Russia,' she wrote. 'We think and speak of you, every day, and pray for safety on your journey. John and Jane send their best wishes to you. The children are growing fast; the house is full of life and laughter, but we speak of finding a home of our own; I wish so much for my own house and my own nursery, but feel guilty at such thoughts, for Jane is like a sister to me.'

Cave Thomas sat with the letter open in his hand, struggling with the emotions Emily's guileless comments had released. He'd held himself in check throughout the journey thus far, but a few simple lines from his sister had succeeded in removing all the effects of distance and extremity. His thoughts raced to Jane and he realised that he was no nearer conquering his love for her than he'd been in London. His heart, he discovered, was not made of ice, but of flesh and blood. Would he make the arduous journey back and find everything unaltered, after such trials, such self-control and determination? And Jane, did she too have feelings of which she was ashamed? This he doubted. She had given him no reason to question her position. He might regard her as being a prisoner in an unassailable citadel, but for Jane, a marriage promise was a living bond. If she had believed anything less, he could not have loved her. Cave Thomas cast the letter down in frustration and stood up, scraping his chair across the floor in his haste. He was in an impossible position, at war with himself and with God. He grabbed his coat and boots and, pulling them on with little care for the fastenings, left the hotel, to walk off his mood.

Outside, the sky had cleared, and a thin watery sun was trying to penetrate the last wisps of cloud. At first Cave Thomas stepped out without direction, wishing only to escape the thoughts crowding in upon him from home; but after he'd been walking for a few minutes, he realised he was nearing the Neva. He turned along the south bank, away from the English church, his feet taking him towards the merchants' quarter. He entered the street where the fur merchant lived and went to find him. The same welcome awaited him, but with a look of concern, Pyotr Kobyzev asked if his mended boots had failed to reach him, or if the work had been faulty. Cave Thomas reassured him:

"They arrived this morning and the work is excellent. I came about another matter."

The merchant looked puzzled.

"I come to you as a painter," Cave Thomas explained, suddenly inspired. "I paint portraits and scenes from history. I make sketches too, to aid me in my work. I wonder, would it be possible to draw you and your family? I would pay for the privilege."

141

Kobyzev looked non-plussed. Cave Thomas, eager to reassure him, took out the small sketchbook that always lay in his pocket. He showed it to the merchant, who turned the pages with a solemn face. Cave Thomas watched his hands, marked by his work, as they lingered on each drawing, communicating far more of the man's appreciation than his face. The merchant's eyes betrayed nothing of his thoughts. However, handing the book back to Cave Thomas, he gave a brief nod and said,

"I admire your work. Come at the end of the day and eat with us. Please, bring your book of drawings with you."

Cave Thomas was delighted. He asked what time would be convenient and promised to come that evening. They parted with smiles. Cave Thomas had made a friend.

Leaving the merchant quarter, Cave Thomas looked at his watch and began the trudge back to the hotel. The exercise had done him good, and the prospect of a few hours with Kobyzev's family had raised his spirits. He turned up the steps into the hotel, stamped the snow off his boots and pushed the door open. He had to pass the desk to get to the stairs up to his room. As he approached it, he was greeted by the man on duty.

"Mr Thomas, I have a note for you." He held out a folded sheet of paper. Cave Thomas took it and asked whether there had been any verbal message. There had not. When had it arrived? An hour previously, brought by a lad.

Cave Thomas thanked him and started up the stairs.

"Oh, Mr Thomas," the voice called after him, "I showed your visitor up. He awaits you in your room."

Cave Thomas retraced his steps. "I beg your pardon?"

The man faltered. "He said he was your brother…come from Berlin."

"A slender man with a beard and spectacles?"

"Yes, he said that you were expecting him. He showed me your letter – the one about the luggage. He explained that you had taken his box by mistake. He said, 'Tell Mr Thomas that I have brought his gloves, which he left behind when we last met.' I hope that I did the right thing?"

"Of course," said Cave Thomas, "How stupid of me. I'd forgotten he was coming today. Thank you. I'll go up to him in a moment – I think I may have left a book in the residents' parlour yesterday. I'll just take a look, before I go up."

He left the desk and crossed the hallway to the parlour. It was empty at this time of day so, after a quick search for his non-existent book, he took the note to the window and read it carefully. It was from Evans.

'WCT, I have collected the paperwork you asked about and will bring it to you at midday. Wait for me in the dining room. We can discuss it over lunch. Arthur.'

The man had used code. Something had happened. The fact that he had signed himself Arthur was significant. Cave Thomas was torn – should he go up to his room and discover who was waiting for him there, or wait for Evans and recruit his assistance?

He might have wasted precious minutes in indecision had not Evans suddenly appeared. The man at the hotel desk showed him into the parlour.

"Mr Thomas, you have another visitor," the man announced, and then withdrew, closing the door behind him.

Evans looked around the room and seeing it empty, took off his coat and sat down by the fire. Cave Thomas joined him.

"I've had one hell of a morning," Evans began, "Not least because of you!" He was clearly very angry. "What were you thinking of? After all we've been through, surely you have more sense than to wander off on your own, without a by your leave to anyone!"

Cave Thomas felt the impact of his words. He could say nothing.

"Think man, think! We're dealing with all manner of undercurrents here – we have no idea who our enemies are or where they might be hidden. We've been scrupulously careful in all we do, ever since we met up on the train. We've been followed, held at gunpoint, tricked and misled, confused at every turn. We are deep in enemy territory and surrounded by who knows how many spies, and then you take it into your head to go for a walk. My God!" He collapsed back in the chair, unable to continue.

"What can I say?" asked Cave Thomas. "I'm sorry. I didn't think."

"No, you didn't. And now I understand why Sir Henry had such doubts about you. Just because we've delivered the money, it doesn't mean we're out of the woods. Surely you must see that?"

"I do. I do. I don't know what came over me," Cave Thomas lied, knowing that his reaction to Emily's letter had been little short of disastrous.

"Luckily for you, I followed you."

"And was I under observation?"

"Yes. I recognised one of the two men who tracked your movements. I'd seen him before, on the road. He's based here in St Petersburg. I encountered him when I was last here." He stopped abruptly, as if he had said more than he'd intended.

This was sobering news. What a fool he'd been. Cave Thomas shook his head to focus his dull thoughts.

"I'm sorry. What can I do to make things right?"

"Why did you go to the merchant?"

Cave Thomas thought for a moment. How should he answer? A partial truth came to mind.

"I went to thank him for the work on my boots and to pay his bill. Then he asked me if I would care to join his family for a meal tonight. He knew I was an artist and wondered if I would make a likeness of him."

Evans considered this carefully. At last he said,

"Go, as planned. This might help as a cover story – particularly if the merchant tells his friends about you. You're supposed to be an artist, so I see no harm in acting like one."

Cave Thomas felt the humour in this but kept a straight face. He knew he'd been a fool, risking them all, and was lucky to be getting off so lightly.

"Very well, I will. I'm expected there at six."

"Then I'll follow you and keep watch," said Evans, in a quieter tone, his anger purged. "What time is lunch?"

"Twelve-thirty, but I have first to investigate my room. I gather I have a visitor waiting there. Unless I'm mistaken, the elusive Herr Finkel has arrived in St Petersburg."

Evans was immediately alert and eager to act.

"I'll come up with you."

"Do we expect Russell?" asked Cave Thomas.

"Yes, but I'm not sure when. If it's only one man, we should be able to deal with him alone."

"Very well. Let's go up."

The two men left the room. The hallway was empty, so Cave Thomas didn't have to explain his failure to find his book. At the door to his room, Cave Thomas paused. Evans took out his gun and flattened himself against the wall.

Cave Thomas tried the door. It was unlocked. He opened it and stepped to one side. Evans entered swiftly, gun in hand. Herr Finkel sat in the armchair by the stove. His hands lay palm upwards on the arms. Opposite him stood Russell, also gun in hand. The four men froze, then Evans moved slowly across the room to cover Herr Finkel from the other side. Cave Thomas entered the room and shut the door behind him.

"Lock it," said Russell. Cave Thomas obeyed. "Well, Herr Finkel, we are all gathered. Now tell us why you're here."

Herr Finkel sat very still but appeared relaxed. Cave Thomas watched his face, looking for signs of the man's character, probing to see whether he would speak truth or lies.

"Gentlemen," Herr Finkel began, "I fully understand your misgivings regarding me and my behaviour. I am happy to explain all, but for now, I think it best to give you the shortest version possible, as time is of the essence. I am Prussian. My family connected to the oldest and most royal family in the land, and to the royal family in England. I told the truth when I said I had been schooled in England. What I did not say was that I was also educated in Prussia – I work for the secret service of that blessed realm and I have been assigned to assist my royal cousins in their endeavour to help fight against Russian Imperial ambition in Prussia. We have men in St Petersburg, and elsewhere, who are seeking to avoid military confrontation. Any war would destroy our country and send us into a dark age of chaos."

The three men listened to this in silence, but at this point Russell stepped in with,

"Proof, we need proof."

"I have none, other than the safe word given by our leader." He then uttered a word in his own language. Cave Thomas couldn't recollect its translation, but it made sense to Russell and Evans.

"Very well. Continue," said Russell, still gun in hand.

"I was instructed to carry funds to our underground network, to buy arms and food. Their task is to harry the Russian troops should they attack our country. The network is commanded from St Petersburg. The money was in the box. I argued that it was too obvious a target, but to no avail, so I travelled with it as it was. Once I was discovered, I knew my only chance was to pass it on to you," he turned to Cave Thomas. "Your mission was clearly doing better than mine."

"What do you expect us to do now?" Cave Thomas put his question simply.

"I need your help to get it to where it's needed. The network in St Petersburg is being watched. If we split up the money, it could be carried less obviously and, hopefully, some of it would get through."

"Are you asking us to help deliver it?" Russell inquired.

"I am."

Russell lowered his gun, made it safe and returned it to his pocket.

"Evans, you and Mr Thomas must go down to lunch, as planned. I'll stay here with Herr Finkel and work out a plan. Keep a lookout for strangers."

"You intend us to do this?" Cave Thomas's shock was audible.

"I believe we should consider Herr Finkel's request and see what we can do to help. I have been expecting this, ever since Tauroggen."

Cave Thomas and Evans left them to it, locking the door after them.

"I hope it's a good menu today," said Evans. "I'm always hungry before a journey."

19

Portraits and Plans
Tuesday 31st January 1854 (afternoon)

Cave Thomas led Evans to his usual table in the dining room and ordered a second place to be laid. They chose from the limited luncheon menu and engaged in a casual conversation, suited to this public place. Evans had seated himself where he could watch the room. He seemed satisfied with the clientele, not seeing anything or anyone to disturb him.

"So, you're dining with the Russian merchant this evening," he said. "He's a fine workman. An interesting job – busy through the winter and not much doing in the summer."

"I'm not sure you're right," said Cave Thomas. "Summer must be dedicated to buying the furs and preparing the coats and other items ready for the autumn."

Evans grunted agreement, saying that he'd spoken without thinking.

"I'm hardly in the position to object to that," said Cave Thomas, with a wry smile. "Shall we return to my room?"

Evans looked at his watch and stood up.

"I'll follow you in a moment," he said quietly.

Cave Thomas folded his napkin and pushed back his chair. What had Evans spotted? He left the room and started up the stairs. Evans followed him into the hallway and then paused, as if he had forgotten something. He retraced his steps to their table and bent down to retrieve a slip of paper from the floor. This he folded and put into his waistcoat pocket, then he joined Cave Thomas and the two went up together. Outside the room, Evans took out the paper and showed it to Cave Thomas. It bore a single word:

'TONIGHT' and the picture of a small bird – possibly a hawk. What did it mean?

"We must be alert. Something is about to happen. Say nothing yet." Evans signalled to Cave Thomas to unlock the door, and the two men entered.

Herr Finkel had unfolded a map on the table and he and Russell were poring over it, identifying potential rendezvous sites. They looked up as the others entered and waited for the door to close.

"Herr Finkel has been showing me the locations of some of the muster points for the Russian Army, which he has received from other agents along the way," said Russell. "Our friends, the deserters, were close to one of the points – which might confuse matters, unless they've moved on. We'll hope to gain intelligence regarding that before we set out."

"The plan," Herr Finkel explained, "is to split the money into three or four parcels, each to go to a different unit. The largest parcel will stay here in St Petersburg. If anything goes wrong with the mission, it will be needed to buy arms and to use as bribes, should that become necessary."

Cave Thomas was worried. It appeared that the discussion had moved on several steps whilst he and Evans had been lunching. He raised an eyebrow in Russell's direction.

"We assume nothing, here, Cave Thomas. You can join us, if you wish, or keep out of it. Your choice."

"Given that I know something of your plans, I consider that I am already involved. But I also have my duty to Robertson. His mother's illness has changed everything. It's unlikely that he'll be free to return to England when I do. I must speak to him before I commit myself to anything, but if he agrees to my leaving him behind, I'll be a free agent."

Herr Finkel fixed him with an appraising stare. "Do you agree that our country has the right to defend itself in this way?" he asked.

"To harry the Russian army? Only if your country is directly threatened by it, and as a last resort." Cave Thomas dreaded the prospect of war.

"When an army passes through a territory, there are many innocent casualties. Any civilians who get in the way are regarded by the enemy as totally expendable. This is what we seek to prevent, or at least defer. If, by our actions, we can buy time for our countrymen, an exodus of the most vulnerable might be possible." Herr Finkel looked at Russell, who nodded in agreement.

"It's a race against time, Cave Thomas," said Russell. "With the spring will come the thaw. Once the rivers are in flood, it will be too late. We need to delay the march of the army in any way we can and give the native population time to move out of its way."

It looked like an impossible task. But he had succeeded in one impossible task already – why not another?

148

"I'll leave it to you. Tell me what you want me to do and I'll try to do it. But I shall need a little time. I must keep my appointment this evening. Will I be needed tonight?"

Evans took up the question. "Is something planned for tonight?" he asked, handing Russell the slip of paper he'd shown to Cave Thomas.

"Who gave you this?"

"I don't know. I had a feeling that we were being watched. I tried the old trick of returning to the table. The pepper pot had been knocked over, so I looked on the floor and found this. It's one of ours, isn't it?"

Cave Thomas and Herr Finkel watched the interplay between Russell and Evans, with interest. There were shades here that neither of them fully understood, but each sensed that the note had made a significant difference to the two men's thinking. At last, Russell took the lead.

"This note is of great significance. It is what we call in the service, a bugle cry – a call to arms. All has changed. The Czar has possibly ordered his men to action." The four men sat in silence.

"Cave Thomas, keep your appointment this evening, but be back here by eleven at the latest. Evans, you must stay with Cave Thomas – and watch your back. Herr Finkel, once you have sent your message to your superior, use this room and get what sleep you can. I'll keep watch and try to contact Mr Ellis. We'll meet again at eleven."

Cave Thomas's return to the fur merchant was made in a quite different frame of mind from that in which he'd made his visit earlier that day. He hailed a troika and asked to be set down at the end of the street where the business lay. Evans accompanied him and as they alighted, melted into the shadows cast by a tall building. He would be near, but invisible, for the next few hours. Cave Thomas made his way down the street, fighting the impulse to look over his shoulder, and determined to place his trust in Evans's skill. Having caused such fury in the morning, he was keen to redeem himself, especially under the new pressures.

He knocked and was invited in, as before, only this time the merchant welcomed him with a smile. He bade Cave Thomas come through to the living quarters and there he was welcomed by the Kobyzev family - wife, brother, sister and children of the merchant. There was an aged woman, huddled in a corner,

149

wrapped in shawls and dozing by the stove. Kobyzev whispered, "My mother," and placed a finger on his lips.

The faces of the gathered family were lit by the gentle light of oil lamps, suspended from the beams and placed on the table, upon which plates were set, ready for supper.

"We will eat and talk first," said Pyotr Kobyzev. "I will tell you our names. This is my oldest son, Leo Pyotrovitch; my second son – who mended your boots - Iosif; my daughter, Natasha - named after her mother; her little sister, Galina, and my two little ones, twins, Borya and Artyom[4]. I named them badly, for now they are always arguing."

This last comment was lost on Cave Thomas but caused some amusement in the family. Their faces relaxed and he had hopes of making more natural likenesses than had seemed possible, at first.

The meal was simple but well cooked. It was eaten in silence by the women and children, allowing the men to talk of business and other male concerns. However, as the empty plates were removed and the children settled by the fire for a story, Cave Thomas began to see that these old-fashioned manners concealed far more complex relationships between family members. Although quietly spoken, Natasha Kobyzev was clearly respected and loved by her children. Kobyzev had told him that Natasha was English, but it was clear to Cave Thomas that this had been a half truth. Her strikingly beautiful face betrayed her Slavic ancestry. Her father had been English, but her mother, Russian. She smiled at her husband's guest, her warmth and intelligence lighting up the room. Cave Thomas slipped his sketchbook out of his pocket, found his pencils and began to draw. Leo Pyotr and Iosif , who had stayed at the table with their father, watched as he captured the rapt gazes of the children and the expressive face of their mother, the lamplight softening their skin. The sketching lasted for as long as the tale. Story-time ended, and their mother sent the younger children to bed. She and her elder daughter, Natasha, followed to hear their prayers and tuck them in. Cave Thomas handed Pyotr Kobyzev the sketchbook. He nodded approval.

"May I make a likeness of you, too?" Cave Thomas asked, adding, "just as you are."

Pyotr agreed, returning the book. He sat very still, with a slightly conscious expression, as Cave Thomas drew. Sensing that

---

[4] Borya and Artyom mean 'fighter' and 'butcher'

the man was ill at ease, Cave Thomas suggested that he make a sketch of the two sons, who had stayed at the table. They agreed, and Cave Thomas set to work.

"It will take a little longer," he said, cunningly turning his sketchbook sideways and holding it so that none of the sitters could see what he was doing. He worked steadily for twenty minutes, then pocketed his pencils and turned the sketchbook around. The three Kobyzevs leaned forward to look, then cried out in surprise. Cave Thomas had captured them all. To the left, the two sons, Iosif and Leo, and to the right, watching thoughtfully, their father, Pyotr, who had been totally unaware of being sketched. There was much laughter and cries of congratulation. Pyotr Kobyzev went to fetch glasses and filled them, to toast the work. His wife and daughter returned and were shown the likenesses. A blush of pride transformed Natasha's face. She took the book and went to show it to the old woman, who, all this time had sat, unnoticed, in the corner. The woman stirred and held the book close to her eyes. A torrent of Russian poured from her hitherto silent lips. Natasha Kobyzev turned to Cave Thomas.

"My mother-in-law thanks you for your talent. She asks you to come to her. She does not see well so she wishes to touch your face."

Cave Thomas approached and bent down. Natasha took her mother-in-law's clawed hand and lifted it towards Cave Thomas's face. The hand opened like a withered flower with petals about to fall. Then, so gently that Cave Thomas was deeply moved, she ran her sensitive fingers over his face. He gazed into her clouded eyes – only a small part of which could still see. The face was wrinkled and ancient, although she couldn't have been more than sixty or sixty-five. He reached out, instinctively, and cupped his hand against her cheek. The skin was soft, and she smelt of fresh herbs, a clean, good smell. Her hand moved to cover his, pressing it gently to her face. Then she let it go and Cave Thomas straightened up. The woman was speaking too quietly for him to hear clearly. All were quiet.

"My mother blesses you," said Pyotr Kobyzev. "She says that she will pray for you. She says 'You have a heart that is sore. Healing will come, good fortune and a loss. You will be sad, but you will find a deeper joy.' That is all."

Cave Thomas thanked the old woman. Her words had found their mark. There was no need to write them down – he had committed them to heart. They could only be about Jane.

151

He looked quickly at his watch. It was time to leave. He thanked them all and made his farewells.

"I wish you a safe journey," said Pyotr Kobyzev as he saw his guest to the door. "Take good care. The land will soon be riven by war."

The door was shut and locked behind him. Cave Thomas, turning the events of the evening over in his mind, set out for the hotel. Evans slipped into place behind him. He would be safe.

20

'Pack Your Bags.'
Tuesday 31st January (late evening)
– Wednesday 1st February 1854

Evans and Cave Thomas reached the hotel without incident, at ten minutes before eleven. Finkel and Russell were ready for them.

"I've heard from Robertson," said Russell, "he's waiting for us."

"Do we all go?" Cave Thomas wanted to know.

"Yes, but not together. Cave Thomas, stay here and pack your bags. You must be ready to leave at short notice. I'll travel with Herr Finkel to the studio. Evans will go ahead to spy out the land."

Herr Finkel nodded agreement. Cave Thomas watched his face. How reliable was he?

"Very well. And, once I've packed?" Cave Thomas wished to be a part of the mission, conscious that Robertson might be glad of his presence.

"Wait until one. If we've not returned by then, try to reach Robertson. Otherwise, stay where you are and only open to a known visitor. I'll send word, if I can."

Cave Thomas yielded to Russell's command, but regretted that he'd not be there for his friend at this critical time.

Evans set out just after eleven, leaving by the back stair. Russell and Finkel left a few minutes later, making their farewells in the corridor, so that their leaving might be noted by any watchers, and draw attention away from Evans. Cave Thomas locked his door and began to pack, only then realising that his portmanteaux had been returned to the hotel by Robertson's messenger. 'There are many hidden hands in all this,' he mused, as he folded his clothing and pressed it into the bags. He crammed his art materials into a satchel. He would try to keep them with him throughout his return journey. Sketching eased his tension and focused his mind, allowing his subconscious to work on the problems that lay ahead, without troubling his conscious mind. To be an artist, he mused, was to live two lives. Realising that the wait ahead might be difficult, he opened the sketchbook and began to draw, from memory, the merchant's house, with the family gathered around the table and the old woman in the corner. His thoughts turned from her to her words, and from those words to Jane, the face that dwelt at the back of his mind and troubled his dreams. As he drew, his dilemma crystallised into sharp focus. Jane, the unreachable, ice-cold Jane... no, that wasn't fair. Her heart wasn't cold, but neither was it his. He might never be able to reveal his feelings to her, but he could capture her elusive beauty in his paintings. Was it a sin to think of her? Possibly. But if he were to place her always within a pure and sinless setting, perhaps he could learn to love her as a sister? His conscience pricked. No, he was a fool to believe this. His only hope was to forget her – and that, he knew, he never could.

He put down his sketchbook and wrapped his pencils in their leather cloth. He was indeed a fool, to idle away these precious minutes in fruitless dreams. He tucked the final items into his bags, closed them, and placed them by the wall near the door. Then he knelt beside his bed and began to pray.

The call came at a little after one. Cave Thomas was ready. The tap at his door announced the hotel manager. He opened to him and received the note he'd brought, thanked and tipped him, and then closed the door, turning the lock once more.

'Take your luggage to the English Church. E. will meet you there. R.'

The English Church? In the middle of the night? He turned the note over, seeking further confirmation that the note was genuine. There, in the corner, was a tiny mark. He took it to the lamp. It was Russell's cypher G{}R in the minutest hand – easy to miss unless one were looking for it. He checked the room thoroughly, running his hand over every hidden surface and peering into drawers and under the bed. Confident that no trace of him or his visitors remained, he donned his coat and boots, slung his satchel over his shoulder and ventured out into the corridor with his luggage. He locked the door behind him and descended to the hallway. The manager sent a lad in search of a troika whilst Cave Thomas paid his bill. His explanation of his abrupt departure was that his friend's mother had been taken suddenly worse and that he had called him to the bedside. He'd been asked to stay with his friend for the next couple of weeks.

The manager, who'd heard many tales and encountered many kinds of men and women in his work, accepted these excuses and handed Cave Thomas a receipt. The lad returned and helped him carry his luggage to the troika. Once seated, Cave Thomas loudly commanded the driver to take him to Robertson's address. However, as soon as they were at a safe distance, he reached out and tapped the man's arm, indicating that he wished to go to the English Church instead. The driver shrugged and drove on. He was accustomed to the vagaries of British visitors. A good tip would resolve any difference in the fare.

At the English Church, Cave Thomas disembarked from the troika and carried his bags into the deep shadow by the door to the building. He knocked. The door opened a crack and a voice inquired as to his business.

"William Cave Thomas," he said, "On George Russell's orders." The door opened a little wider.

"Your note?"

Cave Thomas fumbled in his coat pocket for the note and placed it into the outstretched hand. The hand withdrew and the door closed. He waited, pulling up his collar against the icy wind, from which the building gave little shelter. After two or three minutes, the door opened, and he was asked to step inside. He picked up his bags and slipped through the narrow gap before the door was shut and locked behind him.

"Come with me." The man who had opened the door to him was dressed in priest's robes. He'd not seen him before. The man led Cave Thomas along the corridor leading to Mr Cattley's room. However, they passed that door and turned into the room beyond it. The priest, if he was one, closed the door behind them.

"Mr Thomas, I am Father Ambrosius. I serve here. Please, make yourself comfortable. Mr Cattley, who has an apartment in the building, has been informed of your arrival. Please, sit down. I will make us tea."

So, Cattley was living at the church. Cave Thomas shrugged off his thick coat, sat down near the stove and watched Father Ambrosius make tea in a small samovar standing on the top. He was glad of the warmth. Was this priest the agent of whom Evans had spoken?

"A bitter night," said Father Ambrosius, handing him a cup of black tea. Cave Thomas refused sugar. He waited, unwilling to initiate conversation.

"Mr Cattley is on his way," Ambrosius said, and a moment later Cattley, who had been working late into the night, entered the room. He held out a welcoming hand to Cave Thomas, who took it and shook it politely.

"So, you have come to us," said Cattley. "Matters must be progressing." Cave Thomas eyed him cautiously. How much ought he to say?

"We are ever grateful for the service you have performed for the English Church," he went on, "so, of course, anything we can do to help you, we will. You had to leave your hotel in a hurry?"

"Yes," Cave Thomas felt he could give the man an explanation without revealing too much. He glanced at Father Ambrosius. Could the man be trusted? "Mr Russell received information from London. It was felt best for me to move lodgings."

"So, how can we help?"

"May I leave my luggage here for safe keeping? I need to go to my friend. His mother has been taken worse. But it was felt that I should travel light, and leave my options open, in case there are…difficulties."

"I see," said Cattley. He turned to the priest. "Mr Thomas must have our guest room placed at his disposal. His luggage can remain there, and he must return whenever necessary." He turned back to Cave Thomas. "Will that arrangement suit you, Mr Thomas?"

"Perfectly," Cave Thomas smiled. "With your permission, I'd like to go to my friend now and find out what needs he has. I could stay there tonight and return at lunchtime tomorrow. Would that be in order?"

"Father Ambrosius acts as our '*hospitalier*'. He will ensure you have all you need. Ambrosius, take Mr Thomas and his luggage to his guest room, and then return to your other duties."

'*Hospitalier,*' mused Cave Thomas. 'Then he is the man.'

Father Ambrosius bowed. "Come," he said, and Cave Thomas rose to follow him.

"Leave your coat here, Mr Thomas," said Cattley, "and come back and see me before you leave."

Cave Thomas agreed. He followed Father Ambrosius from the room, down a staircase and along another corridor. He was shown into a cell-like room, simply furnished, but clean and warm. The door had a lock, to which Father Ambrosius gave him the key.

"Your belongings will be safe here," he said, before leading him back to Cattley and leaving the two men together.

Cattley hadn't moved. He gestured to Cave Thomas to be seated by the stove, once more.

"Father Ambrosius is entirely trustworthy. He's worked for me for several months. Your secrets will be safe with him, and with me." Then he asked, "How much are you able to tell me?"

"I don't know," was Cave Thomas's honest answer. "Matters are moving apace. I think I must leave St Petersburg very soon if I'm to get back to England."

"I agree," Cattley replied. "Messages reach me from various sources. I gather that a group of British unofficial peace makers are on their way to St Petersburg. I believe they're likely to arrive today. I understand that they wish to address the Czar."

"I'd heard something of the sort as we travelled," Cave Thomas replied. "Quakers, I believe."

"Yes, three of them. They come without the blessing of the British Government. They appear determined to deliver a letter to the Czar."

"Is it likely they'll succeed?"

"Perhaps. Anything's possible at these times, and the Czar is here in St Petersburg at present - he and his son. I believe the three Quakers have friends in high places – Count Nesselrode's name has been mentioned."

"Count Nesselrode? Does he have influence with the Czar? I understood that the two had fallen out."

"Don't believe everything you hear. Count Nesselrode may have annoyed the Czar with his honest opinion of the campaign, and the possible outcomes of war with the Four Powers, but the Czar has relied on his judgement in the past, so may listen again."

"Is Count Nesselrode against a war?"

"Nesselrode is in favour of what is good for Russia. He sees that, in the long run, keeping on good relations with people in the West might be of greater benefit than taking over a port or two in the East."

"Interesting," said Cave Thomas.

"Mr Thomas, I stand very much in your debt, so I'll be completely frank with you. I'll help you all I can, but you must recognise that time is running out for us here. Soon, very soon, we will have to lock the doors to all who are not of our household. I've already set in motion the first steps in that direction. We're to lock the water gate, double the locks on the safe room, and withdraw to the most secure parts of the building. If matters turn against us, we'll defend the church to our last breath. All this I tell you in confidence. We'll watch what happens with this Quaker business and we'll be prepared. But for yourself, if you wish to return to England, I advise you to expedite your business and leave as soon as you can. Your belongings and your person will be safe here for as long as we can make them."

157

"I understand completely, Mr Cattley, and I hope that my presence won't bring you into danger."

Cattley waved a dismissive hand, "No, no. Stay while you need to."

"Late though it is, I must go to my friend," said Cave Thomas. "I'll send word to you if I can. If I fail to return, you must feel free to dispose of my belongings as you see fit."

"Very well, Mr Thomas. Thank you for your openness. We'll do our best for you and pray for your safe return."

The two men stood. Cave Thomas put his thick furs on once more, picked up the satchel, which he'd left with his coat, and shook Cattley's hand.

"Go with God," Cattley said. Then he himself showed Cave Thomas out, locking the outer door quickly behind him.

Cave Thomas set out for Robertson's apartment. The streets were deserted, but Cave Thomas felt eyes at every corner. He stepped out more quickly. As he crossed the street, he was aware of a man approaching him from behind. He glanced round.

"Cold night," said Evans, "better not linger,"

The two continued at a swift pace. Twenty minutes should bring them to Robertson's door.

21

Difficult Decisions
Wednesday 1st – Thursday 2nd February 1854

Robertson and Cave Thomas had discovered that it was easy to make plans, but far more difficult to carry them forward. Their situation kept changing. Hazards they couldn't possibly have imagined had reared up before them when least expected. People, of whose existence they'd been entirely ignorant, would suddenly appear, sending them off at a new tangent. Perhaps they should have become inured to it, but each new assault on their nerves increased their level of tension and this had begun to affect their vigilance. Cave Thomas wondered how Russell and Evans managed to retain their sang-froid, facing each new development with such iron nerves.

As they turned into the courtyard entrance to Robertson's apartment, Evans stumbled. He flung himself against the wall and Cave Thomas, acting entirely on instinct, did likewise. Evans's face was rigid with pain. He clutched his upper arm.

"Gunshot," he muttered, through gritted teeth. "Go back."

Cave Thomas had heard only a muffled 'crack' – the gun had been silenced, perhaps with a cloth. He slid silently backwards until he reached the corner of the archway. Here, he stopped. They'd approached it boldly. Anyone could have seen them. Was there someone waiting outside, a gun trained on the archway?

Cave Thomas removed his hat and held it out at head level. Silence. He slipped his satchel off his shoulder and swung it round so that it covered his chest. Then, inching his way forward, cautiously, he bent low and peered around the corner. There was no sign of life. He felt Evans behind him.

"They're at the back. They must know about the secret stairs."

"Are you able to run?" Cave Thomas whispered.

"I think so. It's a flesh wound, I think."

"We'll go together. Now!"

The pair dashed out of the shelter of the archway between them and the front entrance to the apartments. Knowing full well that there might be an enemy awaiting them in the entrance hall, they pulled open the door and slid inside. Cave Thomas had his revolver in his hand, but it wasn't needed. The hallway was empty. They

159

approached the staircase and looked up. No sign of life. Keeping to the wall, they climbed the stairs slowly, ears strained for any slight sound. They reached the landing. Robertson's door was shut. Cave Thomas gave the agreed signal and it opened a crack. Robertson let them in and closed it behind them, securing it with a double lock and placing a bar across it.

"You're hurt," he said to Evans, who was slumped against the wall, clutching is injured arm. "We heard a shot."

"Not badly, but it hurts like hell," said Evans. "I should have taken more care."

"Never mind that," came Russell's voice. "Come into the studio. I'll sort out your wound."

Robertson went for water and cloths. Cave Thomas helped Evans to a chair and eased his wounded arm from his now damaged coat.

"Damn!" Evans permitted himself to say. "That cost a month's wages."

The next few minutes were not pleasant for the wounded man or his friends but were mercifully soon over. The wound was not, as Evans had declared it, a mere 'flesh wound'. The bullet had passed straight through his arm but had missed the bone. They cleaned the wound, packed and bandaged it. They'd need to keep an eye on him. It could easily become infected. Evans put on the clean shirt Robertson offered him. He pulled a blanket around him.

"This may change our plans," said Russell.

"What's been going on here?" asked Cave Thomas. "Did you know they were there?"

"We didn't know, but certainly suspected. They must be getting desperate to take a shot at you like that." Russell handed Evans a glass of brandy, which he was glad to drink, there being nothing else to dull the pain.

"Who do you think they are?" asked Robertson. "Are they after you or after the gold? And, if the gold, which lot of gold?"

"Good points," said Russell. "I'm not sure how we'll know – unless they show their hand."

"It could be someone who's followed us all the way," mused Cave Thomas, "or someone who's followed Finkel. It's going to make our next steps far more dangerous. Do you think the note we received is anything to do with it?"

"Maybe," said Evans, his face white and his hand shaking as the shock of what had happened began to set in. "I don't think there can have been many of them out there."

160

"I think you're right, Evans," said Russell. "If it were the state police, you'd both be in custody; if a common thief, he'd be more likely to break in. I think it's more likely to be someone working alone. If so, who?"

"Let's get Evans to bed," said Robertson. "He can have my room."

A grateful Evans accepted the offer and Robertson helped him down the corridor to his bedroom, saw that he had everything he needed and promised to return in a while, to see how he was. He left Evans to get what sleep he could and returned to the studio.

"I'll keep watch," said Russell. "If he's going to get a fever, it will be tonight. Sorry to bring all this upon you Robertson."

"Would you like Thomas and me to take turns to guard the place tonight?"

"Would you mind? With Evans down, I'll need your help."

"What about Finkel?" Cave Thomas had missed out on that man's plans. "What's happened to him?"

"He came here… yesterday, after we left the hotel. We spent the best part of the afternoon planning our route and sorting the gold into parcels. He left to take the first parcel to the St Petersburg agent." Russell's expression spoke his doubt.

"Do you think he's tricked us?" Robertson asked.

"Funnily enough, no. I think he's genuine. But we must remember that he was followed across Europe. That's why he had to discard the gold in the way he did. He thought he'd shaken off the men following him, but maybe they were biding their time. If they've got Finkel, then we're in even more danger than we thought."

"So, Russell, what are we to do about the rest of the gold?" Cave Thomas asked.

"We'll wait until the morning. Finkel may return. If he does, it may throw some light on who took the shot at Evans." Russell left them then, to take up his post by Evans's bedside.

"Toss for it?" said Cave Thomas.

"No, you sleep first, my friend. You've had a rough night. I'll take first watch. I'm only sorry I can't give you a better bed."

Cave Thomas gathered the drapes and blankets, used the previous night. He gave a wry smile.

"I'm getting used to your floor," he said, and settled down by the stove.

161

Thursday morning dawned, dull and cold. There was a thin fall of snow covering the street. When Russell ventured out to examine the yard for signs of their midnight visitor, any signs had been covered. What was certain was that the gunman had gone to ground. He returned to the apartment and told the others what he'd failed to find.

"Where does that leave us?" Robertson wanted to know.

"Much where we were last night. Unless Finkel turns up. Let's have some breakfast. A plate of porridge will help me think."

The door opened and Evans appeared, "Is there some for me?"

"Evans! How are you this morning?" asked Cave Thomas, thinking the man still looked very pale.

"Not too bad, thank you. I've been through this before. The first couple of hours are the worst."

This lie fooled no-one, but since the porridge bowls arrived at that point, it passed unchallenged.

Marie-Claire looked shocked when she saw Evans. Her hand shook as she handed them their breakfast, but she said nothing. Then, noting the shirt and jacket, she offered to wash them. Evans thanked her and she picked up the bundle and left.

Once she was gone, the four men discussed their situation. There was still no news from Finkel. The longer that went on, the worse matters looked. If they were to go ahead with the plan to take the gold to the Prussian resistance forces, they might be putting their lives in jeopardy, for nothing.

Evans was keen to be included in any plans, but until his wound had healed a little, it would be foolish to set out on such a journey. Cave Thomas, eager to return to England whilst he could, was torn two ways. This additional mission had been somewhat foisted upon him. His conscience told him that he should see it through, but he was undecided. He had no wish to delay his journey but his friend couldn't leave his mother. Ought he to stay and keep Robertson company?

The conversation went along these and similar lines for the best part of an hour. They appeared to have met an impasse. Something would need to happen to make the way forward clear. Robertson left them, to sit with his mother. Russell set to work cleaning his and Evans's firearms. Cave Thomas did the same. The guns had just been reassembled ready for firing, when there came a strange thud behind the locked door to the back stair. Russell was at the hidden door in an instant, gun in hand. Evans moved near to the stove; it would give him some shelter should an enemy rush them.

Cave Thomas crouched behind the dais, gun in hand. Russell eased the key in the door lock and the door slowly opened. On the floor, lay Finkel. Somehow, he'd managed to get through the lower door and mount the stairs, before passing out in the storeroom. Leaving Cave Thomas to see to Finkel, Russell took the stairs down to the back door. There was nothing to show that the door had been forced. He closed it, pulled down the bar across it and returned to the studio. Finkel was lying on the dais, a pillow under his head, a blanket over his body, senseless.

"He's breathing," said Cave Thomas. "I'm not sure what's wrong with him. I can't detect a wound, but he's icy to the touch."

Russell went over to him and examined him carefully. He lifted an eyelid and noted the enlarged pupil beneath it.

"Drugged," he said. "Keep him warm and let it take its course. He can maybe tell us more when he comes around."

"We'd better warm him up slowly," said Cave Thomas, remembering the boy in the snow. "It looks as if he's spent the night outside, his clothes are wet with snow."

"I wonder how he managed to get in – and climb all the way up the stairs?" Russell pondered.

"Perhaps he'll tell us when he's awake. But at least we now know where he is, so that's one step in the right direction." Cave Thomas left Herr Finkel and returned to the stove. He lit his pipe and sat down to wait. He'd not be returning to the English Church that day, after all.

The day wore on. Robertson joined them for lunch before returning to his mother's side. Over lunch he had time to tell them his own plans. He would stay in St Petersburg until the end. His mother was dying but could drift on in her weakened state for weeks or even months. Her powers were diminishing each day. Every lucid hour was followed by hours of weakness and sleep. Each time she rallied it was to a lower mark. Her life was gently ebbing and there was nothing to be done about it.

"I must sort out her estate," said Robertson. "Once she has gone, I'll sell her paintings, shut up the apartment and return home. If all goes well, I'll make it home before hostilities make travel impossible. If not, then I will stay here and make myself as useful as I can. If it becomes unsafe to live here, I'll take refuge at the English Church. Cave Thomas tells me that the accommodation is clean and relatively secure. I would at least be amongst my own people."

"You must do what you feel to be right," said Russell. "Once Herr Finkel has returned to us, we'll know how to act ourselves. I hope."

The light faded; the shutters were closed against the night and the thick curtains pulled across to keep out the cold. They lit the lamps and built up the fire in the stove. Herr Finkel was beginning to show signs of gaining consciousness, so they made up a bed for him nearer to the stove and gently carried him there. As he stirred, they lifted a cup of water to his lips and he sipped it, gratefully. He tried to speak, but his voice failed him, and he lapsed once more into sleep.

"He's gradually recovering. Give him a little longer and he'll be ready to talk. I'll see to our supper." Russell went to find Robertson and the pair went to the kitchen to order more food. Marie-Claire followed them back to the studio and laid places for them all at the table, returning soon afterwards with soup and rolls, and a bottle of wine. She paused to tell Evans that his clothes were dry and that she was in the process of mending the damage. Evans murmured his thanks and turned his attention to the soup. He was glad of the wine to dull his discomfort. The others ate in silence. Russell placed a bowl of soup for Finkel on the stove, to keep it warm. Marie-Claire returned to remove their bowls and brought roast meat and vegetables. It was the best meal Cave Thomas had eaten for some time. They sat with their wine, speaking quietly of anything other than the matters on their minds. Each watched Finkel, waiting to see a change in him. At about ten o'clock it came. He began to stir and tried to sit up. His senses seemed dulled and it took a few minutes for him to fully understand where he was and who was with him. Gradually he became more himself and they helped him up, seating him an armchair and wrapping his legs in blankets. They brought him the bowl of soup and he ate it greedily. As soon as he'd finished it, Cave Thomas took away the empty bowl and handed him a glass of water.

"Thank you," he said. "Thank you."

They didn't hurry him. Nothing he had to say would make any difference to their immediate plans. Whatever he told them they'd do nothing before morning. There weren't enough of them to make a midnight foray worth the danger; they couldn't afford any more casualties.

At length, Russell led the interrogation. He began very gently,

"Herr Finkel. It's good to have you back. Could you please tell us what happened to you?"

164

22

Herr Finkel's Story
Late Thursday night 2nd - Friday 3rd February 1854

Herr Finkel's story was remarkable. It explained something of the mystery of his disappearance and return but not all. It left some questions unanswered. He'd taken a portion of the gold to the St Petersburg men. He'd followed protocol, used all the right codes and made sure he wasn't followed. He began his story hesitantly, but once started, he seemed eager to relate every detail.

"I memorised a message from the cell but destroyed any evidence. I was returning to the apartment when I was set upon. I was bundled into a carriage, held fast, with a sack over my head, and taken some distance. They took me into a building somewhere near the river. I was interrogated but gave no information. I didn't recognise their voices. They were not exactly gentle but didn't injure me, although they threatened violence if I didn't give them the information they wanted."

"Any idea who they were?" asked Russell.

"No. I was searched thoroughly but they found nothing. Then they bound my wrists and put me in a cellar, I think – it was down some stairs and smelt of river damp. I'm not sure how long I was there. I fell asleep for a while, exhausted, but woke when they returned. They promised me food if I told them what they wanted. Somehow, I managed to convince them that I'd been taken in error, that I was an innocent party."

"What tale did you spin them?"

"I said that I'd been visiting friends and knew nothing of any men in a third-floor apartment. They appeared convinced and brought me a meal. They untied my wrists and removed my blindfold so that I could eat. They stood behind me. I couldn't see their faces. I still didn't trust them, so only pretended to eat. Afterwards, I keeled over and feigned sleep. They must have drugged the food as it seemed that this was what they expected. They put the sack back over my head, carried me out of the cellar and pushed me into the carriage once more."

"The same carriage?"

"I think so. It smelt the same. We travelled quite a long distance before they stopped. I don't know whether we travelled in a straight line, or if they went in circles to confuse me. All this time I feigned unconsciousness."

His hearers marvelled at this and wondered how he had sustained it. Finkel smiled.

"I used to do a little acting when I was a student. It was extremely useful. However, I couldn't fool them forever, so I pretended to wake up. They carried me into a warehouse. I could smell tallow and oil. The questioning started again. Again, I managed to convince them that I knew nothing. At this point, they appeared to become worried that I would recognise them and get them into trouble. The next thing I felt was a needle being stuck into my arm. Then I knew nothing until I woke up in the snow, near your doorway. It was late. Whoever dumped me there had gone. I struggled to get up. I managed to untie my wrists as the rope was rotten, but they'd bound my legs so tightly that I couldn't feel them. I dragged myself to the back door and then I fainted. I woke in the night, the pain in my legs was terrible. I struggled to unbind them and finally succeeded in doing so. I tried the door and it opened. Inside, I tripped over the body of a man. I think he may have been stabbed or shot; there was blood. I didn't wait to see if he lived but pulled myself up the stairs. The door at the top was shut and locked. I think I passed out again. When I woke, I tried the door again and this time it opened. I dragged myself in and knew no more until you found me."

It was a lurid tale, full of questionable events. The dead man at the foot of the stairs was a curious feature of the story. They'd found no sign of him. Cave Thomas wondered whether he'd existed or was merely an hallucination brought on by the drug Finkel had been given. Russell was less ready to dismiss it.

"I won't be long," he said, and disappeared behind the curtain covering the secret door. Cave Thomas went over to the corner of the room, leaving Robertson and Evans to guard Finkel. He slipped out of the room and leaned over the rail to watch Russell below. He was examining the stairway and door minutely. Straightening up he shook his head, then paused and bent down. He picked something up and examined it before joining Cave Thomas on the small landing.

"Here's something that shouldn't be there." He held out his hand. On it lay a small fragment of bloodstained cloth. "Somebody missed this."

166

So, it looked as though Finkel was telling the truth. The two men looked at each other, the same question reflected in their eyes: who were they dealing with?

"I'll send a message to Mr Ellis as soon as I can, but we can't expect to hear anything for days, unless, of course, he's heard something already and a note is on its way."

It was not much of a plan but until they knew more, it was hard to plan their next move.

It was getting on for one in the morning when Cave Thomas went to sit with Mrs Robertson for a while, to give her son a break. She lay very still. He hardly knew whether she was awake or asleep. To pass the time he took out his sketchbook and began to draw her. Her maid, still up, came in once or twice to check that all was well, then went back to the kitchen where she was mending Evans's clothing.

After a while Mrs Robertson opened her eyes. She looked at Cave Thomas and smiled weakly.

"Do you find enough to interest you in my old face?"

"You're not old," said Cave Thomas. "Just ill."

"I'm bone weary, William – if I may call you that?" Cave Thomas bowed assent.

"I finished all my most important commissions," she went on, "but I wish I'd done more. My health has betrayed me."

"You've been sorely tested."

"I should have returned to my husband months ago. At the time, I thought I must stay here. I felt there would be time enough to spend with him when I returned. I thought he would recover from his illness. I was wrong."

"It was difficult to judge what was right. In your place, I would have found it hard to leave St Petersburg. I don't wish to leave it now."

"And I will not leave it. I've left it too late once more. Don't make my mistake William."

"You think I should leave?"

"James will stay here with me. Nothing I say will make him go. I'm grateful really. I'm a little afraid, I confess. I'd rather face the end with him by my side."

A spasm of pain gripped her, and Cave Thomas watched, unable to help. She had taken all the laudanum permitted.

"Your paintings will live on," he said; the greatest compliment one artist could give another. "They are very fine."

167

Mrs Robertson lifted a slim hand in dismissal of his praise.

"I know my faults," she said. Then, with a spark of wit, added, "are you quite sure you know yours?"

"Oh yes," said Cave Thomas, his heart full as he caught a glimpse of what Robertson's mother had once been. "I know them, and I repent on my knees."

"Don't waste your life in grief or regret," she replied, her voice weakening as she slipped towards sleep once more. "Go home. Paint. Forget the past. Live for the future."

She slept.

Cave Thomas sat for a while, pencil in hand, but made no marks upon his book. His mind was far away, in a London drawing room, watching a mother holding a beautiful child - who was not his own - and wishing that one day he would experience the blessing of being Father to such a son.

Robertson came to sit with him later and began to speak of home and his longing to return, reflecting Cave Thomas's thoughts and tempting him to open his heart in return, but reticence triumphed. After all, his was only half of the story. He must remain mindful of what he owed to friendship. He must not besmirch Jane's innocent name.

It was proving to be a sleepless night for all of them. When Cave Thomas returned to the studio, Russell was ready with the next part of his plan. It was clear, from his manner, that something had happened. Cave Thomas glanced across to Evans, who mouthed a single word: 'Ellis'.

"Ah, Cave Thomas, we were just speaking of you. It's time for you to leave us. It'll take a few days, but you must set about acquiring the papers you'll need in order to leave St Petersburg. We've agreed that it would be best for you to move to the English Church and remain there until ready to leave. It'll take at least two or three days to sort the papers. Once you have them, return here to say your farewells and then head home for England. Try to reach Berlin in ten days' time - or as near to that as you can. You'll need to be clear of Russia well ahead of any military action."

Cave Thomas sat down near the stove and examined his hands, thoughtfully.

"Are you all agreed in this?" he asked.

"Yes," said Russell and Finkel in unison.

"Evans?" Cave Thomas turned to him.

Russell interrupted before Evans could answer, "Evans isn't well enough to travel. He'll remain here with Mr Robertson. Herr Finkel and I have a few more details to sort out and then we'll follow you."

"What's to happen regarding the deliveries?" Cave Thomas couldn't quite grasp what had been decided about the extra gold.

"Herr Finkel and I will do all that's necessary. You needn't trouble yourself with it, further."

"Very well. When should I leave here?" Cave Thomas chose not to challenge Russell's decision in front of Herr Finkel.

"First thing in the morning," said Russell. "You should return to the English Church and then make an appointment to go to Police Headquarters. I gather it's best to arrive there between eleven and twelve. They'll probably fit you in quite quickly."

"Very well. I'll leave after breakfast." Cave Thomas spoke calmly enough, but his mind was full of questions he felt impossible to ask in front of Finkel.

"I've set up a bed in my room," said Robertson. "You can catch a few hours' sleep there."

"Excellent," said Russell. "Evans, Finkel and I will sleep here, in the studio."

Finkel had remained silent through all this. Looking at him, Cave Thomas thought he could detect an aura of resignation. He seemed to have gone beyond himself, to have yielded to powers greater than his own. 'Something has changed,' Cave Thomas thought. 'Whilst I was with Mrs Robertson, they must have heard from Ellis,' certain that only this could have set these plans in motion. It certainly fitted with Evans's signal to him. He stood up. Finkel watched as he collected his satchel, coat and boots.

"I'll take all these to your bedroom, Robertson," he said.

"I'll come with you Cave Thomas," said Robertson. Russell nodded approval.

"I'll be along in a few minutes," said Evans, "There's something I'd like to ask you."

Finkel leaned back in his chair and opened a book. He appeared to start reading. Russell walked over to the stove and threw in more fuel. The slight bulge in his pocket showed that his gun was to hand. Cave Thomas was glad to leave the studio and gain the comparative peace of Robertson's room.

Once there, with the door closed, he asked, "What's happened Robertson?"

"Ellis has been in touch – obviously without knowing what's happened regarding Finkel. He knew there were conflicting factions at work and warned us about the people trying to interfere with Finkel's mission. It's still not entirely clear, but the gist of his message was to help Finkel deliver the money to the Prussian agents, but not to let him out of our sight. Ellis wants him brought back to England. He thinks he'll prove useful."

"Does Herr Finkel know this?"

"Yes, and he seems relieved. I think he'd got in deeper than he'd planned. He's glad to have us with him and I believe he'll be of use if the return journey is to be made safely. He knows useful people along the way."

"And with Robertson staying in St Petersburg, do I no longer have a part to play?"

"Not exactly. Ellis wants you to be a free agent. He thinks that if you travel separately, you'll be able to move ahead of them. They'll try to connect with you at Berlin."

Cave Thomas, who'd much rather have been a part of the discussion, said nothing. He needed time to think matters through.

"What's happened to Evans?" he said, "I thought he wanted to ask me something."

"I expect Russell's kept him. He'll catch you when he can. None of us feels that we can talk freely in front of Finkel."

"That's true enough."

"Look," said Robertson, "If you follow Russell's advice – or orders – you'll be outside this place and away from the gold. That must make matters safer for you. You can keep your ear to the ground, too. Cattley, at the English Church, is no fool. I'd lay bets that he has his own eyes and ears picking up intelligence."

"You have a point, Robertson," said Cave Thomas. "But what about you? I hate to leave you like this."

"You've spoken with my mother. You know how matters lie. It's February now, I don't think she'll see April. I must stay with her. If I miss my opportunity to leave – if the thaw comes - I'll just have to stay until the roads are clear. I'll travel home as soon as I can, never you fear."

"Very well, my friend. I'll go along with Russell and leave as soon as I can. I'll come as planned to say my farewells to you and your mother, and I'll bring what news I manage to garner. Come, we'd best re-join the others, or they'll think we're hatching our own plans."

"In a sense, we are," said Robertson.

170

'Yes, we are,' echoed Cave Thomas's thoughts, 'and some of mine are for no-one's ears but my own.'

"You go," said Robertson, "I'll sit up with my mother and relieve Marie-Claire."

"Very well. I'll tell them what we're doing and then turn in."

The two men parted.

They all settled to get what sleep they could. Around seven, Cave Thomas woke and quickly packed what small possessions he had into his satchel, ready to leave after breakfast. A knock on the door announced Evans, come for a word before he left.

"I wanted to catch you alone. I didn't get a chance yesterday."

"Robertson's still with his mother. We won't be interrupted."

"I can't say I like Russell's plan. I still don't trust Finkel. I never trust a man who goes under an assumed name."

"I'm not sure that knowing his real name would make much difference," said Cave Thomas.

"Maybe you're right. Look Cave Thomas, I don't like being left here with Robertson. He could be here for months. I'd much rather be on the road. My arm's improving all the time. I think I could make myself useful to you."

"What, come with me?"

"If I can."

"Against Russell's orders?"

"If I wait until he's gone, he won't know I've set out. He'll take much longer than us to get out of Russia, so we'll be ahead of him all the way. He doesn't need to know before we reach England."

"We?"

"I'll come with you. Tip me the wink when you're ready and I'll join you."

"Are you sure?" Cave Thomas would be glad to have Evans at his side but didn't wish him to get into trouble. And he only had Evans's word for it that his arm was mending.

"If you stretch out your stay until Monday or Tuesday, I ought to be able to meet you on the outskirts of the city."

"Very well. It's Friday today. I'll move to the English Church, as planned, and see about getting my papers tomorrow. It'll take at least until Tuesday to sort out all the permissions – maybe even Wednesday. How will you manage?"

"I'll make the usual arrangements," Evans grinned. "I tend not to use the Police, if I can find another way."

171

'Forgery. Of course,' thought Cave Thomas but said nothing. The reference to 'usual arrangements' also jarred, Had Evans been in St Petersburg in the recent past? The thought took seed. It would explain a number of things that had been puzzling Cave Thomas.

Evans opened the door a crack and looked out. The corridor was empty, so he slipped out and headed for the kitchen to hurry the breakfast.

When breakfast was finished, Cave Thomas made his farewells and left for the English Church. There, he was received calmly and without question. He was in time for morning worship, so climbed the stairs to the unusually crowded church. The congregation was drawn from every rank; the rich gathered near the front, the less affluent further back – all driven there by their increasing anxiety. He found a place on the end of a row and gave his full attention to the service. Afterwards, he returned to his room, before joining the small number who were to eat together that day. They comprised the chaplains and priests, a handful of clerks and two or three visitors. Not wishing to be pestered, he ate his meal quietly, responding to his neighbours' inquiries but not engaging in conversation. He left the table as soon as he could.

His visit to Police Headquarters couldn't take place until the next day, so he decided to take a short walk in the weak afternoon sun. As he approached the door, he found Father Ambrosius beside him.

"Are you intending to go out, Mr Thomas?"

"Yes. A little exercise will do me good."

"Please would you permit me to go with you?"

Cave Thomas couldn't find a reason to refuse him, so welcomed his company. Father Ambrosius fetched his coat and the two of them set out along the English Quay.

"How long have you been here?" asked Cave Thomas, thinking it polite to start a conversation.

"Six months. My home is fifty miles away. I came here to study."

"A wonderful place," said Cave Thomas.

"A beautiful city," Father Ambrosius agreed. "I think the view across to the island is perhaps the most impressive in all of Russia."

"Have you travelled much?"

Father Ambrosius looked a little shamefaced. "Not since I arrived here, but I hear of other places from the people who come to the church."

"I expect they're drawn from all over the world."

"Yes, like you, sir. You come from England?"

"Yes."

"Is London as beautiful as St Petersburg?"

Cave Thomas took in his surroundings, the wide river, the stately buildings, the streets white with snow. In his mind's eye he saw the dirt of London, the choked streets, the beggars, the poor.

"No," he said. "St Petersburg is more beautiful than London."

Father Ambrosius seemed satisfied with this reply. They turned back towards the church. Cave Thomas pushed thoughts of London from his mind and allowed his eyes to take in the magnificence of the architecture, the grand scale of the buildings and the incredible light, setting its seal of beauty on the city. As they approached the church, a beggar thrust his begging cup towards them, asking for alms. Father Ambrosius pointed to the side of the church and addressed the man rapidly in Russian. The man turned away and went towards a line of ragged people which was forming beside the church.

"I told him to join the queue," said Father Ambrosius. "They will be fed at five."

They parted in the church's vestibule, Father Ambrosius to his duties and Cave Thomas to his room. There, he took out his sketchbook and began to draw – not the beautiful buildings he had seen, but the ravaged face of the beggar. As he drew, he pondered upon his impressions of Russia. So far, he'd viewed it from beneath, focusing on the darkness and the hardship, barely noticing the opulence around him. It occurred to him that, had he not been watching the shadows, he would have been so dazzled by St Petersburg's magnificent light, that he might not have seen its other story. How very strange.

173

23

Rumours
Saturday 4th – Sunday 5th February 1854

Saturday dawned clear and cold. Cave Thomas joined the small resident community for breakfast, after which he checked through his documents ready for his appointment at the Police Headquarters. He set out in good time, knowing that he'd probably waste an hour or two waiting to see someone who'd eventually sign to say that he was a good citizen of Britain and had behaved impeccably in St Petersburg. Once armed with these essential papers, he was likely to spend the next couple of days taking them from one place to another in order to arrange his journey. Only then would he be free to leave.

He emerged from the headquarters building at about two, the precious permission papers lodged in his deepest pocket. It was too late to do any more that day, so he found himself returning to the merchants' quarter, and to the shop of the Kobyzev family. There, he was greeted as a family friend and ushered through to their living quarters as before. No-one was surprised when he pulled out his sketchbook and began to draw. When the shop closed, Kobyzev brought in friends from the neighbourhood to see this marvel. Cave Thomas worked hard, drawing each of them and then giving the drawings to the merchants. He soon found himself firmly embraced in their friendship, completely at ease. Over a pipe, they talked freely about the situation in St Petersburg. Most spoke English, although one or two resorted to Russian at times, which Kobyzev translated when Cave Thomas didn't quite catch the meaning. As he listened to their talk, he began to realise how well-informed they were, and how prepared for what might follow should Russia go to war with England. In the event of such a conflict he couldn't possibly view such men as his enemies, nor they regard him as anything but a friend. If only the whole world could operate under bonds of friendship! Time passed and it appeared that all were expected to stay for supper.

When he left, three of the men came with him, swearing that it wasn't safe to be out alone at night. They saw him to the English Church then quietly slipped away in the darkness as he waited for

Father Ambrosius to open the securely guarded door. Ambrosius greeted him in a friendly fashion and offered to bring him supper but Cave Thomas refused, saying that he'd already eaten.

"A letter has arrived for you," said Father Ambrosius, handing it to him. He thanked the man and took it to his room. It was from Evans and was in code.

He took a little time to read it, realising that he must be sure to unpick all its nuances. Once the task was completed, he sat for a while, wondering what he should do. Evans had news for him. The three Quakers had arrived and were making their presence known in the city. They'd been seen visiting several influential figures. It looked as if they would succeed in their mission to see the Czar. Cave Thomas wasn't sure what their advent would mean for him. Sir Henry Loughton had viewed them as a huge risk to the British mission. It occurred to Cave Thomas that Sir Henry's demise, although blamed upon a mixture of his weakened constitution and the stress and worry surrounding the mission to take gold to St Petersburg, might well have much wider causes. He was a significant man in the secret world of government intelligence, working behind the scenes to manage the British Government's dealings in a complex world. Ministers couldn't be expected to know all the minutiae of international politics. It took men like Sir Henry, with workers in the field such as Russell and Evans, and Cave Thomas, the 'enthusiastic meddler' assisting in this instance. There were no official titles, no public faces, just men committed to serving their country and their countrymen overseas. Since meeting Herr Finkel and gaining some understanding of the involvement of British interests with those of Prussia, he couldn't help wondering what deeper waters had passed him by. Was it possible that the Quaker gentlemen represented some kind of threat to the balance of secret activities in Russia and Europe? Were there more agents working here than they'd been led to believe? How deep did British involvement with Russia go? How much had been hidden from them by Sir Henry? From his lodging at the English Church, Cave Thomas might learn more about the Quaker deputation. It certainly wouldn't do any harm to keep his ears open for news of their progress. But if he was watching them, who else might be doing the same, and where would that leave him and his friends?

Over breakfast, the next morning, Cave Thomas found himself seated by Father Ambrosius. He wondered if he'd be able to raise the matter of the three Quakers with him and was just looking for an opportunity when Father Ambrosius brought up the subject himself.

"Your countrymen – three men from England – wish to meet with our Czar. Do you have ambitions in that direction?"

Cave Thomas paused, his fork halfway to his mouth.

"No, not at all. What have you heard about them?"

"I hear that they are churchmen, but from the Quaker Connection. I thought that those men were silent, but it seems that these want to talk to His Imperial Highness."

"Will they succeed, do you think?"

"I think that for a man to travel all the way from England to St Petersburg, in the middle of winter, he must have a good reason for coming here. And he would wish to return home as quickly as he could. For a man to do that, he must have friends in high places. Therefore, yes, I think they will succeed."

Cave Thomas continued to eat his breakfast. Father Ambrosius's words were heavily loaded. Was he answering Cave Thomas's question, or posing one of his own, regarding Cave Thomas himself? Was Ambrosius a friend or a spy?

"Well, good luck to them," Cave Thomas said, folding his napkin and placing it beside his plate. "Quakers can be very determined, and these men must truly be committed to peace to have travelled so far, especially in these uncertain times."

"All men who take such risks must either be committed to a cause or in fear for their life. Or both."

"Some people wander into danger without realising it," said Cave Thomas.

"But you are not such a man," Father Ambrosius replied. "I imagine that you think hard before you do anything. You are an artist. An artist does not proceed with a painting without giving it much thought."

"That's true," replied Cave Thomas, "but it's hardly the same as acting as a peace envoy."

"But to be a peace envoy – or an artist, travelling with an artist friend – these are good cover stories for people coming here for different purposes." Father Ambrosius's eyes did not waver as he gazed intently at his neighbour.

"I don't follow you…" said Cave Thomas.

"I think you do," Ambrosius replied.

Not sure how to respond to him, Cave Thomas stood up and pushed his chair away from the long table.

"I must go. I have matters to attend to."

"Allow me to accompany you," said Father Ambrosius, "I have something to ask you."

Unable to throw the man off in public, Cave Thomas allowed Ambrosius to go with him to his room. He closed the door and stood by it, ready to escape if need be.

"I am your friend," said Father Ambrosius. "I trust you. Will you trust me?"

"Explain please." Cave Thomas felt that he should allow Ambrosius free rein if he were to hear all that the man had to say.

"I told you that I come from a village fifty miles away from St Petersburg. I was not truly accurate. I come from Prussia."

'Another Prussian!' thought Cave Thomas. 'Be careful.'

"Whereabouts in Prussia?" he asked. Ambrosius told him the name of a village, but it meant nothing to him.

"Where is that, exactly?"

"Ten miles over the border."

"Why are you really here?"

"I am here to study. That part was true. What I did not tell you was that I try to serve friends in Britain. I help the British here in St Petersburg and in Britain. I try to help Prussia too. My family are all in the village. I would like to return there to be with them. There will be a war. My family needs me there, not here, where I can be of no help to them."

"Does your superior here know your wishes?"

"No. I dare not tell him. If I say I wish to go, he will refuse to let me. If I don't, but leave without his knowledge, he will not be given the opportunity to forbid me, and so I'll not be guilty of disobeying him."

The logic of this argument echoed that of Evans. Instead of questioning him further on the subject, Cave Thomas decided to read Ambrosius's face. He relied on his artistic perception to see the man beneath the skin. Father Ambrosius met his gaze unflinchingly. He put a hand in his pocket and withdrew a small locket. He flicked it open and showed it to Cave Thomas. Inside was a miniature portrait of a young girl.

"This is my little sister. It was painted for her fiancé who perished in battle. When I came to St Petersburg, she gave it to me so that I would pray for her. My father is dead. If war comes, my mother, sisters and brothers will need me. I must go home."

"And you want to travel with me?"

"Sir, with you, I know I could get there. Alone, I don't think I would succeed."

Cave Thomas moved away from the door and sat down on his bed. This was an added complication. What ought he to do?

"Please sir," said Father Ambrosius, "take me with you."

"What about papers?" asked Cave Thomas.

"I can get those. I have status as a Russian national as well as a Prussian. My mother was born here."

"How soon could you be ready to travel?"

"Three days."

"Very well. Make your preparations. I'll think about your request and then tell you my decision. But be clear, I have not said yes, only, perhaps."

"Perhaps will become yes, I know it," said Ambrosius.

"Then you know more than I do," said Cave Thomas, dismissively.

"Ah, but I have prayed," said Ambrosius, "and God sent you to help me."

With such an argument, Cave Thomas could not contend. Ambrosius left Cave Thomas to his thoughts and went about his daily duties.

If Cave Thomas were to decide to travel alone, he'd have to creep out when Ambrosius was otherwise occupied. No-one was meant to know that Evans intended travelling with him. Would Ambrosius imperil their plans? And what would Evans have to say on the subject?

It being Sunday, Cave Thomas joined the church household for a brief service at a quarter past eight, not wishing to be part of the main service later in the day. Mr Cattley was also present. As the service ended, he stopped Cave Thomas and invited him to join him before lunch, in his office. He went, as invited, at twelve thirty, and found Cattley with a glass of sherry in his hand, and with another poured out ready for his visitor.

"Mr Thomas, I gather you intend to leave us," he said, handing Cave Thomas the glass. "You must tell me if there is any way I can help you."

"I'd certainly welcome your advice regarding transport. The carriage that brought me here is long gone. Can you recommend a company?"

178

"Of course. We have good contacts and can certainly help you with that. It's the very least we can do. How is your friend's mother? Will she be well enough to travel?"

"Of that I'm uncertain. It was definitely my friend's intention to bring his mother home to England." He saw no reason to tell Cattley more.

"It would be good to do this. Allow me to help. I can write letters that will expedite your journey."

As Cattley went on to explain what a difference such letters might make to the speed of a journey, an idea formed in Cave Thomas's mind. If they were to take an invalid back to England and carried papers to help them on their way, it might be possible to smuggle Ambrosius out of the country – or even Finkel. If the papers didn't stipulate the person's gender, they might be able to pass off one or the other as the elderly invalid. Wrapped in sufficient shawls, anyone could pose as Robertson's 'relative'.

Cattley promised the necessary letters by the morning. He called his secretary and asked him to bring Father Ambrosius to join them.

"Father Ambrosius is keen to be of assistance to you. To be frank, we don't have enough to keep him busy here, so he'd be quite free to go with you to arrange transport."

Father Ambrosius arrived, and Cattley explained the plan. Cave Thomas admired the man's ability to hide all emotion. He received the news with calm agreement. He would be pleased to help Mr Thomas. They could go the next morning, taking with them Mr Cattley's letters and the permissions Cave Thomas had received from the Police. The secretary said he would be happy to prepare Mr Cattley's letters directly. He would bring them to Mr Cattley to sign that afternoon. With everything falling into place, Cave Thomas left Cattley and went, with Ambrosius, to eat the midday meal. Ambrosius went to sit by another guest, so Cave Thomas was free from his immediate scrutiny and was able to slip away alone at the end of the meal.

He spent the afternoon poring over the map which had travelled with him all the way from London, worn and crumpled now, after its adventures en route to St Petersburg. The place names were faint and only the major towns were labelled. He tried to find the Prussian name Ambrosius had given, but it was too small to feature on the map. A couple of other names stood out though - places Russell had mentioned in connection with Finkel's Prussian

179

resistance troops. He mapped the route Russell and Finkel might make, including the loop to the east of St Petersburg. Evans was right; it would take time for Finkel to find his contacts and thus create the opportunity for them to leave after Russell and Finkel, and still manage to get ahead of them. It could work – but a map is flat and this one gave Cave Thomas no idea what the terrain was like and how difficult the travelling conditions might be. He looked again and tried to work out where they would cross the border. He wondered how well it would be guarded, away from the main routes, how many troops might lie between them and Prussia, how many rivers must be crossed and whether they would be able to trust their drivers. There was much to think about. But first he must wait for Evans to work out where it would be safe for them to meet – and when. Without a secure rendezvous, the plan might fail before they'd left St Petersburg. If there was no further note from Evans by the next morning, he must return to say farewell to the Robertsons and find out what was happening. He folded the map carefully and put it in his satchel. Then he tidied his room, put on his coat and set out for a brief walk ahead of the evening meal. He needed to clear his head.

When Father Ambrosius appeared at the door to accompany him, he realised that he was being carefully watched. He resolutely set aside all further thoughts concerning the future until after supper. As he and Ambrosius walked by the Neva, he limited his remarks to the view and the weather.

24

An Interesting Encounter
Monday 6th February 1854

Cave Thomas woke around six thirty the next morning. The atmosphere was dank. Damp river air seeped through the ill-fitting window. There was a change in the temperature, another slight thaw. This was not a good sign. It might delay his journey. He wanted to be away as soon as possible. He washed, dressed, and went to breakfast at seven. Father Ambrosius slipped into the chair beside him.

"Good morning Mr Thomas. I hope you slept well."

"I did, thank you."

"This weather is a blow to your plans."

"How do you mean?" asked Cave Thomas, helping himself to tea.

"The temperature has risen above freezing. The rivers must be tested before they can be used for travel."

"I don't imagine it will last," Cave Thomas replied with a nonchalance he didn't feel.

"Perhaps."

They ate in silence.

"I am busy this morning," said Ambrosius at last. "Will you go out?"

"I thought I might."

"Perhaps you will visit your friends?" Ambrosius seemed to be in step with Cave Thomas's thinking.

"Perhaps," he echoed.

"It would be good if you could do so today."

They parted. Nothing had been said, but it seemed clear to Cave Thomas that Ambrosius wanted him to expedite his plans. He collected his satchel and coat, changed into his boots and headed out to visit Robertson, and whoever else remained at the apartment.

The way was busy with men heading to work. A few troikas were still to be seen but most men walked, so Cave Thomas joined the throng and made his way steadily towards Robertson's apartment. He approached the entrance with confident step and pushed the outer door open. Having entered, he stepped sideways and waited, alert for footsteps following him. There were none.

Perhaps he was no longer of interest to the anonymous watcher – or watchers, or maybe he had lost them in the crowds. He climbed the stairs to Robertson's apartment and knocked, waited, and knocked again. There was the sound of a bar being lifted and a key in the lock. The door opened a crack and then swung wide to admit him. Russell greeted him warmly as he shut and locked the door, barring it once more. As ever, he appeared calm and contained.

"Best to be safe," he said. "It's good to see you. Have you breakfasted?"

Cave Thomas told him he had but would welcome coffee if there was any. They walked down the corridor to the studio, where Evans, Finkel and Robertson were finishing their breakfast. He noted that Evans looked very pale and Finkel quietly confident. Robertson bore the signs of a night spent by his mother's bedside.

"How is your mother?" Cave Thomas asked him.

"Sleeping now but she spent a restless night. The pain is at its worst around two and three in the morning."

"I'm sorry to hear that," Cave Thomas put his hand on Robertson's shoulder. "If I can do anything to help while I'm here…"

Robertson's look was one of gratitude and exhaustion. "You're very kind, but she's sleeping now. I'll leave nature to do its work. Sit down. There are still some rolls warming by the stove."

Cave Thomas sat down, tempted to enjoy a second breakfast, whilst Russell brought him up to date with their plans. He unrolled a map on the table.

"Everything is in place for tonight. Finkel and I will leave St Petersburg as late as we can. Under cover of darkness we'll make our way to this village." He pointed to a spot not far from St Petersburg, about two or three miles from the edge of the city. "We'll spend the night there and then go on, just before dawn, so that we can reach our rendezvous by mid-day. Once we've made our delivery, we'll continue east until we get to…" He pointed to a spot with a name in Cyrillic beside it. Then tracing the route on the map, he showed how they could confuse anyone following them by making a zig zag journey from village to village before setting out directly towards their next rendezvous south-west of St Petersburg.

"Evans will stay here with Robertson. What are your plans, Cave Thomas?"

"I have most of my papers. I'm just waiting for my 'permission to leave' certificate. I've advertised my intention at the English

Church – publicly but not too publicly if you follow me. According to the Civil Governor, that will be sufficient. I must still visit the Military Governor's office for a final paper and to collect my passport. After that, I'm allowed a week in which to organise my journey."

"How soon do intend to leave?" asked Russell.

"As soon as I can get away, but with some of my papers still in the hands of the Military Governor, I may be delayed a little."

"So, we could be in Berlin ahead of you," said Russell. "May your travels go well."

"I wish I were coming with you," said Evans.

"Impossible," Russell retorted. "You must stay here with Robertson. When he's ready to return to England will be soon enough for you to think of travel. I'm not happy about your arm."

Cave Thomas glanced across at Evans and noted his frustration as he replied,

"You're in charge, Russell. I'll just have to concentrate on getting fully fit once more."

Finkel had remained silent throughout this exchange, but at this point he added his own thoughts.

"My countrymen may well need further help. If you are free to travel in a month or two, you could be of use to them and to me."

Evans, who had no wish to become embroiled in a Prussian resistance movement, said nothing. He was wise enough to realise that the less he said, the less likely he was to betray himself and his plans. Cave Thomas watched them all and wondered how he had managed to become caught up in this complex web. He'd be glad when it was all over – if things went well, of course.

"I'm going to my mother for a while. Would you like to come with me, Cave Thomas? She'll be awake by now."

"Of course," said Cave Thomas. He brushed the crumbs from his jacket and rose to follow Robertson.

"Don't be too long," said Russell. "There's something we need to discuss before you leave." He walked past Robertson and opening the door, peered down the corridor to ensure all was quiet.

Cave Thomas and Robertson moved towards the door but were stopped by Evans.

"Take Mrs Robertson my apologies, will you? In all the upheaval, I forgot to post this letter she gave me." He fished in his pocket and drew out a folded sheet of paper, addressed and sealed. "Here."

He reached past Cave Thomas and handed it to Robertson, who took it and slipped it in his pocket.

"I hadn't realised she'd asked you to do this. I'll ask her what she wishes to be done about it."

Evans walked away and sat down once more near the stove. His face was unreadable. Russell reappeared.

"All's quiet. Go ahead." Russell's increased vigilance underlined the seriousness of their situation.

Robertson and Cave Thomas left the studio and went down to Mrs Robertson's room. They knocked gently and entered the room, dismissed her maid and then sat together at the foot of the bed. Robertson took out the letter and looked carefully at the handwriting.

"This is not my mother's hand," he said.

"I didn't expect it to be, did you?"

"No." Robertson slid his finger under the seal and unfolded the letter. It was in code, as they had expected. He handed it to Cave Thomas, who slowly unpicked the meaning.

"I am watched day and night. I cannot speak and am not sure I'll be able to get away. I'll try to get a message to you before I leave, but if not, meet me at the 'Eagle with the Broken Wing' in…" he passed the letter to Robertson. "What does that say?" he asked, pointing to the name.

Robertson thought for a moment. "I think it's a suburb at the edge of St Petersburg, out on the road to the south. The houses are little more than shacks, but I believe there's some kind of inn down there. It must be the place Evans told us about in that note – the one we received at that post house. I never thought to ask him about it, did you?"

"No, I'd quite forgotten about it."

"I expect it will be easy enough to find."

"I'll need to be able to trust my driver," said Cave Thomas.

"May God go with you," said a faint voice from the bed. Mrs Robertson was awake.

"It is my prayer," said Cave Thomas. "I go tomorrow, early. Will you pray for me?"

"Yes," it was as much a sigh as a reply. "And will you pray for me, and for my son?"

"You have my solemn promise."

"It is enough. And my son will follow you… when I am done."

Robertson's expression told all his thoughts and emotions. 'Everyone can master a grief but he who suffers most,' Cave

Thomas thought, wondering as he did so whether it was his own thought or a half-remembered quotation.

He concentrated on the letter. "Cave Thomas, it mentions a time – dawn tomorrow, the seventh."

Cave Thomas looked. Yes, it did.

"I'll destroy it," said Robertson. He walked across to the stove and threw it into the flames. "We'll tell Russell that my mother decided not to send it after all."

"Send what?" came that thin voice once more.

"A letter, Mother. One you wrote and asked Mr Evans to post for you. Do you remember?"

"Ah, yes. The letter. I remember now. It was to my dressmaker."

"I'll explain it all to Mr Evans," said Cave Thomas. "Now, I ought to be on my way." He approached the bed, lifted Mrs Robertson's hand and bent to kiss it. She turned to him and smiled.

"Such a pleasure to meet you, William. Remember me, and paint, paint, paint."

"I will. I will." he replied. He placed her hand gently on the counterpane and stepped back to Robertson.

"My dear friend," he said. "Forgive me for bringing trouble upon you. I had hoped it would all be very different."

"We'll meet again in London," said Robertson, "I promise."

"Of course. In London then."

The two men embraced as brothers. Circumstances had forged a friendship that would last for years to come.

Cave Thomas returned to the studio. No mention was made of the letter. Russell hadn't seen it and Finkel had kept his thoughts to himself.

"How is Mrs Robertson?" Russell asked.

"She's very weak, but still lucid. It can't be long now. Leave her to her son."

"We'll all be gone very soon, and with us, the gold and any danger it brought with it. We'll make sure we leave the place clean, and Evans will remain to guard them once we're gone." Russell was placing a lot of faith in Evans's ability to keep the Robertsons safe. Cave Thomas realised that any danger would take time to dissipate once they'd gone. There was no guarantee that the Robertsons would be spared a search by the police – or, worse, a criminal gang. Since none of them really knew where danger lay, all they could do was keep to their plans and hope for the best.

185

"I'll send a message to the telegraph office in Berlin," Russell went on. "As soon as we've completed our mission, we'll make our way there to see you. If anything goes wrong, don't wait for us beyond the 20th. You'll need to be back in London before the end of the month if you can."

"Very well," said Cave Thomas. "I'll do my best. Good luck and God speed to you. We'll meet in Berlin, I hope."

With this, he left.

As he neared the Neva, Cave Thomas slowed his steps in order to examine the state of the ice. The temperature was dropping once more, and he noticed sledges and people on the frozen river. So, the thaw was nothing to worry about. All would be well for the next day. His path took him past the English Church and up the street to where the Governor's Office was located. When he arrived, he was directed into a waiting room; the Governor's staff were busy. He sat down on a bench and looked at the other people waiting. They were mostly businessmen and merchants, but three stood out as different. He quickly realised that they were English. Two were men aged around sixty, the other looked ten or fifteen years younger. They were soberly dressed and spoke quietly to one another. It was clear from what Cave Thomas could catch of their conversation that they were recently arrived in St Petersburg and were there about their papers. A clerk came into the room and called their names: Mr Sturge, Mr Charleston and Mr Pease. The three men followed the clerk for their interview with the Governor. 'These must be the famous Quakers' thought Cave Thomas, 'they can be no other. Hardly dangerous-looking but looks aren't everything.'

Another clerk came out and called Thomas's name. Cave Thomas followed him into a large room within which lay rows of desks, piled high with boxes of papers. He noticed that the three Quakers were standing at separate desks, on the other side of the room. His clerk led him to a desk and sat down behind it. A few quick questions settled matters. There was no need to trouble the Governor. Cave Thomas received his passport and permits to travel, thanked the clerk and turned to leave, almost colliding with one of the Quakers as he did so.

"I beg your pardon," he said.

"Not at all. I should have been paying more attention myself," said the Quaker. "Robert Charlton," he added, holding out a hand.

"William Cave Thomas. Pleased to make your acquaintance." Cave Thomas took the proffered hand and shook it.

"I've heard of that name," said Mr Charlton, thoughtfully. "Do you have anything to do with the Thomases of Bristol?"

"I'm afraid not," said Cave Thomas. "My family resides in London. My father is a picture framer and gilder. I am a painter by profession."

"Ah, it must be another branch of the family – but you have a look of someone I know." He called to the other two gentlemen, who had also completed their business and were ready to leave. "Don't you think this gentleman has a look of Mr Francis Thomas of Horfield?

The two gentlemen appeared a little at a loss.

"I cannot say," said one, "never having met him."

"I met him once, but cannot see the likeness," said the other.

"He's from England, as we are," said Mr Charlton, "Mr Thomas. May I introduce my friends, Mr Pease and Mr Sturge."

"How do you do," murmured Cave Thomas. "Are you recently arrived in St Petersburg?"

"We are. Just a few days ago. We are staying at Benson's Hotel."

"I stayed there myself, when I first arrived, but since then have been staying with an old friend." He mentioned Robertson and his mother but avoided the English Church connection.

"We're finding it very comfortable," said Mr Charlton, "although I don't entirely trust the water."

Cave Thomas was tempted to suggest he add some spirits to it, but recalled, in time, that the Quakers were abstainers.

"Are you here on business?" he asked, hoping his innocent question might unlock a flow of useful information. He was not disappointed.

"We are here to see the Emperor," said Mr Sturge, "and to bring him greetings from the Society of Friends, together with a message entreating him to choose the way of peace."

"We've been travelling for two weeks, through every kind of weather. We hope that he'll see us very soon and then we can return home." Mr Pease looked as if he was starting a cold.

"A singular feat of endurance," said Cave Thomas. "I congratulate you all and wish you success in your mission. My own is of sadder nature. I accompanied a friend to visit his mother, resident here in St Petersburg. We had hoped to bring her home to

187

England, but it appears that we have left it too late. She is too frail to travel."

"That is sad for you both," said Mr Charlton. "Do I gather from your presence here that you intend to return to England?"

"Yes. I have family commitments there. I must leave my friend to do his duty here and return to do my own duty in England."

"Then God speed your journey, sir," said Mr Pease.

"Perhaps we will meet in London?" said Mr Sturge.

"It would be a pleasure, gentlemen. I must leave you and return to my lodgings. I wish you well and hope you, too, have a safe journey home." Cave Thomas bowed and left them.

An interesting encounter. He wished he could be there when they addressed the Czar. He wondered what, if anything, might come of their mission. It was a long way to travel with so little chance of success. He returned to the English Church aware that his feelings about the Quaker deputation had changed. Instead of seeing them as a meddling irritation, as Sir Henry had done, he now viewed them with respect. Their motives for travelling had been purer than his own and, he hoped, the outcome of their venture of more lasting value than anything bought with gold.

25

Westward bound
Tuesday 7th – Friday 10th February 1854

Cave Thomas's bags were packed and ready. He'd taken Mr Cattley's letter of introduction to the carriage hire business and booked a carriage-sledge, slightly smaller than that which had brought him into Russia, for early Tuesday morning. An hour or two had furnished him with supplies for the journey, which he'd had parcelled up and delivered to the English Church. Father Ambrosius, fully aware of these preparations had brought his own small bag down to Cave Thomas's room, asking if it could stay there until the morning as he didn't wish to draw attention to his plan to leave. He'd brought a letter too, addressed to Mr Cattley, to leave behind, explaining his departure. Cave Thomas was not happy about this, but Ambrosius was adamant. A letter must be left. It was his duty to treat his superior fairly. Unable to change the man's mind, Cave Thomas had yielded, only once Ambrosius had left him, he pocketed the letter with the intention of posting it after they left St Petersburg, rather than leaving to chance how soon it might be discovered.

He was up and dressed, ready to leave, by five thirty. Ambrosius arrived silently and the two men carried their belongings to the side door to the church. Ambrosius took out his keys and unlocked the door. In the darkness it was hard to make out the carriage, but trusting that it was there, they made their way out to the street, locking the door behind them. The carriage-sledge was waiting. Cave Thomas walked round to talk to the driver. He slipped Ambrosius's letter into his hand, together with a few coins. The man, who introduced himself as Otto Bauer, would make sure it was posted in the first town they reached. There was an exchange of papers and then the driver's mate – his son - dropped down to open the carriage door for them. Ambrosius clambered up into the carriage. Cave Thomas took a moment to remind the driver of his additional passenger, waiting in the suburbs. It was all in hand, he was assured, in broken English, so he climbed up to join Ambrosius and the door was shut and secured behind him. With a crack of the whip, they set off towards the south-western approach road to the city. After half a mile or so, the driver turned the equipage into a narrow side road and began to zigzag around to the southern district. Acutely aware of the need for vigilance, Cave Thomas strained his ears to listen for any pursuit but, as far as he could tell, there was none. After they had been travelling for twenty minutes the carriage slowed and they drew up in front of a ramshackle building which the pre-dawn light revealed to be a drinking house. The driver whistled and a figure emerged from the dark shadow of the building. The door opened and in clambered a heavily muffled Evans, preceded by his travelling bag. The door was closed by the driver's son and they were soon on their way once more. Evans settled himself and eyed Ambrosius with surprise.

"Who's this and why is he here?" he asked.

Cave Thomas introduced the two men to one another.

"Evans, this is Father Ambrosius – he'll be travelling with us for the first part of our journey. Ambrosius, this is Mr Evans. I'm to accompany him home to England. He has been unwell."

The pair peered at one another in the gloom and muttered a greeting. Evans spoke briefly to Cave Thomas to assure him that he'd not been followed. Unless they were both mistaken, their departure had been of no interest to the authorities – nor to anyone else.

The carriage-sledge gradually left all signs of habitation behind it and headed out into the countryside to the south of St Petersburg. The road was not one of the main routes to the city, but one used by farmers to bring their produce to market. Consequently, the going was rough and the lurching and noise of the carriage, creaking on its sledge platform, made conversation difficult. Evans, whose arm still troubled him, slid into a doze. Ambrosius appeared to do likewise. Cave Thomas stayed wakeful, waiting for the sun to rise so that he could assess his companions properly, and the terrain through which they were travelling.

Dawn gradually crept upon them through leaden skies. There was clearly more snow on its way. Cave Thomas cleaned the small carriage window with his glove. Through the small aperture he could discern trees and snow-covered fields. There were houses dotted around the landscape; buildings skirted by ramshackle barns and sheds. Horses, cattle, goats, their breath steaming the air, waited patiently as farmers forked fresh fodder for the day. The carriage swept past each smallholding, leaving the workmen standing, staring after them, arrested by sight of a lone carriage. The animals, restricted to the open barns, would not see pasture for months to come. Cave Thomas wondered how much would be seized by the army, how many men forced to fight, how many hearths lose their masters, how many widows be left to mourn. Contemplation of the effects of war made for bitter thoughts. He tried to think of other things but found little respite as he considered his companions and wondered what new difficulties might lie ahead because of them.

The day wore on. The promised snow began to fall, thin but persistent. They left the country roads and joined the main route to the south-west. Every few miles the driver stopped to change horses. Papers were examined and Mr Cattley's letters acted like magic. The post houses were happy to speed them on their way, honoured to do them service. Cave Thomas wondered at the power wielded by such a seemingly ordinary man. The British Factory must have influence over a large area. For this he was grateful. Nobody commented that they were not accompanied by an out-rider. Such precautions appeared to have been abandoned in the current upheaval, for they saw none on the road. A smooth journey was what they all three needed. In this way the day passed. The light began to fail and on they went, into the night, sleeping and waking, eating when they were hungry, the provisions they'd brought with them, the hours slipping away. Morning came and still they travelled, putting as much ground as they could between themselves and any potential pursuit.

At one of the larger post houses they bought hot food and stayed in the relative shelter of the carriage to eat it. Both Evans and Ambrosius were fully awake. It was time to plan their strategy for the rest of the journey. Cave Thomas brought out his map and spread it on their laps as soon as they had finished eating. Ambrosius looked with interest. He pointed out two or three places that they would need to travel through if they were to find a safe entry to Prussia. They could not return the way Cave Thomas had come.

"There will be troops between us and the border," he said. "The main border crossings will be guarded, but we could slip through unnoticed if we were to aim further south."

"Are you sure?" asked Cave Thomas, wondering how the man received his intelligence.

"Fairly sure," he said, "Unless the army has moved that way. We'll need to watch the road ahead."

Evans looked carefully at the map. Some of the place names were familiar to him.

"We could cross the first big river here," he said, pointing to a narrow gorge marked on the map. "As far as I know, it is still frozen. There is a bridge, but it's likely to be guarded. We'd need to cross the river upstream of the town."

Ambrosius looked where Evans was pointing. He nodded agreement.

"I know that place. It would be good. We could leave the main road here," he pointed to a small village. "This track would take us near the town on the river, without drawing attention to ourselves. If we continue at this pace, we should arrive there at dusk and could cross the river by night."

"Is that safe?" asked Cave Thomas.

"We would need a guide," said Ambrosius. "Perhaps the driver knows of one."

"Can we trust him?" asked Evans.

"Of course," said Ambrosius, with a wide smile. "He's my cousin Bertha's husband, Otto Bauer. His son is called Paul."

'Of course,' thought Cave Thomas. 'We are hedged about and directed in this venture. I don't believe anything has been left to chance.'

Before they left the next horse post, Ambrosius spoke to his relative and returned to the others with good news.

"The way ahead is clear. There have been troops, but they have moved through the area and have set up camp about twenty miles to the north. Their scouts are unlikely to come this way. Otto knows of a guide. He'll pick him up in his village before we divert to the south."

On they went, ever closer to the border. With a taxing night ahead, Cave Thomas yielded to sleep. He'd need his wits about him later.

Towards dawn, Cave Thomas woke with a start, certain at once that all was not well. Ambrosius was leaning over the prostrate form of Evans, loosening the man's clothing and feeling for a pulse.

"What's wrong?" he asked.

"I was woken by Mr Evans," said Ambrosius. "He has a high fever. We must get help."

192

Cave Thomas reached over to lay his hand on Evans's forehead. The man was burning. The wound must have become infected. Between them, Cave Thomas and Ambrosius removed Evans's furs and revealed the festering wound on his upper arm. They wondered how long the man had hidden his pain.

"You're right. He needs medical help. Where are we?" Cave Thomas looked out of the window at the passing terrain. They'd left the main road once more. Why, he couldn't be sure. He wondered how long they had been travelling blind. Until the carriage stopped, they'd have to make do with what they had. He reached into his satchel and withdrew some clean painting cloths. Ambrosius produced a water bottle and took the cloths from Cave Thomas.

"I am used to this," he said, and gently tended Evans's wound. Evans moaned as the pain roused him from his semi-stupor.

"Have you anything to dull his pain?" Ambrosius asked.

Cave Thomas produced a small bottle of laudanum and passed it to Ambrosius who measured out a draught. He trickled it into Evans's mouth and gradually the man lost consciousness. As the carriage carried on relentlessly, Cave Thomas wondered what they should do.

At the next stop, Ambrosius left the carriage and went to talk to the driver. After a few minutes they both came to the carriage and Otto climbed up to see Evans for himself.

"He must have help," was his verdict. "We can't go on. We must turn back towards Riga. I'll drive to my uncle's village. It's a few hours from here but is the nearest place of safety."

"Very well," said Cave Thomas. "I agree. Where is the place?"

When he heard the name, he could hardly believe their luck. Unless there were two villages with the same name, he felt certain that it was the very place he'd stopped on the way to St Petersburg – the village where the boy under the handcart had been taken. If so, they would be amongst friends.

The sledge swept into the small village at about nine that night. It pulled up in the centre and Otto jumped down, whilst his son went to hold the horses' heads. He then left the carriage in these capable hands and went to a nearby house and knocked loudly. It was answered by a man, with a child at his feet. An exchange of words in Russian was followed by the door being flung wide and the entire family spilling out into the snow. The driver returned to the carriage and reached up to open the door. Cave Thomas was ready.

193

He leapt down into the snow and went over to the family, certain now that he knew where he was. God had directed his path from the very beginning. Cave Thomas accepted this coincidence as His ordained will – too engrossed in what had to be done to waste time in feeling surprised.

He was greeted as an old friend. It was the family he had helped, the family who'd sworn that they owed him a life.

"I bring you a sick friend," he said. "Please, will you help us?"

"Of course, of course," said the woman. "Bring your friend to us."

Cave Thomas returned to the carriage and found Ambrosius cradling Evans in his arms, ready to be lowered gently to the ground. Between them, they transferred him from carriage to house, where a place was made for him near the fire. By now the poor man was shaking with cold, the fever having intensified in the past hour.

"I will nurse him," said the woman. "First we must cool the fever. Peteris, fetch water and cloths. We will soon make him well again."

A lad brought water for his mother and a hot drink for Cave Thomas and his companions. It was the boy whose life Cave Thomas had saved.

"Pyotr," he said. "You are well?"

"Yes sir, but my father calls me Peteris," said the boy, schooled in English by his mother. "I am glad I can help your friend as you helped me."

"Thank you, Pyotr. But may I call you Peter, for that is your name in my language?"

"Oh no, sir, the Great Czar was called that. Call me Peteris, as my mother and father do. Like them, you gave me life."

"Very well. Peteris. I'll give your mother money to pay for my friend's needs. When he's well, will you help him to find his way to join me in Berlin? Perhaps your father can help."

"I will ask him, sir."

The boy went to his father and brought him to Cave Thomas. The man held out his hand in friendship and spoke rapidly in Latvian, or Lettish, too fast for Cave Thomas to catch his full meaning, He wondered where the father's alliances lay and whether they had brought trouble to the house.

Peteris allayed his fears once more. "My father is pleased to help. He is not happy with the Russian army coming this way and taking what is not theirs. He will help your friend and keep him

194

safe. He says that we are not on a big road here – the army will pass us by."

"I hope that's true," said Cave Thomas, addressing the father and waiting for his son to translate, sensing that his Russian would not be welcome here. He gave the man money, with Peteris explaining what it was for. It was accepted and placed in a jar on a shelf.

"My father will give from his own purse if your friend needs more. He thanks you for the money. He will spend it to buy medicine."

"We must leave," said Cave Thomas. "I'll say goodbye to my friend."

He went to Evans who, although very feverish, seemed able to understand his situation.

"Stay until you are well. You won't be discovered here – these are friends. They'll help you on your way when you are well enough to travel. Here..." he gave Evans a purse with more money and promised to wait for him in Berlin.

"Get well, my friend. Send me a message, post restante, when you can."

"I will," said Evans, his voice ragged with pain. "I'm sorry Cave Thomas, I meant to help you."

"And you will again. I'll wait for you. We'll make the rest of our journey home together, just you see."

With that, he took the food package prepared by the family and, with vows to write in due course, he and Ambrosius climbed back into the carriage. The horses, walked and fed during this interval, were ready to go. Trusting to Otto Bauer's knowledge of the road, the two men slumped back in their seats, exhausted. On they swept, into the night, trusting that the way ahead was clear and hoping that no enemy pursued them through the dark.

At last they found their way back to the crossing point, reaching the river at about midnight. All went as Ambrosius had predicted earlier – before their plans had been throw awry. The guide was found in the nearby village. He was willing to travel at night. The town was quiet, its gates still open. The roads were clear and as they reached their crossing point, a thinning of the cloud allowed enough moonlight to filter through to show the way - but not enough to betray their presence. However, it was not without bated breath and heightened anxiety that the crossing was made, and all three were glad to reach the other side. Their guide, receiving Cave

195

Thomas's generous tip with gratitude, set out to walk the three or so miles back to the town, where he had kin. He'd wait for the town gate to open and then stay with them for a few days.

The seemingly tireless horses pulled them onwards. They still had many miles to cover before they'd reach the Russian border. Cave Thomas and Ambrosius dozed, overcome by prolonged fatigue and tension.

26

Into the Forest
Saturday 11th – Monday 13th February 1854

It was impossible to know how far they'd travelled through that night and on through the following day. The landscape was wild and seemingly empty. They met nobody on the road. The weather had closed in and the country peasants seemed to have taken shelter until the storm passed. The snow fell with thin persistence. Cave Thomas feared for their safety but Ambrosius remained confident. Otto was a good driver. He was reliable and knew the country well. He was confident that they'd get through.

In their enforced isolation, it was inevitable that the two men became better acquainted. Ambrosius spoke of his family - his wish to become a priest, his father's death, time away for military training, how his mother had insisted that he followed his vocation and how the death of an uncle had left his mother without male support. He told Cave Thomas how he'd met the leaders of the Prussian resistance group, formed when Russia began to appear a threat once more. (This came as a surprise to Cave Thomas. He wondered whether Ambrosius had been working with Herr Finkel and, if so, what that might mean.) He explained that he'd been recruited whilst on military training – the movement had been in existence for some years, but never become widely known. "Every nation has its secrets," he told Cave Thomas, challenging him to reflect on the secrets behind Britain and British interests overseas. "Look at yourself," he went on. "Are you not part of that secret force?"

It had been an unsettling conversation, echoing, as it did, so many of Cave Thomas's own thoughts. He began to see that Ambrosius combined zeal and commitment to his country with an incisive mind and high intelligence. He'd been right not to underestimate the man. He was a man who was capable of many things, including – perhaps – a reluctance to be entirely honest about his actions. Cave Thomas realised that his new respect for the man hadn't entirely remove his earlier mistrust.

Evening came and they stopped to change the horses. The two passengers clambered down from the carriage and sought shelter in the inn. Hot soup was brought, and they huddled by the fire, easing their cold stiff joints, and enjoying the brief respite from the discomfort of the journey. The soup warmed them, and the coarse bread satisfied their hunger. Otto joined them, asking their host to make up a parcel of food for his son, who was seeing to the horses. He asked the innkeeper what he knew of troop movements in the area – a common enough question it appeared, as the man sat down with them and spoke at length of all that he knew.

"There've been no soldiers in the district – we're too far from the main route through to Riga – but I've heard talk of troops twenty or so miles north of here. Take my advice - keep to the road south-west. Stay away from any turnings to the north – they'd bring you back to the main road. From what I've heard the soldiers are hungry. I fear for my business if they come this way. I fear for my wife and daughters, too." He left them, returning a few minutes later with a jug of warm spirits and water, mixed with herbs and spices.

"This will warm you up," he said, pouring some into their cups.

Otto wanted to know more about what might lie ahead, so he questioned the innkeeper. Unable to follow all that was said, Cave Thomas turned to Ambrosius, seeking a translation. Ambrosius looked sombre.

"He says that there have been rumours about men living wild, ahead of us, in the forest. They're deserters. They steal from travellers and sometimes kill or leave them to freeze to death. He warns us to take guard against them and avoid travelling if the sky clears and the moon is up. That's when they hunt."

This was bad news. Having encountered such men on his way into Russia, Cave Thomas had hoped to avoid them on the return journey. He'd been lucky once; to ask for a second stroke of luck was perhaps expecting too much.

"We must offer to stand guard through the forest. I have a handgun. Can you still remember how to use one?"

"Yes," said Ambrosius. "Military service leaves an indelible mark. I can use a handgun and a musket. I am trained to kill in other ways, too."

Cave Thomas digested this information. It was always useful to know the abilities of one's companions in such a tight place, but to be reminded that he'd been travelling with a trained killer was sobering. He was glad that Ambrosius had become his friend.

Otto finished his discussion with the innkeeper, who left them and returned to his work in the next room. The driver turned to

Ambrosius, wishing to explain in his own language, what he planned to do. Again, Ambrosius translated for Cave Thomas, who'd followed the gist of what was said, but not every detail.

"He says that he's familiar with the landscape ahead of us and has friends in the forest, who work as charcoal burners and hunt for meat and furs. He's confident that we can escape the attention of the 'vagabonds' - that's the word he used - especially if the bad weather holds. He says it's a well-known fact that feckless outlaws like to keep their feet dry and their backs warm."

Cave Thomas laughed. "A good expression – let's hope he's right."

"He'll take the trail that leads to his friends and, if necessary, recruit them as guards," Ambrosius continued. Then he turned to Otto and spoke quickly.

"I've told him that we're armed and that we're ready to defend ourselves," he said, turning back to Cave Thomas.

Cave Thomas nodded his agreement and then brought out his gun to show them. Ambrosius said that he'd be happy to use a musket if the driver could produce one. This was quickly done. Otto reached into his bag and brought out oil and rags so that they could clean their weapons and prepare for the journey ahead. As they were doing this, Otto's son Paul appeared, sent in to warm himself for a while, whilst an ostler looked after the horses. He too was drawn into the discussion and said he'd fight anyone who dared to attack them. His father, with a look of pride, cuffed him gently and told him to keep his head low and stay out of trouble. There'd be time enough for heroics in the months to come.

They set off at last, travelling through the night, peering into the darkness as the light of their lamps picked out the way ahead. The snow was still falling, and the wind was such that drifts were beginning to form. They were torn between a desire to reach the forest, where there'd be shelter from the wind, and fear of what the forest might conceal. An hour brought them within sight of the first trees. The landscape was bleak and empty as before, with no sign of life, no wisp of smoke to betray a dwelling or a campfire. Ambrosius wrapped himself in another scarf and, as they paused at the top of a slight hill, emerged from the carriage to join the driver and his son, musket to the ready. Cave Thomas remained inside the carriage, watching through the windows, his revolver in his hand. Thus prepared, they set off down the hill towards the trees.

199

As the branches closed in around them, the wind dropped dramatically, and little snow fell through the thick interlaced canopy above them. The wind moaned through the firs, buffeting their topmost branches, but at ground level, the sound was more muffled, and they felt protected from the worst of the storm. They proceeded through the trees along a track used by foresters. There were few signs of life; a coniferous forest doesn't yield much sustenance for wildlife, especially in the depth of winter. The horses were unable to fan out very wide, despite the track being well-established and far from narrow. Otto's hand had to be firm as the horses were easily spooked and were better trained for travelling across wide open spaces. All four men remained alert, ready to act if necessary, ears pricked for the sound of human activity, guns to the ready, hardly bearing to breathe.

They travelled thus for more than an hour. Then gradually, Cave Thomas became aware of a slight change in the trees. There were fewer firs and more deciduous trees, naked at this time of year. With this change they travelled across more difficult terrain. The snow, with less to impede its fall, was lying ever thicker on the track ahead. It was clear to him that they were unlikely to be able to proceed through the forest as planned but would be forced to stop before they'd reached their goal. They'd been aiming to reach a village thirty miles the other side of the forest, near a river. They'd hoped that the horses would last that long, but they were nearly finished.

After another fifteen minutes of struggle, the carriage sledge came into a clearing, about which lay a straggle of wooden huts and shelters, belonging to the forest workers. A door opened at their approach and a figure stepped out, carrying an ancient musket. Two more figures followed him, similarly armed, and then a fourth, holding an axe. Otto called out to them and straight away the figures lowered their weapons and greeted him with evident pleasure.

The man with the axe leaned it against the doorpost and came to help with the horses. Cave Thomas emerged from the carriage and climbed stiffly down. Introductions were made and they were welcomed and taken inside the hut. Amidst much talking and many questions, they gradually told the forestry workers of their journey and how they were trying to avoid both the army and the deserters. They learnt that the outlaws were encamped about ten miles to the southeast. They'd done well to take the road they had as the men seldom came this way, knowing how well-armed the foresters were and how much better they knew the forest.

"They leave us alone," Otto's friend told him. "They don't like our muskets or our traps." Ambrosius translated this in case Cave Thomas had failed to catch the joke, amidst the laughter of the foresters. One of them showed them a trophy, gained in a skirmish. It was an army weapon. So, the deserters had taken their weapons with them. It was an uncomfortable thought.

It soon became clear that it would be impossible to go any further before morning. The track ahead was deep in snow. The last of the men to return from work that day had struggled to get back to the camp. Otto and Paul left the warmth of the fire to assist in the task of stabling the horses. They pulled the carriage sledge into a building and concealed it with wood, taken from a stack lying ready to build another shelter. Some straw thrown over their footprints completed the task, and, unless a thorough search were made, the carriage would remain hidden. They returned to the fire, bringing blankets from the carriage, and then all, apart from those on guard, settled down for the night.

Morning brought with it a stillness which meant the storm was past. Over a breakfast of rough rye bread, the men discussed what should be done. The road ahead would be hard to follow and there'd be places where they'd have to dig themselves out. Slow progress would put them at greater risk. The deserters had horses and could move about much more easily than they could, although the forest workers didn't think they'd move far from their camp in such weather. At last it was decided that they would move on, with a guard of foresters to see them safely through the next few miles. Once they reached the edge of the thickest part of the forest, they would find the way easier, perhaps. Cave Thomas couldn't see the logic in this, but kept quiet, knowing that he must trust the men who knew the landscape.

They set off as soon as it was properly light, to make best use of the short day. Five foresters came with them, all mounted. As they left the clearing, Cave Thomas waved farewell to those left behind and said a brief prayer as the carriage sledge took the snow-filled track to the southwest. Ambrosius sat with head bowed. He was holding a cross and his lips moved as he read the daily office.

The next hours were hard work for them all. The sledge moved well over flat ground, but each time it met a hollow, the snow

201

became too deep and they had to dig their way out. Ambrosius and Cave Thomas took their turn in the work and, at all times, one or more kept watch. After a few hours spent in this way, the landscape began to change. The close-planted trees had larger breaks in them, and the land seemed to become a plateau. Around noon, they reached the edge of the forest and stopped. They gathered in a circle to share bread, before separating, the foresters to make their way back and Cave Thomas's party to proceed to the border. He shook each man's hand and thanked him for his service, handing each money 'for his family'. This was accepted as their due, although Cave Thomas sensed that they would have done the same for nothing. He watched, as the riders disappeared between the trees, grateful for their generous assistance.

The road ahead was empty. They set off at a faster pace and were soon able to travel as quickly as before. From time to time figures, too far away to be seen clearly, appeared on the horizon. They seemed to be riders, keeping their distance, travelling in the same direction and never far from view. It was unsettling to think that their progress was being watched and that they may at any moment become the victims of an unknown enemy. These feelings of unease increased as the light began to fail. They neared the small village they'd been aiming for and paused there to change their horses, deciding not to stop. Otto asked about troop movements in the area and brought back news that the army was mustering to the northeast. The outriders they'd seen were probably scouts, sent forward to spy out the land. This chilling news made them quick about the change of horses. They bought food and took it to the carriage. It was no time to linger. Off they went again, trying to put as many miles between them and the soldiers, as possible. They crossed the frozen river and drove on; they'd have no sleep that night. Cave Thomas sat with his pistol in his lap. Ambrosius had kept the musket. It was propped by his side, ready to fire. They sat in silence. This was a night for watching and listening.

A little before dawn, the movement of the sledge slowed dramatically, and Cave Thomas heard the driver cry out. The horses came to a halt and stood shivering and pawing the ground. There followed a cry of fear from Paul and rapid words in Russian.

"What is it?" cried Cave Thomas. "What has he seen?"

"It's one of the horses – it's gone lame," Ambrosius explained.

"But he shouted out in terror…what is it?"

"He cried 'we're surrounded'," said Ambrosius. "Look!"

Cave Thomas opened the door a crack and peered into the darkness. He was aware of activity as Otto and Paul tried to hold the horses and deal with the one that had gone lame.

They were indeed, surrounded, but by whom or what, he couldn't tell.

"Quick, we're needed," Cave Thomas called back over his shoulder, and dropped down into the snow. Ambrosius took the door on the other side of the carriage and did likewise, musket held firmly and already raised in defence as he regained his balance. They could both hear and sense movement all around them. Cave Thomas scanned the landscape trying to make out how many of the enemy had come upon them. He crouched by the sledge and held his gun steady. Then, without warning, the horses took fright. The driver and his son, taken by surprise, nearly lost control of them, but, at that moment, the lame horse had been cut free. As the sledge lurched forward a couple of yards, Cave Thomas perceived their enemies moving towards them, closing in. The dark shapes moved slowly, and he was aware of the hairs going up on the back of his neck as the air filled with their hunting cry. He shouted to Ambrosius.

"Get back in the carriage!" and to Otto and Paul, "Climb back, quickly. Leave the horse!"

He swung himself back up onto the sledge and both heard and felt Ambrosius's return to the safety of the carriage. The sledge began to move, and he hung onto the open door with his left arm and levelled his gun ready to shoot. As the sledge passed the injured horse, the enemy surged forward and there was the sickening sound of attack and the never to be forgotten cries of the stricken animal. One of the figures, still intent upon claiming the carriage and its passengers as well as the horse, left the group and ran towards the sledge. As Otto and Paul struggled to control the terrified horses, the carriage juddered and swung about dangerously, its fixings emitting shrieks in objection to such treatment. The figure came on, intent upon a kill. Cave Thomas took as steady an aim as he could and fired. The leaping form dropped to the ground, dead. Cave Thomas hung onto the door and managed to swing his leg inside the carriage. Ambrosius grabbed his coat and pulled hard, and he found himself inside. He pulled the door fast shut behind him. He was panting hard, all energy spent. Ambrosius helped him to sit up and handed him a water flask.

"How many were there?" he asked.

203

"I don't know. Too many to count."

"Were they the deserters, do you think?" Ambrosius's question surprised Cave Thomas, but, on second thoughts, it had all happened so quickly, and Ambrosius had been on the other side of the carriage.

"No," he said gently. "Not deserters – wolves."

27

Prussia
Tuesday 14th – Thursday 16th February 1854

Leaving the wolves to satisfy their hunger, they drove on. The remaining horses gradually eased their pace and, out of danger for the time being, settled into a steady rhythm. It was clear that with one horse gone, their speed had been reduced, but they couldn't stop. They needed to put more miles between themselves and the wolves… and the army scouts. If the troops found evidence of the kill, they'd know that the carriage was one horse down and might come in pursuit, but as the minutes stretched into hours, it seemed that they'd left that danger behind them.

The carriage sledge reached the Russian border an hour before dawn, crossed it, and continued into Prussian territory, still going well on ice-packed tracks. In this desolate spot there were no guards, no customs buildings, no indications that they'd left the Russian empire. The road was too insignificant to guard. Ambrosius and his relatives had chosen their route well. A few miles further on they neared a village. All was quiet, but as they slipped between the houses, lights were beginning to appear as people prepared for a new day. At the end of the village they found an inn and stopped there to see about hiring fresh horses. The welcome was guarded. The ostler wanted to know where they'd come from. He called for his master. Three men emerged from the building and gathered by the horses. Two seized the harness, whilst the third questioned the driver. Then he approached the carriage and demanded to see inside. Ambrosius laid a hand upon Cave Thomas's arm and put a finger to his lips. He quickly reached for his bag and pulled some papers from the top. The carriage door opened, and a command was given for them to descend. Cave Thomas sat back and allowed Ambrosius to go first. As he emerged, he allowed his crucifix, on a chain about his neck, to drop forward into view. The man stepped back a pace and bowed. Ambrosius gained the ground and held out a hand in greeting. He spoke quickly in German. Cave Thomas strained his ears to hear what was being said. Then Ambrosius turned to him and invited him to come down. He introduced Cave Thomas as his friend, a painter, an Englishman, here to help the Prussian kingdom. Mr

Thomas had travelled to Russia to help Englishmen there, and was now bringing him home, to defend Prussia. He showed the innkeeper a letter of introduction and pointed out the address and the signature. The man, who clearly couldn't read, appeared impressed. He called an order to the ostlers and invited Ambrosius and his friends to enter the inn for refreshment. The driver and his son were included in this invitation, so Ambrosius accepted and indicated with a gesture that Otto and Paul Bauer would be wise to join them. Inside the inn, they sat down near the hearth where a woman was preparing breakfast. She poured boiling water into a jug and the smell of coffee rose into the air. Rye rolls were warming in a basket, and butter and sausage were set on a table. A young girl brought a basin of batter and the woman began to make pancakes with one hand whilst turning bacon on a griddle, with the other. She glanced up at the new arrivals and instructed her daughter to bring more plates.

Cave Thomas allowed himself to relax and enjoy the meal. Being fluent in German, he was able to follow the conversation as the men discussed the state of the roads, rumours of troop movements and their concern for their families should the Russian army march into Prussia. Ambrosius gave a brief explanation for his journey, similar to the one he'd given Cave Thomas. When at last it was his turn to speak, Cave Thomas found himself able to give plausible reasons for his own journey, spoke of the help he'd been afforded by Ambrosius and how he intended to return to England to urge the Government to support Prussia in its hour of need. This was received with nods and smiles - and offers of more coffee and fresh horses.

They parted after an hour or so, purses lighter but stocks of food replenished and a full set of horses to pull the sledge. As they travelled south, the roads became busier and the towns and villages they passed were full of activity. The whole country was preparing for war. The day passed slowly. At an evening halt, Otto told them that they should reach Ambrosius's home by morning. Soon Cave Thomas and Ambrosius must part. The roads were clearer now, so an hour was spent removing the carriage from its sledge to enable them to progress on wheels. As they moved off, Cave Thomas found himself regretting the gentle swish of the sledge runners, as the heavy rumble of wheels became their new companion. It made Russia seem further away. Feelings of detachment began to come between Cave Thomas and all that had taken place over the past two weeks. It would be easy to forget the menace and continued

206

danger through which he was passing; easy to leave it all behind. He must force himself to remember, to keep alert, to be aware that national boundaries might mean nothing to the men who'd tried to harm them in St Petersburg.

Glad of something to distract him from such thoughts, he encouraged Ambrosius to talk about his home in more detail; they'd reach it later that day. Ambrosius required little encouragement, eager as he was to see his family once more.

"My village," he told Cave Thomas, "lies between Oels and Breslau. My father, Nicolas Meyer, was a farmer, but my mother left the farm after his death and now keeps house for a cousin, Artur Schneider, whom I call Onkel Artur. He's a merchant, and lives above the business, in the village. My sisters, Sofie and Else, live there too, employed as embroiderers. You have seen the portrait of Else. Our land is being worked by a family who own the neighbouring farm. They rent it from my mother, but the rent is low. The house was shut up when my family left, but I intend to go and live there, work the farm, and bring my mother and sisters back home. I'm young and strong and can do this. It will help my country."

Cave Thomas wondered what other plans he might have to 'help his country'. He felt increasingly certain that the farm might become a cover for quite a different kind of activity. After all, his calling had been to become a priest, not a farmer – unless, of course, that too had been a cover for something else. He again mused on the coincidence of both Ambrosius and Finkel being Prussian. Ambrosius's confession regarding his connection with the resistance movement had not been followed by any further revelations. Cave Thomas wondered whether he'd ever discover the truth. He was surprised to realise that the young man who'd entered his life so recently, had become almost like a younger brother. He'd be disappointed if he were to learn the man had lied to him. But many questions had been raised on this journey which would probably never be answered. Once they reached the village, he and Ambrosius would part. He wondered whether he'd ever hear from him again.

The plan, once they reached Ambrosius's family, was for Otto Bauer to take Cave Thomas on to Breslau, where he'd board a train for Berlin. The driver and his son would return to the village and help Ambrosius move his family, then stay and work on the farm, it being unsafe to travel back into Russia.

"I understand that Otto has no desire to return there, in any case," said Ambrosius. "He has close family living not far from here. He'll probably give up driving for the time being."

'And join you in whatever you plan to do,' thought Cave Thomas. War was coming and all lives would be affected.

Pleased to have a plan at last, Cave Thomas prepared his papers for the next stage of the journey. They reached their destination just after seven the next morning, drew up at the inn and stabled the horses. They made their way to the merchant's house – just a few dozen yards – on foot. It lay halfway along the main street. The front of the building, given over to the merchant's shop, still had its shutters closed. A gateway led to the rear and it was through this that Ambrosius led them. A door opened and a woman came out onto the step.

She stared at Ambrosius for a moment and then ran towards him, arms outstretched, to hug him. She cried out in delight and relief.

"Nico, Nico! My son!"

Ambrosius's two sisters joined them and there was much laughter and some tears as the family was reunited. The yard was icy underfoot, so they were glad to be admitted to the house.

They were shown into a spacious hall, which acted as eating and cooking space. Ambrosius's mother introduced her cousin, Artur Schneider, who joined in the welcome. Her thanks rained down +upon Cave Thomas, as if he alone were responsible for bringing her son home to her. Ambrosius managed an embarrassed shrug of the shoulders and abandoned Cave Thomas to her attention.

At last, all welcomes done, they were invited to remove their coats and sit by the fire. Breakfast was laid and they moved to the table to eat. It was the second hospitable breakfast Cave Thomas had eaten in as many days, and memories flooded back of his years in Germany, as a student. He felt very much at home.

After they'd eaten, plans were made for the next day's journey to Breslau. Cave Thomas retrieved his copy of Bradshaw from his bag and studied the timetable. There were four possible trains. Two involved an overnight break along the way, one went straight to Berlin, but left at a quarter past eight in the morning – too early unless he travelled to Breslau that day and found a hotel for the night. The fourth would leave the following afternoon and arrive in Berlin early Friday morning. He could book a sleeping berth and arrive fully rested and ready for the day ahead.

Ambrosius begged him to catch the afternoon train and stay with them another day, rather than stop in Breslau. He wished to return the generous hospitality that Cave Thomas had shown in paying for his journey home and helping him along the way. Ambrosius's mother added her voice to the argument, so it was agreed. He'd be taken into Breslau in plenty of time to catch the Thursday afternoon train, which left at a quarter to six. This settled, he was free to enjoy this break from travelling. A bedroom was quickly prepared for him and none was surprised when he asked if he might go to bed for an hour or two, not having slept properly since they'd left St Petersburg. Ambrosius's mother then became conscious of her responsibility as housekeeper, and with her cousin's approval, persuaded all four travellers to take a rest, promising that they'd be woken in time for the mid-day meal. She insisted on showing them to their rooms, herself.

The house was comfortably yet simply furnished. Cave Thomas's room was high up in the eaves. The bed was narrow but the linen well-aired, and the jug of hot water, basin and towel, provided for him, meant that he was able to wash away the dirt of travel before he lay down. As he drifted into sleep, the shutters were taken down from the shop beneath him and the comforting sounds of commerce drove away all images of wolves and hostile forces.

The household gathered in the hall-kitchen for lunch. All four travellers felt better for their rest, and the remainder of the day passed in conversation and industry. Ambrosius's sisters went back to their work, sitting by the window to make best use of the winter daylight. They were embroidering wedding garments for the daughter of a rich family who lived just outside the village. Ambrosius helped his mother, by bringing in dry logs for the fire and making himself useful in ways which impressed Cave Thomas. The shop was busy all afternoon, selling fabrics, lace, ribbons and all the accoutrements necessary for household furnishing and dressmaking. The cousin, a man in his sixties, had run the business for thirty years. He was a widower and glad to have three women in the house to take charge of its smooth running. He spent his time in the shop stitching, as he had a reputation as a tailor, although it was not his first interest - that was buying and selling. He took full advantage of Cave Thomas's presence to retell the story of his life and work. The sisters smiled at one another, amused that their visitor should fall into this trap, but Cave Thomas, taking out his

209

sketch book, sat listening and drawing the merchant who was busy with his needle, gesticulating and punctuating his speeches with stabs of needle or pins.

Assured that there would be no difficulty in finding a berth on next day's train, Cave Thomas surrendered himself to this domestic holiday. He'd be travelling once more, soon enough. He wondered if he would ever be free to return to Prussia. A war would probably have swept across the land before then, leaving who knew what scars upon lives and landscape?

The following morning, having talked late into the previous night, none of the visitors were eager to be stirring, but the sounds of the family starting another day added speed to their preparations and they arrived downstairs for breakfast only five minutes later than Herr Schneider. Cave Thomas would be ready to leave at whatever hour was thought best. After some discussion, it was felt that the sooner the journey was made, the better. It wouldn't do to delay in case Cave Thomas missed his train. So, it was with sadness that Cave Thomas took his leave of Ambrosius's family and set off for Breslau. He answered Frau Meyer's sincere entreaties to return to them one day with genuine warmth and hoped that he would be able to do so once the world had lost its madness.

Ambrosius decided to travel with him, keen to make sure that he had done all that he ought to bring Cave Thomas as far away from Russia as he was able, He pulled out the end of the musket, which had been hidden under the seat.

"You see, I can still defend you if the wolves are hunting."

As they headed towards the city, Cave Thomas hoped that this jest would remain hypothetical and that no human 'wolves' were following their trail.

The carriage pulled into Breslau station yard at about two thirty. The roads had been clear and, although crowded as they neared their destination, were in good repair – a luxury much appreciated after weeks on wild Russian roadways and tracks.

"Cave Thomas," said Ambrosius, as they parted at the station, "I would like it very much if you would write to me once you have reached London. I shall pray for your safe arrival there and it would give me great pleasure to hear of your work as a painter. I have enjoyed your company and I owe you so much…"

Cave Thomas shook his hand and told him to think nothing of it. "We have been companions on a difficult journey. I will ever be grateful for your help, and your friendship and hospitality."

Ambrosius brushed this aside, "It was the least I could do."

"There is something I would like to know," said Cave Thomas. "Your mother called you Nico when we arrived at your village. I have known you only as Ambrosius. Will you trust me with your real name?"

Ambrosius smiled. "If you are to write to me, then I must. My name is the same as that of my father. I am Nicolas Meyer, one-time feudal lord, now, merely a farmer. Maybe, one day, I will be Father Ambrosius once more, but not until the coming war is over."

"Meyer," Cave Thomas tried it on his tongue. "It suits you, Nicolas Meyer."

"I am equally pleased with Ambrosius," Nicolas Meyer replied, "but sometimes one has to wait for the things one loves most. Goodbye."

Cave Thomas shook hands with him again, and then with Otto and Paul, their fearless drivers.

"God speed, and may we meet again in happier times," he said. Then they were off, leaving him to find somewhere warm to wait for the overnight train to Berlin.

211

28

Russell's Explanation
Thursday 16th - Friday 17th February 1854

Cave Thomas entered the station and went in search of a paper. He bought the local newspaper and a ten-day-old copy of The Times, strapped them to the top of his satchel and made his way towards the waiting room. Seeing a bar was open, he stopped to buy a hot drink, which he carried to a table outside, under the station canopy. He opened his satchel and took out the parcel of food Frau Meyer had pressed upon him, glad that he needn't leave the station in search of a meal. Whilst he ate, he watched the platforms. There were a few passengers waiting, like him, for the evening train. Elsewhere all was quiet. It would become busier at the end of the day when workers left for homes outside the city. He was conscious of being alone for the first time in his travels. Remembering that he was still in potentially hostile territory, he scanned the faces of his fellow passengers, looking for any he might recognise, and noting styles of dress, what luggage was carried - anything which might help him pick out a man – or woman – whose presence jarred, who might be following him. Nothing. But just because he'd failed to note anything unusual or out of place didn't mean that it wasn't there. He thought of Evans's patient vigilance, his determination to keep the 'meddler' safe. He'd have appreciated Evans's company now. The two had worked well together. But Evans was far behind. Cave Thomas hoped the man was recovering from his wound and would be able to make his way safely to Berlin before the 20th – the date by which he'd told Evans he must leave. It would be good to know that his friend was safe.

Loosening the strap holding the papers he'd bought, Cave Thomas and pulled out The Times. As he cast an eye over the news pages, his eye was drawn to a piece about Baron Brunow, Russian Minister to London. It appeared that he had left for Darmstadt on the 4th and that all diplomatic relations between Russia and the British Government were now suspended. He turned to the report for more details. There had been a statement in the House of Lords. Orders were going to St Petersburg, by courier, directing the

212

British and French Ministers at the Court to 'place themselves in the same position', whatever that might mean. Negotiations at Vienna were at an end. Count Orloff had returned to St Petersburg… 'it is almost superfluous to add that no attempt was made by the Government to disguise their full conviction that the country is on the brink of war'.

Baron Brunow – that was a name he knew. The man had been Minister to London for years – ever since '39 or '40. If he had gone, then things were about as bad as they could be. Cave Thomas thought back over the past few days. What had he been doing whilst all this was happening? Thursday 2nd whilst he had been moving his bags to the English Church, Baron Brunow had been visiting the French Ambassador to say farewell. The Quaker Peace Delegation had seen the Czar on the 3rd and Finkel had appeared on the 4th – the same day that Baron Brunow received his marching orders. Cave Thomas wondered at the complexity of it all and how he'd stumbled into this strange confluence of events at such a pivotal moment. Each of these players had connections linking them to others, whose strong beliefs or powerful patrons held the destiny of Europe in their hands. He folded the newspaper and pushed it, and the local paper, deep into his satchel. There would be time enough once he'd boarded the train to go over them in fine detail, but first he must buy his ticket. He took up his bags and made his way to the ticket office, where he managed to secure a place in a sleeping compartment. The train would be ready for boarding at four fifteen. He looked at the clock – an hour to fill. He went to the waiting room and made himself as comfortable as he could, then took out his sketch book and began to draw.

Lost in his work, Cave Thomas was surprised at how quickly that hour passed. The flinging open of carriage doors and the shriek of the engine releasing some of its steam, alerted him and he quickly put away his book and pencils and made his way to the train. His ticket checked and the compartment found, he waited to see who was going to join him. The compartment held two. His was the lower bunk. He tidied his bags away and took out the newspapers to read more thoroughly. No-one came, and as the train pulled out of the station, he folded the newspapers, swung his legs up on the bed and settled down for a nap. He was still weary from the long journey out of Russia and was glad to be able to seize an opportunity to rest before dinner.

213

He woke about half an hour later, as the Inspector came to check his ticket. He inquired as to whether he would have a companion. The Inspector checked his notebook and told him that the berth had not been taken. He would have the compartment to himself. For this, Cave Thomas was extremely grateful. His life had been so full of people that to have some time to himself was a relief. He waited another hour and then made his way to the restaurant car for a meal. The efficiency of the service and the cleanliness of the table linen were exemplary. He wondered how they managed it with the engine spewing out smoke and cinders. It must make plenty of work for the staff. He ordered from the menu and waited for his meal to arrive – hot soup, with seared steak to follow. All was prepared to perfection. As he drank his coffee, Cave Thomas counted out a generous tip for the steward.

Back in his compartment, he made a check of his belongings. He'd been well trained by Evans and had left snares to betray any interference with his bags. Nothing had changed. No-one had taken advantage of his absence to look through his things. He felt a little safer, but then realised that he'd been travelling via an unlikely route. Once he reached Berlin, he'd be moving into more familiar and potentially hostile territory, taking train services which were used more regularly by international travellers. Having been hidden from view, he was walking straight back into public gaze, and thus, into danger once more. He would need to stay alert. The frustration of not being able to identify who had been involved in the attacks in St Petersburg once more clouded his mind. He wished that these enemies would come out into the open – like the wolf that had attacked them. A known enemy he could face but not knowing who they were added to the strain of the journey and forced his thoughts into an unending circle. He shook his head and determined to banish doubt and fear, took out his New Testament and began to read; he hoped this would lead to a better night's sleep.

The train pulled into Berlin on time, stopping at the terminus near the Stralauer Platz. It was just four-thirty on a cold Saturday morning, but Cave Thomas was ready to alight. He tipped the carriage steward and made his way through the station and out to the street, where he secured a drosky. He named "Hotel de Russie" as his destination, but once they were on their way, called to the driver and changed the address to a small *pension*, a few streets away from that bustling hotel. The habits instilled in him by Evans weren't forgotten; he'd chosen an obscure boarding house, used by students and commercial travellers. He wished to avoid the busy footfall of a hotel frequented by Russian and British visitors. He needed to time to think and plan. If he was going to meet with any others, here in Berlin, he wanted it to be on his own terms.

The drosky dropped him at the *pension*. He was glad that he had so little luggage – it was all quite different from his journey out to Russia, carrying the precious cargo of cases and parcels which had made everything so difficult. The proprietor was already up and opened the door to this new guest, welcoming him with a surprising degree of amiability, considering the hour. Cave Thomas handed the man his passport and booked a room at the back, for five nights, saying that he wished to see the sights whilst he still could. This opened the subject of war and its possible effects, and the man held forth at length about the conflicting reports in the newspapers and the effect it was having on business. All this was in German, Cave Thomas having greeted the proprietor in his own tongue. Herr Ziegler clearly warmed to him, telling him that the British were seldom visitors in his house, but on the rare occasions they stayed, tended to keep to their own language. It was refreshing to find an Englishman willing to try German.

'A little friendliness is always worth the effort', Cave Thomas thought as he settled into his room. This belief was confirmed a few minutes later when he was brought hot water for washing, and a breakfast of coffee and *brötchen*. He consumed these hungrily and then lay down to get another hour or two's sleep before going out into the city.

His first stop when he ventured out, was the telegraph office to discover whether there were any messages awaiting him. He was surprised to find two. He took them to a bar just off a main street and found a seat towards the rear, where he could watch the door. He ordered a beer and opened the messages. The first was from Russell. He was already in Berlin. He would meet with Cave Thomas in the vestibule of the Hotel du Nord. He would be there at eleven each morning for the next three days. Cave Thomas checked the date and time of the message. It was a day old. The proper code words were in place, so he could trust its reliability. He checked the time – ten thirty - he'd make that his next stop. The second message came as a complete surprise. It was from Evans. He'd sent it from Dirschau the previous day. He'd missed the afternoon train so would stop there overnight and catch the next day's train. He hoped to be in Berlin the following morning. The train came in at 5.15. Could Cave Thomas meet him at the station and find him somewhere to stay. He didn't want to see anyone else at present. Cave Thomas stared at the message. If it had been sent on Thursday, the train Evans was hoping to travel on would arrive Saturday morning. He'd need to check in Bradshaw, but he wasn't certain that the train would go at the time Evans had written. There was something not quite right about the telegraph. He folded the paper and placed it in his pocketbook. He finished his beer, looked at his watch and, slipping Russell's message into his pocket, set off to find him.

Russell was waiting for him, seated in a corner, reading a newspaper and keeping an eye on the hotel entrance. Cave Thomas walked over to the desk and enquired whether a fictional friend was staying at the hotel. Having received a negative, he turned to leave, ignoring the figure who was folding his newspaper. Outside, he turned to the right and set off towards a small public garden he'd noticed on the way to the hotel. He entered and slowed his pace, appearing to admire the dismal statuary which lined the path. Finding a seat away from other people, he sat down and took out his notebook. The damp chill of the morning was beginning to dissipate, and the sun had come out, making it quite pleasant to sit and while away a little time in the garden.

A shadow came between him and the sun.

"May I join you?" Russell's easy tones betrayed no anxiety. He sat down beside Cave Thomas. "Not a bad morning for this early in the year."

"It can't last," said Cave Thomas. "How are you?"

"Well. All is well. Our friend managed to see all his connections and deliver their presents. The journey was a little exciting at times, but here I am."

"And our friend?"

"Ah, yes, our friend. He has been delayed."

"In what way, delayed?"

"Shall we take a walk?"

The two men stood up and set off, walking slowly, in the direction of the river.

"Tell me what happened after you left." Cave Thomas was keen to hear Russell's perspective.

"For your ears only…"

"Of course."

216

"We travelled out of St Petersburg, as planned. The group outside the city appeared to be well organised. We left a parcel of money with them and they helped us find our way around the edge of the city, without drawing attention to ourselves. Once we were properly on our way, the journey went well, until we neared the Prussian border. The countryside was riddled with soldiers and peasants on the move. We kept having to retrace our steps and try another route. After three or four false starts, we finally managed to cross the border into Prussia. Then the fun really began. The Russian unit had given us directions to find the Prussian groups, but they'd all been forced to move. We wasted hours heading in the wrong direction. Twice we were held up by the military. They took quite a bit of persuading that we were bona fide travellers. Eventually we managed to deliver all the packages, but I must say, I wasn't impressed by their lack of organisation, and their idea of secrecy was a joke. I don't give them long, in a state of war, before they're discovered and eliminated."

"That bad?"

"Yes, that bad. They appeared to be led by men whose claims to noble birth gave them the right to lead. They were, to a man, arrogant and meddlesome."

Cave Thomas smiled inwardly. He'd been accused of meddling himself. As if conscious of his *faux pas*, Russell went on to describe some of the 'better men' and added high praise of Herr Finkel, who'd remained 'focused throughout'. But he didn't envy Finkel his task.

"Did you ever get to the bottom of what happened to Finkel in St Petersburg, and who was behind it?"

"I can't be certain, but it looks as if there were two different factions within the St Petersburg secret police. It's a complicated story, and I'm not sure we'll ever quite understand what was going on, but my belief is that whilst one lot of police were watching all foreigners, and seeing who they met, another lot were following a different path, supported by a small group who don't agree with the way the war is being conducted in the East. They appear to be a rough crowd, out for monetary profit and political power. But like all things Russian, it's hard to tell who's who. I think poor Finkel was mistaken for somebody else. Certainly, there were no obstacles to our meeting with the resistance group outside St Petersburg, but we were meant to be meeting another group inside the Russian border, and that never happened."

"Do you know where Finkel is now?"

217

"No idea. I left him outside Berlin. He wouldn't say where he was headed, only that it would be safer if I went my own way. I said he was delayed but perhaps waylaid is closer to the truth. It's my belief that the resistance forces refused to let him go. He has links with people in positions of real power, so they want to hang onto him and use his connections to their own advantage. But it's no longer any of my business and, since I have other matters to attend to, I left him and arrived in Berlin a couple of days ago."

'No mention of taking Finkel to London,' thought Cave Thomas, but he avoided the subject, instead, bringing Russell up to date with his own activities. Not wishing to divulge Evans's decision to leave St Petersburg, he restricted his report to the swiftness of the journey and the help they'd found along the way, which meant they were kept safe from deserters and wolves.

"You were not alone?" Russell asked. He missed nothing.

"There were four of us – me, Ambrosius and the driver and his son."

"Ambrosius?"

"A priest, from the English Church. He wanted to get home to his family, near Oels. I spent the night there before coming on to Berlin, via Breslau. Without Ambrosius, I'm not sure we'd have managed to cross the border."

Russell remembered him. "An unpromising hero – but, if you're telling the truth, he had qualities I didn't see."

"I found him to be a remarkable man," Cave Thomas replied. In an attempt to distract him, he added, "with two very attractive sisters."

Russell laughed, "Trust you to note a pretty face."

"I didn't just note them, I drew them." He pulled out his sketchbook and opened it on the page he'd drawn in Ambrosius's home.

"Very pretty," said Russell.

Cave Thomas's ruse worked. Russell asked only one more question: "Do you have time for lunch?"

29

An Unexpected Rendezvous
Friday 17th - Saturday 18th February 1854

Russell left Cave Thomas after lunch, saying that he looked forward to meeting him in London. As they parted Cave Thomas congratulated himself that he'd managed to satisfy Russell's curiosity without betraying Evans. He'd handled Russell rather well, he thought, and put the matter from his mind. The rest of the day passed pleasantly enough, exploring parts of the city he'd visited as a student. He couldn't help noticing how much had changed, even in these few years. Perhaps he'd changed as much as Berlin. Although the place was as busy as he remembered it, he noticed how tense people appeared to be, their faces grey with worry. He picked up a few odd words as he passed people deep in conversation. They, and the newspapers on sale in the streets, all spoke of war. To the residents of Berlin, Russia was a looming shadow. People knew its power and feared for themselves and their city. Most of the fighting was likely to take place in the East, but conflict in the West was also a possibility. News of troop movements appeared to be common knowledge. Britain had for centuries considered itself safe from danger, its shores well protected, remote from the turbulent Continent – that melting pot of petty rivalries, vaunting Imperialism and wars. But where boundaries were fluid and ownership swung from one nation to another, there were good reasons for unease. Cave Thomas's thoughts flitted to St Petersburg. He wondered how his friend Robertson was faring, and his mother. And he wondered whether the Quaker peacemakers had managed to leave the city yet. They'd need to act quickly if they were to reach home safely. He might have worried less had he been aware of events in St Petersburg. Even as he was thinking of the Quakers, letters ensuring that their return journey would be both expedited and safe, were being written by a secretary, on behalf of the Czar. They would receive them the next day.

Towards early evening, Cave Thomas ventured out to a restaurant. He sat where he could watch the door, but no-one disturbed him, and he ate his dinner in solitude. He stopped to buy

219

a copy of an evening paper on his way back to the *pension*. He'd have plenty to read that evening, and he felt no need for company. He read for an hour or two and then turned down his lamp, knowing that he must be up early the following morning. He was soon asleep. His room was safe – he'd locked the door and wedged the back of the chair under the handle.

The nearby clock struck four. It was Saturday morning and Cave Thomas was awake. Evans's train was due in at five fifteen and he intended to be in place well ahead of then. He'd need to be cautious in case this was a trap. He unlocked his door and quietly left the *pension* as the clock sounded the half hour. Unable to find a drosky, he walked to the station and made his way carefully to the platform where the Dirschau train would arrive. He found a good place to stand, hidden from view by a stack of freight awaiting collection. The station was almost empty. A few railway workers were hanging around at the end of the platform, but apart from that there was no-one else on his side of the track. Aware of movement to his left he glanced sideways and saw three men emerging from a luggage office on the opposite platform. One man was pushing a barrow; the other two walked behind him, deep in conversation. It all appeared innocuous, but Cave Thomas decided to stay near the entrance and looked around him for a way out, should he need to make a quick exit.

The sound of the train approaching triggered a flurry of activity as several people came out of a waiting room in search of the passengers they'd come to meet. Steam and smoke enveloped the train and platform and for a few moments obscured his view. As the atmosphere cleared, doors opened, and the platform filled with passengers and luggage. A door not far from Cave Thomas was opened by a steward and a woman descended the steps, carrying a single portmanteau. She paused on the platform and looked about her, then, seeing Cave Thomas, she approached him hesitantly.

"Monsieur Thomas?" she said, raising anxious eyes to his. "Do you remember me?"

Expecting Evans, Cave Thomas was momentarily taken aback. He glanced quickly about, to make sure he was not being approached by anyone else, then gave the woman his attention. Her face was familiar but what was she doing here? He struggled to recall her name.

"I am Marie-Claire Monceaux, Madame Robertson's maid. She send me."

"I…" Cave Thomas was lost for words.

"You expect Monsieur Evans?"

"Yes."

"I send you a telegraph. I think that you will come to the station if you think your friend Monsieur Evans arrives. I know that you and he become separated and you wait for him. I am not certain you will come to the station for me."

"Mademoiselle Monceaux, you've taken me by surprise. Why are you here? I understood that you were to stay with Mrs Robertson, in St Petersburg. And how did you know that Mr Evans was meeting me here?"

"We cannot talk here, Monsieur Thomas. Please, can we go somewhere safe? I have nothing to eat since yesterday."

"Of course, of course. Come, hand me your bag and we'll go and find a café."

The bag was heavy. Was this to be a one-way journey?

They left the station and Cave Thomas helped Marie-Claire into a drosky and climbed in beside her. They set off and shortly arrived at a café Cave Thomas knew would be open at that hour. He paid the driver and the pair found a table away from the window. Cave Thomas waited for Marie-Claire to begin her explanation, but her first remark was a question.

"How is Monsieur Evans?"

"I'm afraid I don't know," Cave Thomas watched her face. Her expression betrayed her true feelings. "You are concerned for him?" he asked.

For a moment, Marie-Claire's inner battle was clear. She wanted to trust Cave Thomas but feared the outcome should he disapprove of her. All this was obvious to a man who painted portraits.

"How did you know that Mr Evans had come with me and that we had parted company?" he asked.

"A message comes to Monsieur Robertson. It is from the priest – Père Ambroise. Monsieur Evans makes him promise to tell Monsieur Robertson that his plans change."

This was news to Cave Thomas. He wondered again just how important Ambrosius was and what game he had been playing. He wondered too what part Marie-Claire had played. He decided to give her as much of the truth as he safely could.

"Let me help you," he said, after a minute or so. "Evans is a good friend of mine. As you know, he came with me when we left St Petersburg, with Mr Robertson's blessing. On the way, he became ill. I left him with good people in a village near Peneviej. They will keep him safe until he is well and then help him to cross the border."

Marie-Claire listened intently. She flinched when Evan's illness was mentioned and then began to weep silently. Cave Thomas watched and waited. At last she conquered her tears, wiped her eyes and with a slightly unsteady voice began her explanation.

"It is all my fault," she said. "Oh, Monsieur, I am so sorry. I cannot help myself – Monsieur Evans is so kind and then all I do - it brings harm to him."

"Was there an attraction between you?" Marie-Claire remained silent but nodded slightly. "As I thought," Cave Thomas went on. "So, you spent time with Mr Evans and perhaps he made promises to you?"

"Oh no," Marie-Claire protested, "He promised nothing, but I know that he likes me. He say that if things are different, he will take me with him, back to England. But then I do a terrible thing and it ends with poor Monsieur Evans *blessé*." Tears threatened once more, so Cave Thomas waited for the mood to pass.

The waiter served their order, gave a discreet bow and left them. He obviously thought they were lovers.

"Have something to eat," Cave Thomas bade Marie-Claire. "There's plenty of time to tell me all about what happened, but you need some food to steady your nerves."

She smiled a little and accepted the roll he offered her. Cave Thomas drank his coffee and watched her covertly. At length, Marie-Claire began her tale.

"I have worked for Madame Robertson for seven years. She employed me when she was staying in Paris. When she returned to Russia, six years ago, I went with her. Then she became ill and I promised I will stay with her, no matter what happened. When Russia went to war with Turkey the news began to be full of rumours that the war will spread. Then you and your friends arrived, and our lives were, how do you say it… turned upside down? I know that an important box was hidden under Madame's bed, and that I must not touch the other boxes… in the *atelier*. Madame told me to see nothing and to say nothing. She said that we will be in great danger if anyone learn the boxes are there. When you and your friends come to… unpack… the boxes, I stayed with Madame, but I knew that something important was happening. I trust Monsieur Robertson, so I did as I was asked, but then something happened, and then I did not know who to trust."

She sipped her coffee and gave Cave Thomas a searching look. "You, I do trust, for Madame said that you are a good man. That is why I came to find you."

"Go on," said Cave Thomas, wondering what had happened to frighten her so much and why she thought it was her fault.

"Père Ambroise came to see Madame. Monsieur Robertson was out, so I let him in. He asked to see Madame and then he said that I must leave them so Madame can make her confession. I left them together. Later, I returned and listened at the door. He was still there. I heard him tell her that he is from *l'Église anglaise*. I could hear Madame speak but her voice was low, and I could not hear her words. Then she rang her bell and I went back in. She told me that Père Ambroise must leave but cannot go by the front door because the house is watched, so I am to take him down the back stair and let him leave that way. She gave me her key. I took it and went to see if the *atelier* was empty. It was, so I took the priest down the secret stairway and unlocked the door. He left and I went upstairs again. I took the key back to Madame and went to make her supper."

"What happened next?"

"On the night when Herr Finkel came back, I must have forget, no, forgotten to lock the door properly. Or perhaps someone else opened it… I do not know. I was cleaning *l'atelier* when I heard a strange sound coming from the corner where the secret stairs come up. I took my broom and opened the door to the little room. There were sounds on the stairs. I was very afraid, but I opened the door and looked down the stairs. At the bottom was man bending over something on the floor. The man looked up and I could see that it was the priest. He said, 'Come down Marie-Claire. This man needs help!' So, I went down, still holding my broom. There were two men on the floor, at the bottom of the stairs. One is dead. The priest said, 'We can do nothing for this man,' and he covered the man's face. Then he said, 'But we can save the other.' He asked me to help him lift the man who is *inconscient* – I do this – and we move him away from the stairs. Then the priest said he will take the dead man *à l'église*. He said, 'I will get a man to help me. You must clean the stair, so there is no sign of the dead man, then go up and lock the door at the top. I will come back for the other man. You must forget what you have seen.' I was so afraid! I did exactly what he said. I went back upstairs and locked the door at the top. After a few minutes, I heard voices – one was the priest and the other I did not know. I think they were taking *le cadavre* away, but

I was frightened and covered my ears. Then everything was quiet. I put my broom away and waited."

It was obvious to Cave Thomas that the horror of that night still lay upon her. He thought hard. The unconscious man must have been Herr Finkel. What Marie-Claire had told him explained why the bottom door was unlocked and why Finkel's mysterious dead man had disappeared. But Ambrosius's presence was another matter.

"What happened after that?" he asked.

"I don't know what time Monsieur Robertson returned. I think that Monsieur Russell was with him. I did not see him in the apartment until you came with Monsieur Evans. I was making a hot drink for Madame when I heard a sound like a gun. Soon after, you arrived, bringing Monsieur Evans with you. Monsieur Evans *a été blessé …et c'est de ma faute!*"

Marie-Claire began to weep again.

"No, Marie-Claire, it's not your fault. What you did, you did quite innocently. Whoever fired that shot is to blame for Mr Evans's injury, not you. Did you tell Mrs Robertson about what happened?"

"No. At first, I was too afraid, but when you left and took Monsieur Evans with you, I was troubled, and I told Madame Robertson everything. I thought the box was stolen – but it was not, so I didn't know what to think. Madame Robertson told me to come and look for you. She said that you need to know the truth because if the priest knows Herr Finkel, you might be in danger. She said, 'I will explain everything to Monsieur Robertson after you go'. Then I found out that Monsieur Evans was no longer with you – Monsieur Robertson received a message from one of Monsieur Russell's friends and I heard him speak of it to Madame - and so I made my plan. And you received my message and came to meet me."

Ambrosius… a murderer? Cave Thomas found that hard to believe, although the man himself had said that he knew how to kill. But, somehow, Cave Thomas didn't believe it was true in this case. It was far more likely that Russell was right – that there had been a falling out between different factions in St Petersburg – either in the police or the resistance movements – or spies, depending upon one's point of view. Without more to go on, it would be impossible to untangle the allegiances amongst the people he'd met. But one thing was obvious, Mrs Robertson had had good reasons to send Marie-Claire to find him. He should certainly be on his guard, and there was something else he must do – he must do what he could to make sure that Evans came safely home.

"Monsieur Thomas," said Marie-Claire, "Can you help Monsieur Evans?"

"I don't know," Cave Thomas replied, "but I'll try. What will you do?"

"I have done what I come to do. Now I can go to Paris. Madame gave me money and said to me, *'rentrez chez vous en famille'*. "

"Then I will help you to get there safely," said Cave Thomas. I must wait here in Berlin a little longer - just in case Mr Evans manages to find his way here. I promised I would stay until this coming Monday. If you are happy to wait, you may travel with me on Monday. I can make a detour to Paris – I'd like to see it, whilst I'm this side of the Channel." Cave Thomas had no idea what he'd do if Evans failed to arrive in Berlin, but he'd face that problem if, or when, it arose.

Marie-Claire's relief was obvious. "Thank you, Monsieur Thomas! *Merci, mille fois!*"

"This is a bad time for a woman to be travelling alone. Let's go to my lodgings and see if we can find a room for you."

He paid the bill and they left the café and made their way to the *pension*, where Cave Thomas booked a room for Marie-Claire, for the weekend. She left her bag there and the two of them went out for a walk. Whilst they were in Berlin, they could at least see the sights. Now that she had found Cave Thomas and told her tale, Marie-Claire appeared to have let go of her burden of guilt. However, as they wandered through the streets and gardens, and found another café for lunch, Cave Thomas was aware that, far from feeling relaxed, he was looking for danger at every corner.

30

Evans
Sunday 19th February 1854

Cave Thomas spent Saturday evening alone. Marie-Claire retired to her room after supper and they agreed to meet for breakfast the next morning. This they did, going to a small café to eat, after which, Marie-Claire returned to the *pension* and Cave Thomas went to the Hotel du Nord, to attend the English Episcopal Church service held in a large room there. The familiar words of the service freed him from his immediate problems. He managed to sit near the back and slipped away at the end without drawing attention to himself, ready to confront the deeper battle he'd been fighting throughout his journey. He decided to walk by the river, thinking this might restore his peace of heart and mind. The nearer he drew to England, the sooner he must face Jane once more. Her heart was not an unassailable citadel, neither was his own, but their lives were founded on a strict moral code. Each had responsibilities and purpose. No matter how tempted he might feel, he could not bring himself to test Jane's love. He feared the abyss that such an action would open at their feet. He knew he must somehow remain determined to do what was right, but could he do this and retain a feeling, responsive heart, rather than one of stone? Jane was intelligent; it would be impossible to persuade her of a peace which he didn't truly feel. There was still much for him to overcome before he dared to see her.

He turned his thoughts to Marie-Claire. Her arrival had added much to his worries. He hoped that Evans would appear soon. He didn't relish the idea of escorting Marie-Claire to Paris and then having to retrace his steps to find Evans. He might have to visit a bank and withdraw more money to pay for extra train tickets. He'd been spending what he'd brought with him at an alarming rate. His thoughts circled once more, and he knew he must concentrate on something else in order to clear his mind. He found a bench near the river and sat down. It was cold, but to be outside was better than to be confined to the stuffy air of the *pension*. Once more, he took out his sketchbook and pencil and looked about him for something to draw.

The pencil remained mid-air, for, walking towards him with a slight limp, was the man he longed to see – Evans! He jumped up and ran to greet him, seizing Evans's good hand and shaking it joyfully.

"My friend! How glad I am to see you! How did you know where to find me?"

"I arrived late last night," said Evans. "I found a place to stay and then went to look for you. It being Sunday, I knew you'd go to church if you could, so I waited near the Hotel du Nord and then followed you here."

"Of course, you did! My dear friend – you may have been wounded but you never cease to be vigilant and resourceful!"

"We must talk," said Evans. "I'm not so well recovered that I wish to sit and freeze here by the river. Can we go somewhere more comfortable?"

Cave Thomas agreed at once, gathered his belongings and set off with Evans in search of lunch. Marie-Claire would have to make her own arrangements – he'd given her no promises regarding the time of his return. Evans could have no idea that she was here, and he must find a good way of telling him. But first, Evans had his own tale to tell.

The restaurant was crowded, but they managed to find a corner where a partition separated them from a noisy family party at the next table. They could talk freely, knowing that they'd not be overheard. Their order was taken, and as they waited for it to arrive, Cave Thomas took stock of his friend. He'd left Evans sick with fever eight days previously. The marks of his illness were clear. He was thinner, paler and his arm was still awkward. The waiter brought their meal and, once he'd left them, they began to exchange news. Evans couldn't speak too highly of the family who'd nursed him back to health.

"They were good people, Cave Thomas. You chose well. Anton was welcoming and young Peteris made himself my slave. He refused to leave me. His mother kept telling me that she owed you Peteris's life and was glad to repay. I called her Angelica – I couldn't work out her Russian name – because she was like an angel to me. Of course, I left them with money after their escape."

"Escape? What do you mean?"

"They couldn't stay once my presence was discovered by their neighbours. Everything in that region was in upheaval. The army descended on the village on Tuesday and took away all the men of military age. Peteris was too young, so they left him. But the fact

227

that Angelica spoke more than one language had made some of the neighbours suspicious. Someone jealous of her husband's success in business informed against him. The soldiers weren't interested in the legal side, so they just took him away with the others. The moment Anton had gone, the business was confiscated and promised to the neighbour. All this happened incredibly quickly, just five days ago. Angelica hid me when the soldiers came. Afterwards, she managed to convince the neighbours, that I'd run away. She told them that I'd forced my way into the household and held them at gunpoint. They seemed to believe her, and I think most of the villagers would have supported her, but the family who'd been promised the business are powerful. So, three nights ago, we packed our bags and slipped away. I went with Angelica and Peteris, and the younger children. We walked for miles. Eventually we came to a small hamlet where Angelica has kin. They took her and the children in, but I had to leave them. They took me in a cart and set me down near the main road, several miles away. I walked to the next town and then joined a party travelling west. They hid me at the border – I still don't know how they managed it, except that the soldiers were overwhelmed by the number of people returning home and let us through with extraordinarily little trouble. They wanted us out of the way."

Cave Thomas listened to this story, gripped by the horror of what had happened and fearful that his actions had led to this disaster - 'Angelica', Peteris and his sisters, homeless, and the father, Anton, conscripted into the army - that loving family scattered by war, jealousy and fear. What a cruel and pitiless land this was! He prayed that they would survive and return to their home one day. He forced himself to concentrate as Evans went on:

"So, I found my way to Berlin, looked for somewhere to stay and went to the telegraph office to see if Russell had left me any messages."

"Had he?"

"Yes."

"How did he know you were on your way here?"

"Russell makes it his business to know – let's leave it at that. He told me you were here and that I must find you. He wants us to return to England together. He thinks that we'll do better together than we would alone."

"True enough," said Cave Thomas, "but before we start making plans, there's something you need to know." And he proceeded to tell Evans about Marie-Claire.

228

At the first mention of her name, Evans began to look uncomfortable. 'So', thought Cave Thomas, 'she spoke the truth.'

"What did she say about me?"

"She feels badly about your wound. She believes herself responsible for your falling into danger."

Evans seemed to wrestle with his conscience. At last he said,

"I got to know Marie-Claire in St Petersburg last November – ask Ellis if you don't believe me – he warned me off her, but by then it was too late. We met in the market. Her purse had just been stolen and I helped her. Ellis thought it was a ruse, but I'm certain it wasn't – her tears were genuine. The money belonged to her mistress and she was afraid of dismissal. The culprit was caught, and the purse returned. She was grateful for my help and we became… friends. I knew she was working as a maid but had no idea it was for Mrs Robertson. It was a shock when she appeared at their apartment. I wanted to tell you after I was shot – I was afraid for her safety. But each time I tried, something happened to prevent me. Where is she now?"

"Staying with me at my *pension*." Evans looked at him sharply. "In a separate room," Cave Thomas added, and Evans relaxed.

"What did you think of her story?" Evans asked, hoping, as much as anything, to direct attention away from any dalliance between him and Marie-Claire.

"What she said about the connection between Ambrosius and Herr Finkel interests me. Do you think they were working together?"

"Hard to tell, but it's possible. After all, they are both Prussians."

"True. Well, it's no good thinking more about that. We must look ahead and decide what to do. I promised to stay here until the 20th. You've managed to get here a day early, so I think we should leave as early as we can tomorrow."

"Do you still have your copy of Bradshaw?" asked Evans.

"Of course. Shall we go back to the *pension* and consult it?"

"Yes. I'll collect my bag and join you at four if that's in order. Perhaps I could stay the night?"

"As to that, you must ask the proprietor. I think all the rooms may be taken."

"That won't be a problem," said Evans. "I expect we can sort something out."

Cave Thomas chose not to pursue this, and instead paid the bill and the two men left the restaurant. They parted, Evans to return to his hotel and Cave Thomas to find Marie-Claire and prepare her for an addition to their party.

The meeting between Evans and Marie-Claire took place that afternoon. Cave Thomas left the pair together and went out for a walk. By the time he returned, they appeared at ease with one another and had agreed on a plan of action. Cave Thomas, wishing to be included in their plans invited them to join him in his room to discuss this, away from prying eyes.

Evans took charge. "We'll leave tomorrow, travelling together. As you suggested, we must find an early train and go as far as we can before splitting up. You'll need to make the last part of your journey alone, Cave Thomas. I intend to escort Marie-Claire to Paris. I'll be staying there for a while."

"I see," said Cave Thomas. "Are you going to contact Russell about this? He's expecting us to travel back to London together."

"Once I'm in Paris, yes. Not before then. Cave Thomas, will you back me up? I owe Marie-Claire a debt of honour. I must see this through. You can tell Russell that my fever has returned – after all, it's not so far from the truth."

Cave Thomas glanced at Marie-Claire, who had her eyes fixed upon her hands. Her slight blush did something to restore Cave Thomas's trust in her honesty. Perhaps there was genuine love there after all - unless her blush was one of guilt?

"Very well. I'll do my best," he said, then he lifted his Bradshaw out of the drawer and opened it at the Berlin-Paris page. "The train stops at Cologne and Brussels. I could change trains at either. Let's see what connections there are."

After much flicking backward and forward from page to page, they concluded that they must part at Cologne. Evans and Marie-Claire would remain on the train to Paris, and Cave Thomas would take the connection to Ostend. Once there, he'd have several hours to kill before boarding the evening ferry to Dover. He'd arrive in London at about half past four and be home by dawn.

"Can you do it?" asked Evans.

"As long as we're not delayed between here and Cologne. If I miss my connection, I'll have to spend the night on the station. The next train would give me little time in Ostend, and I might have to wait for the next sailing." Cave Thomas smiled. "But don't worry about me. You've done a lot for me and for your country, Evans. I'll manage, and I'm even prepared for a grilling by Mr Ellis when I get home. I'm only glad it won't be Sir Henry, although I'm

230

sorry, none-the-less, that he won't be there. I'd have enjoyed telling him how I'd seen off a pack of wolves."

Evans and Marie-Claire left him, to go out for a walk. They agreed to meet at seven for an evening meal. Cave Thomas made good use of the time repacking his possessions and writing letters, intending to post them at the station the next morning. This done, he sat for a while, going over all the events of the past days. He'd need to write a report, he supposed, but deciding what to put in it and what to omit would be difficult. Much that had happened would need to be left out. He wasn't sure what he'd say about Evans's injury and consequent adventures, not to mention his decision to stay in France. He'd probably leave Evans to explain himself. Much easier. And Robertson? He wondered how he and his mother were faring. Russia was a far from friendly place for the English now. He thought of Cattley and the merchants relying on the gold he'd taken to them; people like Kobyzev and his family – good people who worked hard and loved their families, who looked out for their neighbours and tried to live at peace with all men. What would war bring them? A boxful of gold might help, but it might also make them targets for others' greed. His thoughts went to Angelica's family. Things had not turned out well for them.

He had started out believing that he was simply taking aid to the Christians in St Petersburg, and that he would complete his task and return home. It would be an adventure, an escape from the constraints of his life in London and the conflict between his heart, mind and soul. But this great adventure, crammed as it had been with struggle, success, friendship, pain and betrayal, had left him uneasy – uncertain of himself and of his own motives. Marie-Claire had clearly fallen in love with Evans. She'd risked all to come west and seek him out. Evans had managed to escape, alone, from Russia, still weak from a fever and handicapped by his wound. But the pair had met one another and there was a certainty about them in their decision to go to Paris together, which made Cave Thomas envious.

His thoughts went to his own dilemma and the difficult situation awaiting him in London. Was this the price of love, this anguish and soul-searching? He hoped Evans and Marie-Claire would find happiness but could see no such outcome for himself. Wearily he knelt by his bed and committed his thoughts to prayer.

31

The Journey Home
Monday 20th – Wednesday 22nd February 1854

The first part of their journey was uncomfortably tense. The sense of being watched had not gone away and the three travellers waited on the station platform with heightened awareness, alert to danger and suspicious of everyone around them. They barely spoke, all their concentration fixed upon appearing normal and staying safe. At last the train came into the platform. They climbed up into a carriage and found seats together. They stowed their luggage and waited for the whistle to signal their departure. They were on their way at precisely half past seven. The carriage was full. Everyone who could do so, was going home. Berlin was emptying of foreign visitors. They'd been lucky to get seats.

The train travelled west, cutting through the vast rural landscape, bringing them ever nearer the end of their journey. It would take between fourteen and fifteen hours to reach Cologne. Without discussing it, Evans and Cave Thomas fell back into their habit of taking turns to watch and to sleep. Marie-Claire took out some crochet work and whiled away the time, gazing out of the window at the passing landscape, her fingers busy with her work and her mind fixed – who knew where? The stops for food and exercise were welcome but added to Cave Thomas's tension. He watched Evans and noted that his arm was still giving him pain. Once, as they stretched their legs at a station, he managed to speak to him about it, urging him to seek medical help when he reached Paris.

"I promise," Evans replied. "Marie-Claire will make sure it happens."

Marie-Claire had returned to the carriage.

"Will you marry her?"

"Yes, if she'll have me. I must make sure she is safe and well."

Cave Thomas knew then that there was more to Marie-Claire's escape from Russia than he'd previously thought.

"Can you trust her?"

"I think so. But either way, I'll stay loyal to her. She'll never have to fear my reproach." There was an ambiguity in his words which left Cave Thomas questioning whether they were talking about the same thing. Had they been discussing Marie-Claire's moral position or her allegiances? If it were the former, could Evans be sure he was the father? He only had Marie-Claire's word for that. But he was a decent man. If he'd compromised Marie-Claire, he wouldn't abandon her. He appeared to love her.

"What of your work?" Cave Thomas wondered what Russell and Ellis might have to say.

"The world is changing. A man can become lost in time of war. No-one questions it. Perhaps I'll be useful in other ways."

"Perhaps." Cave Thomas could imagine the tentacles of Ellis's men, reaching out to Paris. Yes, Evans might well be useful. "What does Marie-Claire think about your job?" he asked.

"She only knows a little - she has no idea how deeply I'm committed, only that I report to someone in London. Once we're married, I'll take her into my confidence – as far as I'm allowed."

They re-boarded the train. The engine, water topped up and coal truck replenished, surged on, pulling them further from Russia and danger. As he drifted into sleep, lulled by the motion of the train, Cave Thomas's mind went before him, to London. He walked its streets and entered his front door. His dream took him to his studio. Dust covered his workbench. Cobwebs hung from the paintings which lined the walls. He wandered over to the place where that unforgettable portrait leaned, under its dust sheet. He drew back the fabric and turned the painting to face him. The face was half-twisted away, the rosy cheek and an eyelash all that could be seen. Her neck and shoulder visible, as the robe slipped. His portrait of the goddess - his imagined portrait of Jane. The one George Laws had spotted and mentioned to Emily in Jane's hearing. But as he watched, a seeping rot attacked the canvas. It pierced a hole near her face and it slowly grew, consuming the whole, destroying his work. He tried to shake it from his hand, but it stuck and, as he watched, the mould leached into his flesh and crept slowly but irrevocably up his arm. Soon it would reach his heart…

He woke to find Evans shaking his arm.

"Papers, passports – have them ready please." The official was at the door. They were nearing the end of the journey.

"We're approaching Cologne," Evans said. "We're early. We'll have half an hour here before we leave. Shall we find something to eat before we part?"

They showed the official their papers and he nodded and moved on. "Papers, passports – have them ready please…" as he walked through the open carriage.

"That would be good," said Cave Thomas, still throwing off his disturbing dream. "I was fast asleep. Thank you for waking me."

"You seemed to be having a bad dream," said Evans. "But don't worry, you didn't shout out anything suspicious – just 'no, no, no'."

"I've spent too much time trying to sleep on trains. It's not good for my neck." Cave Thomas lifted down his bag and picked up his satchel. "I'll take all my luggage with me or I'll forget it and it'll end up in Paris."

"Are you coming with us, Marie-Claire?" Evans asked.

"No. You will have things to say before we part. Please accept my thanks and *mes adieux* here, Monsieur Thomas. *Merci pour votre aide et votre compréhension sympathique*."

Cave Thomas took her hand and wished her well. "I'll make sure Evans brings you something to eat," he added. Then they left the train and went to buy food from a stall near the waiting room.

"I've sent a telegraph to Mr Ellis," said Evans. "I've told him that I'm following a lead and going on to Paris. I'll tell him more once I've sorted out somewhere to stay. I also told him to ask you if he wants more information. You'll know what to say."

"Very well. I understand." Cave Thomas was sorry to be parting from Evans. "Ellis is a fair man," he said. "I'll do my best for you. Write to me at my studio if you get the chance. I'd like to know how you get on."

"I'll do that – but don't expect much for a while. All Europe is going to be drawn into war - and for the next few months I'll certainly be busy."

"I'll want to know that your arm is fully mended. I don't like to leave you as you are."

"Marie-Claire will make sure I behave, don't you worry."

"I wish you both well."

"Thank you, Cave Thomas. I wish you the same. And, if you manage to persuade your Jane, let me know – I'll come to the wedding!"

Cave Thomas looked at him sharply. "There'll be no wedding," he retorted, taken off balance. Had he called out her name in his sleep?

"Very well, have it your own way. Can I make you Godfather when the time comes?"

234

So, he'd been right. Cave Thomas smiled. "Of course." He hoped that Marie-Claire had told the truth. If there was another side to her, he trusted that she was loyal to Britain and had acted in good faith - and not merely to entrap Evans.

The Ostend train was announced. The two men parted, and Cave Thomas watched Evans re-join the Paris train. Then he boarded his train, found a corner seat and settled down for the next leg of his journey. He'd reach Ostend in about twelve hours. Weary of travel, he'd be glad reach his destination.

The train pulled into Ostend just after eleven thirty. With seven hours to fill before the ferry left, Cave Thomas made his way to a harbourside café and ordered lunch, making it last as long as possible. At about two, he took his bags and wandered into the town. He found a bar where no one would question how long he sat and ordered a beer. He took out his sketchbook and looked around at the faces of nearby customers. The assortment of men and women provided ample scope for his pencil. He began to sketch, feeling the calm of concentration wipe away the anxieties which had been plaguing him. After a while, he became aware of someone approaching his table. He looked up as Russell said, "May I join you?" and sat down opposite him.

"I didn't expect to see you before London," Cave Thomas said as he closed his sketchbook and slipped his pencil into his pocket. "Can I buy you a beer?"

"I've ordered coffee," said Russell. He paused as the waiter brought over two cups and a jug, then, "How are you?"

"I'm well," said Cave Thomas.

"I've been here for a couple of days," Russell stirred sugar into his cup. "I completed my business in Berlin and came here directly. I hoped we might meet."

Cave Thomas finished his beer and pulled a cup towards him. He poured the coffee and waited.

"Where's Evans?" Russell watched Cave Thomas's face as he sought an appropriate reply. Deciding on honesty, he related what had happened after Russell had left. He left nothing out, other than the possibility that Marie-Claire was expecting a child.

"Paris, you say?"

"Yes. And no, I have no way of contacting him."

"I'm not concerned about that. What does concern me is that he's still injured, with a woman we don't really know, and possibly running into danger."

235

Cave Thomas had nothing to say to this.

"I don't expect you to understand," Russell went on. "Sir Henry was right. Mixing experienced with inexperienced men creates problems. If I'd known…"

But Cave Thomas knew that this was bluster. Russell had lost control of Evans and would have to face Ellis when he got back to London.

"What do you want me to do?"

"Go home to London, Cave Thomas, and paint. I'll come and see you and we'll put together a report for Mr Ellis. After that, it'll be out of our hands."

"War will come. Will Evans be stranded in Paris?"

"That's no longer your concern, Cave Thomas. Leave it to the experts. You'll need to forget about much you've seen, but we'll cover all that when I see you in London. What time is your ferry?"

"We sail at half past six, but I can board from five."

"Then I suggest you make your way there fairly soon. You'll find that there are extra checks. I'll be travelling on it myself, but it would be best if we don't talk to one another. From now on we must be strangers – in public, at any rate."

"Very well. I'll be advised by you."

"I'll watch your back," said Russell. "I owe you that much." Then he stood up, shook hands with Cave Thomas, and left.

Cave Thomas watched his figure disappear down the street. He looked at the clock above the bar – nearly four o'clock – time to be on his way. Gathering his possessions, he left the bar and made his way to the ferry, where he joined the long queue for tickets. Russell had been right. The process took over an hour, but at last he boarded and found a seat. He placed his luggage on a rack and went out to the deck. Scanning the harbour, he noticed how much shipping was entering and leaving. The quay was crowded. As the gangway was hoisted up, he realised that many had failed to board. Once more, he'd been lucky to find a place. Thankful to Russell for urging him to arrive early, he went back to his seat, only to find it occupied by an elderly lady. He returned to the deck. It was a cold night to be outside, but as the swell caught the boat, he was glad to be in the fresh air. It was going to be an uncomfortable crossing. Turning, he caught a glimpse of Russell's face, across the other side of the deck. True to his word, he intended to watch over Cave Thomas until he had landed safely in England.

The crossing was completed with only fifteen minutes delay, because of the weather, steam being more reliable than sail. Cave

236

Thomas boarded the train for London and nodded off within minutes of leaving the port. He arrived in London at half past four. The streets to the markets thronged with carts bringing in produce from the country. Dazed with fatigue, he found a cab and went straight home. He unlocked the door and entered, surprised to find that the house struck warm after the cold outside. He dropped his bags in the hallway and went to his studio, where he found the stove still alight from the previous day's fire. Mrs Trent, his daily help, must have kept the place aired during his absence. He'd been away for five weeks. He'd have a significant bill to pay for all that coal – perhaps he could charge it to Mr Ellis.

He filled the kettle and set it on the stove. He wandered over to where his completed canvases were leaning against the wall, drawn by a compulsion to see the painting of *The Goddess* which had played so much upon his mind during his travels. He lifted the dust sheet covering it and looked at the averted face, the angle of the neck, the smooth shoulder. Jane. There was no nightmare mould, no creeping decay. The colours were vibrant as ever, and his heart ached as it always did, with the intensity of his love for her.

The kettle boiled. He replaced the dust sheet and poured the hot water into a stone bed warmer. Weary from his weeks of travel, he carried it up to his room and slipped it between the sheets, undressed and climbed into bed. But once there, he found sleep elusive. His mind was full of his adventure – over three and a half thousand miles across snow and ice, encountering excitement, secrecy, discomfort and danger. He thought of Robertson, still there in St Petersburg, caring for his dying mother. When would he come home? And Evans, now with Marie-Claire in Paris. Would they survive the upheaval of war? Ambrosius – or Nicolas – courageous and determined, placing family above all else, yet still daring to serve his country. He wondered if they would meet again. He was confident that he'd see Russell and Ellis but was doubtful whether he'd ever learn all that lay behind the mission. Not from them, anyway. Perhaps he'd one day meet the Russian merchants once more – if he ever returned to Russia. He'd made plenty of drawings – it would be good to turn them into a painting. And thinking of painting he fell asleep at last.

He slept until mid-afternoon, then put on his dressing gown and hearing Mrs Trent in the kitchen, went in search of food. She was delighted to see him safely returned. Having found his bags when she arrived that morning, she'd spent the day cooking and cleaning. There was plenty of hot water, she told him, and if he would like to take a bath, she'd lay out fresh clothes for him – she'd had them airing all morning – and would have a meal ready for him when he came down. This seemed an excellent plan, so Cave Thomas did as she said. When his meal was brought to him in the studio, at five o'clock, he found he was ravenously hungry.

There was a pile of letters waiting in the hallway. Mrs Trent brought them in when she came to collect his tray. Cave Thomas leafed through them, looking at the handwriting and setting aside those which could wait. Then he selected one, set aside to be read straight away, and opened the envelope. It was from his brother-in-law, George. Written only a few days previously, it was short. It asked Cave Thomas to come and see them as soon as he arrived home. Emily had been unwell. Their hopes of a child were over. Her life was not in danger.

Cave Thomas sat with the letter in his hand and felt all the brightness of his return fall away. Abandoning the rest of the letters, he grabbed his hat and coat, and with a word to Mrs Trent ran out to find a cab. He arrived in Camden in just over twenty minutes and ran up the steps to Emily's door. The servant who admitted him knew him by sight and showed him into the dining parlour where George was working on some papers.

"I returned this morning. I came as soon as I found your note. How is she?"

"You will see for yourself in a moment. Don't stay long, she's still weak." Then, realising that he ought to welcome his brother-in-law, George asked about his trip. John joined them, just home from the bank.

"It's good to see you back safely, Cave Thomas," he said, "you look well after such a journey."

But Cave Thomas could see that both men had more on their mind than his travels. The huge story of his journey to St Petersburg had been eclipsed, for a while, by the small tragedy of Emily and George's lost hope, so he merely told them he was well and that the trip had been successful. Then he asked permission to see Emily.

"She's in the front room," said George, "she'll be glad to see you back safe and sound."

Cave Thomas left them and crossed the hall to the parlour. There, a very pale Emily sat by the hearth, wrapped in a warm shawl. Opposite her, her needlework in her hands, was Jane. The door closed behind him and Cave Thomas went straight to his sister.

238

"Oh, William, I'm so glad you're back!" she cried, "It's been such a dreadful time. Oh, William…" and he put his arm around his sister as she wept.

Looking across the room, his eyes met Jane's. There were tears in her eyes, too, but whether of grief or joy he could not tell.

Cave Thomas left them soon afterwards and returned to his lodgings. He entered the studio and sat down by the stove. It was over. He had faced the source of his torment. Now he must go on.

What had Madox Brown said? 'Work, man! Work!'

He stood up and went to his easel, placed a fresh canvas upon it and put out his paint palette and brushes, ready for the morning. His travel sketches lay where he'd dropped them earlier that day. He searched the folder and took out three rough drawings of the Russian merchant.

For a while, he stood looking at the blank canvas. Then he spread out the sketches on the bench beside the easel, picked up some charcoal and began to draw.

Lightning Source UK Ltd.
Milton Keynes UK
UKHW041855281020
372396UK00001B/51

9 781839 455155